Born in Scotland and educated at Trinity College, Cambridge, Lauren McCrossan gave up a career in law to work as a freelance writer. Together with her professional surfer boyfriend, Gabriel, she is based in Biarritz and spends most winters in Hawaii. When in the UK, they divide their time between Newcastle and Winchester. Lover of dolphins, football and sweet popcorn, Lauren writes longhand on the beach. This is her first novel.

SERVE COOL

Dumped by her boyfriend, Jack, fired from her job as a trainee lawyer, evicted from her flat by her lecherous landlord, what's a girl in Geordie Land to think but 'Why I?' Jen Summer's life has lost it's spring, until best friend Maz turns her world from black to brown — Newcastle Brown to be precise, with a job as a barmaid in Byker's Scrap Inn. Then Jack puts the ex into exasperating, with a development deal that threatens to bulldoze her new life. Jen is facing upheaval once more, when salvation comes from the last place she'd expect — a daytime TV talk show . . .

LAUREN McCROSSAN

SERVE COOL

Complete and Unabridged

ULVERSCROFT
Leicester

First published in Great Britain in 2001 by
Warner Books
London

First Large Print Edition
published 2002
by arrangement with
Little, Brown and Company (UK)
London

The moral right of the author has been asserted

All characters in this publication are fictitious, and
any resemblance to real persons, living or dead,
is purely coincidental.

British Library CIP Data

McCrossan, Lauren
    Serve cool.—Large print ed.—
    Ulverscroft large print series: romance
    1. Newcastle-upon-Tyne (England)—Social life and
    customs—20th century—Fiction
    2. Large type books
    I. Title
    823.9′14 [F]

    ISBN 0–7089–4739–5

Published by
F. A. Thorpe (Publishing)
Anstey, Leicestershire

Set by Words & Graphics Ltd.
Anstey, Leicestershire
Printed and bound in Great Britain by
T. J. International Ltd., Padstow, Cornwall

This book is printed on acid-free paper

In memory of
Randall — catching waves in heaven
and
Jimmy — who helped me research this
book

Acknowledgements

Thank you to:

Mum and Dad who have helped me so much. Thank you for your amazing love and support and for believing in me.

Anthony and Lucy for ploughing through endless chapters, finding me jobs, lending me your computer and for the giant Toblerone you kept in your cupboard (which I may have forgotten to mention).

Martin, my 'twin', for making me laugh since I was born and my sister Debbie.

Owain my Geordie dictionary, Annette and Peter, prolific readers of the North-East, Jesse, Joel, Davy, Nathan, Cainy, Trev and all our friends in Tynemouth and Newcastle for all your help and humour.

Elaine for being a special friend and for helping to keep me solvent when all I had left to sell was a pair of PVC roller boots.

Naomi, a huge talent waiting to be discovered, and Rob, the bonsai king, the most enthusiastic and fantastic couple I know.

All the wonderful people who have helped me along the way — Alf Alderson, Alison,

Michaela, Ching, Nat and Lloyd, Richie, Lee, Peggy, Mark Fletcher, JDPP Perrin, the Navins, Martyn Diaper, Amy, Rachael, George, Anita Butt and the McCrossan clan.

Anna Telfer for discovering me, Imogen Taylor for your advice and enthusiasm and for putting your faith in my novel, Emma Gibb and all at Little, Brown.

And above all to Gabriel for encouraging me to chase my dreams, for never once saying I couldn't achieve them and for showing me how fun life can be. You are my best friend, my soulmate and my inspiration.

Thank you xxx.

1

1st January, 12:29 a.m.

Less than half an hour into the New Year and my only remaining party buddy was Armitage Shanks, second cubicle on the left, Tuxedo Royale nightclub, Newcastle. I had considered starting up a rendition of 'Auld Lang Syne' among my fellow chunderers, but I didn't think a chorus of 'For the sake of hyurg blurgh yoogh' would be particularly appropriate.

Happy bloody New Year, Jennifer, I thought, just as my inner self decided to show itself for the fourth time already that year.

Only twelve hours before, I had been contemplating the most significant night of my life. New outfit, new hair-do, New Year's Eve and soon a new *fiancé*. Personally, I had always loathed that word: '*fiancé*'. It conjures up images of size-eight Posh Spice lookalikes, sporting diamonds worth more than a small country. Funny how the word had become instantly more appealing when I thought it was finally my turn.

'My *fiancé* and I will probably move to one

of those chic condominiums by the river,' I had told Casey, my hairdresser, as she struggled to control my curls. Condominium? The thought of my own engagement had suddenly turned me into a stuck-up, twin-set, hoise-in-the-Dordogne-darling kind of girl. By the time I had my head between my legs being 'diffused', Casey and I had made hair-do plans for myself, my mother and the 26 bridesmaids. In the car on the way home I had planned the eight-tier cake, vol-au-vents and full lilac colour scheme. By leg-shaving and bikini-line torture in the shower, I had already worked out the hymns, seating arrangements and the requisite number of frilly pouches containing inedible pink sweets. The honeymoon we would plan together during our post-engagement love fest.

What the hell was happening to me? I had always been so anti weddings. After my sister Susie's big do I had vowed never to go through the same scenario. It had taken over eighteen months to plan. Should the colour scheme be peach or fuchsia? Was little Charlotte too fat to be a bridesmaid? Would she unbalance the photos? Should we invite the coffin-dodger relatives and would the iron lungs require separate invitations? Could Dad bear to sit next to Susie's mother-in-law for the whole reception or should she have a table for one? I had suggested a muzzle and doggy chews but my opinion had not been well received. The whole thing had been a complete nightmare for anyone unlucky enough to qualify as a member of the political wedding party. By the time the big day arrived, there were so many divisions in the ranks the atmosphere was more befitting of a wake.

This time, though, things would be different. Jack and I would be the model bride and groom, *Hello!* magazine would beg for exclusive rights to the photographs and 'Love is in the Air' would sing joyously from every stereo in Newcastle in celebration of our perfect love.

When Jack had informed me of our impending important discussion (he liked to speak only in words of three or more syllables), feminine intuition had told me it was my turn. Call it stupidity, call it festive fever or call it one too many peach schnapps at lunchtime. Call it what you will, feminine intuition had got me in the shit again.

★　★　★

Armitage Shanks reached up to say hello for the fifth time as Kim Wilde's dulcet tones bounced off the walls of the stinking cubicle.

I reflected on the fact that when perfectly sober, I would refuse point blank to even sit on a public toilet seat, especially a wet one. I tend to perch above in a Rosemary Conley-style quad-strengthening squat and aim as best I can. Yet here I knelt, cheek pressed firmly against the cold rim, with my arms gripping the wheel of the porcelain bus. Two bottles of wine with a beer, alcopop and vodka cocktail chaser combine to produce the perfect antidote for human pride.

Pride? How could I ever experience that feeling again? Approaching 1:00 a.m. on the first day of the year and I had already been publicly humiliated, dumped and abandoned. Jack had picked a great time to get it all off his tanned, dark-haired chest. While the rest of the party-goers on the floating boat nightclub counted down to Big Ben on the revolving dance floor, Jack was manoeuvring an incredible weight from his shoulders and depositing it squarely on my aching head.

'I just feel we're getting too intense,' he had said.

'Intense!' I had shouted. 'I have to book our dates through your secretary and I practically need a written invitation to visit your flat.'

'I just need space, Jenny, to do my own thing.'

'Space!' Any more space and we would be conducting our relationship from two distant planets. Of course, I pathetically assumed that it had to be my fault.

'Are my thighs too fat?' I had whined.

'No, Jenny, not really.'

'Not really?' Hardly the resounding negative I had hoped for. 'My hair then? It's my hair isn't it? You don't like curls. I'll straighten it. I'll dye it blonde. Whatever you want.'

Why was it that in a crisis I always thought a classic blonde bob would solve my problems? People always described my hair as 'wacky', 'wild' or, worst of all, 'different'. Unfortunately, that inferred chaos seemed to filter through to my personality. General disorganisation was not a particularly appropriate quality for a soon-to-be-qualified solicitor. Girls with perfect hair just seemed so in control.

'It's not your hair, Jennifer,' he had said stiffly. 'It's just . . . I don't want the commitment right now.'

'COMMITMENT!' That little gem. Jack had obviously been reading *Dumping For Beginners* but hadn't got past the second page. Next he would be using the 'I just want to be friends' line.

'The thing is, Jenny, I think I just want to be friends.'

Aaaaaagh! God give me the strength to kick his designer butt. I had felt an immense rage bubbling up from somewhere around my thigh-high boots. How could he do this to me? My beautiful, perfect Jack. So he didn't show his emotions much, I liked a man to be strong. So he wasn't really romantic, but who wanted flowers, chocolates and cuddly teddy bears? So he didn't talk much, but he had a mighty fine bum for black Calvin Kleins. All of the girls in the office, bar the high-powered City lesbians, drooled at the sound of his authoritative yet sultry lawyer voice. How proud I had been when he had plucked me from the admiring throng to be his 'regular date'. My best friend Maz had strongly criticised my 'pathetically non-existent self-esteem' but I hadn't cared. At least I could walk through the office with a swagger, knowing that they seethed with jealousy at my every step.

Oh damn, the office. How could I go back there and face their knowing glances? The gossip would fly faster than a bee on amphetamines. Jennifer had thought he was going to propose. Ha ha ha. Jennifer had been unceremoniously dumped. Ha ha ha. Jack was now available. Every girl for herself! I would be a laughing stock, a mockery, a-lone.

Somehow things had got totally out of

proportion (not a rare occurrence on the odd night that I aim for total alcohol saturation). Jack had stood in front of me, his shoulders wide in his starched blue shirt, his square jaw shut tight with a strange, curious-yet-disgusted look in his dark eyes. I had wobbled in front of him, tears bursting out at all angles sending my apparently waterproof mascara rapidly southwards. I had given up trying to hold in my stomach, which had now broken for freedom between my size-too-small skirt and my sequined crop top.

'But Jacky Wacky, I luv you,' I had slobbered in an attempt to recreate Baby-Spice-esque vulnerability.

That had soon turned into Psycho Spice as Jack had replied coolly, 'But I don't love you, Jennifer. Not at all.'

The rumbling rage had started again, coupled with a real desire to throw up. My legal training skills had eluded me momentarily as all professional negotiation techniques flew out of the nearest window. It would be safe to say I lost my cool. The drink in the face had been a promising start, which led to the attempted headlock and the irreparable damage to the 'This cost £85 you know!' shirt. Shouted obscenities had followed that even Jim Davidson would have had trouble repeating. I had suddenly turned into a deranged, irrational extra from a particularly rough episode of *The Bill*. It was only when I had tried to remove Jack's hair and vital components simultaneously that the bemused bouncers had stepped in to put a stop to the cheap entertainment.

At 11:58 p.m. Jack had been forcefully removed from the club and told, in words of four letters or less, never to set foot on the ship again. By 11:59 p.m. I was slumped over the bar ordering a 'Steamy Passion' and pouring my heart out to Gareth, the adolescent glass-collector.

'Stwas sposed to be a shelabrayshun,' I had slurred. 'I got all dressed up shexy ya know (hiccup) . . . I am shexy 'in I?' I had shouted as 'Boom Shake Shake Shake the Room' blared over the speaker next to my ear.

'Aye,' Gareth had grunted, evidently more interested in the leopard-skin-clad voluptuous breasts that had just slunk into range.

Flippin' heck, I couldn't even interest an 18-year-old spotty Robbie Williams clone whose testosterone levels could overpower the National Grid. At 12:00 midnight, Big Ben had let rip, hugs and kisses had been exchanged beneath the silver disco ball and the DJ had unleashed his 'Songs for Special Occasions' LP on the unsuspecting revellers. I had taken a sip of 'Steamy Passion', got a glacé cherry lodged up my nose and fallen off my stool.

★   ★   ★

My intimate relationship with the toilet bowl was rudely interrupted when a horizontally-challenged Geordie barmaid decided to open the cubicle door with a Shearer-style hoof.

'Howay man lass,' she hollered in my face, 'gan yem will ya. I wanna leave this flippin' joint before next year ye kna.'

I know better than to provoke big lasses in leather hot pants, so I scrambled to my feet, almost losing my left arm down the toilet in the process.

'As you've asked so nicely I'll get going,' I said politely, through gritted teeth.

She stood in the doorway, one hand on each hip, drawing attention to the array of large metallic rings adorning each podgy hand. I wasn't sure whether they would fall within the legal definition of knuckle-dusters, but I was sober enough to realise that they would add a certain amount of kick to her left hook.

'Why-aye it's a gobby southerner who cannat tek her pints. What's the matter pet? Too many shandies?'

All of a sudden, ten replicas of my new

'friend' moved into view.

'Batter 'er man!' they yelled. 'Aye, chin the cheeky tramp!'

I suppressed the tears that were welling up in my eyes. I moved backwards gingerly until my legs touched the toilet bowl. At this point, I thought I'd better make a stand and try to look threatening (not an easy task when facing the oestrogen army).

'I'm not a southerner actually, I moved here when I was twelve.' Bloody hell, why do I suddenly sound like Fergie's sister in these critical situations?

My brain was reaching for the 'mouth shut' button with every word I blurted out. A roar of laughter broke forth from my assailants.

'A'im nort a southerner ayctually,' they squealed.

This is it, I thought. Two hours into the New Year and I was about to get my head pummelled as a bit of après-work entertainment. Not that anyone would care, of course. I mean, it's not like anyone loves me or anything. I was lost in self-pity, and felt warm tears trickling down my face. Mid-wallow, I suddenly realised the raucous laughter had stopped. I opened my eyes and looked up to see that the space in front of the cubicle had cleared. All that remained was my own hideous reflection in the mirror on the wall opposite.

'Blimey, I'm not even worth battering,' I moaned, trying to focus on the repulsive vision before me.

★　★　★

Why is it that enforced singledom has a strange doubling effect on the world? I become single, through no choice of my own, and all of a sudden the rest of the world moves in pairs. I'd found myself outside the nearest kebab shop and everywhere I looked there were couples 'fornicating' (as my mum would say) and, more to the point, enjoying it. All around me they kissed, cuddled, giggled and fed each other chips. Beautiful girls in spangly outfits held hands with their beautiful boyfriends and whispered sweet nothings in each other's ears as they made their way home to their perfect love nests. Even the dogs roaming the streets ran around in pairs, yelping happily. It was a night for romance and I wasn't invited to the party. The rest of the world was shoving it in my face and shouting 'Loser!' Gripped by a sudden urge to stage a large-scale massacre, I decided it was time to leave. I needed my best friend and fast.

★　★　★

Maz was like a breath of fresh air in a curry house kitchen. Boisterous, bold and scared of no man, she always knew the right thing to say to cheer me up. Her goal in life was to be a talk-show host on national television, airing problems and donning out advice. My ridiculously complicated love life had been a constant test of her counselling ability. Maz and I had been friends ever since my first day at high school. I was a 12-year-old Surrey convent schoolgirl with a very blinkered outlook on life. She was a born and bred Geordie lass. A fiery redhead with a checkered history who had fought her way to the position of top dog in the school. Luckily for me, Maz liked me from day one and probably saved me from being totally skinned on many an occasion. We were like chalk and cheese then and, ever since, our lives had taken completely diverging paths, but a hidden link seemed to hold us together and our friendship never faltered.

I instantly felt a pang of guilt at the thought of my friend. Maz and I had planned this night for weeks. Drinks at my flat, drinks in the pub where Maz worked as a barmaid, drinks in town at the Big Market and a general evening of drunken debauchery. Of course, at the last minute Jack's secretary had called and requested that I spend the evening with the arrogant pig. I should have said no but, as they say, love is blind and I am brainless. I had deserted my best, most loyal friend on New Year's Eve in favour of a man who had about as much interest in me as I had in a four-hour cricket special. Maz had warned me about him from the start and she had the annoying habit of always being right. I kicked myself at the realisation that I had become one of those love-struck girlies who would dump her friends at the first opportunity. Poor Maz, she had probably had a terrible night and it was entirely my fault. I vowed to make it up to her and, as I wanted some company, this seemed like a good time.

While deep in semi-sober thought, I walked headfirst into a taxi-rank sign, ignored the queue that stretched for miles down the street, and collapsed on the bonnet of a Vauxhall Cavalier. For the first half of the journey, the taxi driver listened dutifully to the Jack/engagement saga, even adding the odd grunt to prove he was still awake. It was only when I aired my views on castration for the 'soul-destroying bastards' (i.e. men) that he proceeded to swear in my ear, turn Metallica up to full volume and double the already extortionate fare. Ten long minutes later, I was deposited ungraciously outside Maz's front door.

Maz lived in a flat above the Scrap Inn pub (so named because of the scrap yard directly opposite) in a rough area of Byker on the outskirts of Newcastle. The flat was small and admittedly dingy but, as Maz liked to say, 'With less space to spread yer shite out in, you'll make less of a mess of yer life.' The pub was now closed so I made my way around the side of the building and tackled the mass of dustbins, beer crates and car parts that led to the back gate.

As was necessary in this particular area, the ten-foot black double gate was chained and padlocked in a manner reminiscent of the Great Houdini. Not fancying my chances of picking the lock, I chose instead, in my alcoholic wisdom, to climb on the bins and scale the obstacle. I realised my mistake when, with my micro skirt caught on a jagged plank and a PVC boot wedged against the adjacent wall, I looked down to see a small group of teenagers had gathered at the bottom of the gate.

'Why-aye woman,' shouted one Kappa-clad youngster, 'nice knickers yer wearin'. Give ya two pount fer them.' Hysterical laughter followed.

'Aye missus, show wur some more like!'

Shocked by the fact that I was being

sexually harassed by a group of pre-pubescent little runts, I suddenly turned into my mother.

'Don't be so disgusting you little . . . Shouldn't you be in bed by now? . . . Where are your parents? . . . Just wait till I tell them . . . '

'Gladiators ready!' roared the throng as they began to shake the gates furiously.

I held on for dear life as memories of many a PE lesson involving wall bars came flooding back. My pathetic threats and cries for help were lost amid the taunts of my juvenile attackers.

'Nice knickers.'

'Aye, lush shreddies!'

'Gis a shag missus!'

'Howay auld woman!'

'Ha ha ha.'

As the gate shaking became more and more furious, my glitter-varnished nails began to scrape painfully down the adjoining wall. I could feel the Lycra in my skirt straining as my post-Christmas body weight gave in to the force of gravity. One final shake, my skirt gave way and I plummeted headfirst and skirtless into the mountain of rubbish bags on the other side of the gate. My attackers cheered and roared with laughter. Their voices became more distant as they legged it into the nearby housing estate.

'Happy New Year y'auld slapper!' they yelled.

'Bollocks,' I groaned and slipped into darkness.

2

1st January, 10:00 p.m.

Maz and I lounged in my front room, surrounded by an impressive mosaic of comfort food wrappers. Having vowed, only this morning, never to touch alcohol again, we were doing a grand job of polishing off the entire contents of my wine rack. On the television, Julia Roberts was in the middle of a full-scale shopping extravaganza on Rodeo Drive with Richard Gere's gold card.

'How come a prostitute can get a rich lover who treats her like a queen and I can't get anyone?' I moaned through a mouthful of popcorn. 'I get put back on the shelf so much I'll be paying rent there soon.'

'Howay,' Maz sighed. 'You can get a fella, it's just you keep pickin' reet tossers.'

'Like who?'

'Like Jack.'

I was about to jump to his defence but noticed the menacing look in Maz's eyes. I turned my attention back to *Pretty Woman*.

'She's got curly hair but somehow she doesn't look like a walking bird's nest. How

17

does she do it?' I bit into a chocolate éclair. The cream oozed down the front of my sweatshirt.

'Could be somethin' to do with her figure, pet. She's got legs growin' oot of her armpits and a waist the size of an ankle. I doubt it's her personality he's after.'

'Yeah, I s'pose,' I groaned.

'Bitch,' we said in unison.

Maz was struggling with a packet of Jaffa Cakes while trying to balance a full glass of wine on her knee. I glanced enviously at her telescopically long legs. Maz could give Julia Roberts a run for her money any day. I was just considering going out to find a fat, ugly friend to make me feel better when Maz ripped open the packet, sending Jaffa Cakes flying in all directions and emptying the contents of her glass all over my trackie bottoms.

'Ooops!' she giggled.

'Oh my best outfit.' I faked distress. 'These cost £4.99 from Quality Seconds you know.'

We roared with laughter and began throwing any pieces of food we could lay our hands on at each other. I emptied a bowl of tortilla chips on Maz's head. She retaliated with a lemon meringue pie.

'Stop! Not the Häagen-Dazs!' Maz roared. 'I wanna eat that!'

'I'm going to be sick,' I laughed, clutching my stomach.

'You could turn professional after last neet!'

I collapsed back on the sofa and thought back to my New Year's Eve. The nightmare had ended only at eight o'clock this morning when I had woken up to find Maz and a stunning Italian-looking chap gazing down at me as I lay among the rubbish bags in the pub yard. Maz had been considering getting the Italian stallion to give me mouth to mouth but I had stirred at precisely the wrong moment. Bloody typical.

'What the hell are ya doin', man?' Maz had whispered, as if not wanting to break the uncomfortable silence. 'Are ya al'reet like?'

'Me? Yep, fine, morning guys,' I had chirped. 'Fancy a coffee?' (Act cool and no one will notice. Always the worst policy.)

'But Jen, pet, you're sleepin' in our rubbish tip.'

'Mmmm, yep.'

'And . . . and you're not wearin' a skirt.'

I had looked down to see my attempt at seductive lingerie was on show for the world and his uncle. Unfortunately, the slimline pull-me-in knickers and black Lycra hold-ups seemed to have given way to the large volume of flesh shoved inside them. Pasty white thighs oozed out of every possible space in a manner guaranteed to put Maz's incredibly foxy date off his breakfast. He looked like the sort of person who would never have come into contact with cellulite before.

Having muttered something about being mugged, drugged and abandoned, I had been carefully extracted from the debris and shepherded into Maz's car (aptly named 'The Shoe', being smaller than most shoe boxes) much to the amusement of her new friend. 'Paolo' was left to fend for himself in Maz's usual disinterested manner. It was clear that her night without me had not been as terrible as I had imagined.

The first day of the New Year had been spent nursing a hangover and getting in training for another one. Ludicrous amounts of food were consumed and my flat had been turned into a haven of self-pity. It was only when I had suggested playing my entire library of a-ha songs that Maz had realised the extent of my depression. If Maz ever heard the voices of Morten Harket and his two Norwegian friends coming from my flat, she knew things were bad.

'Do you think I should dye my hair blonde?' I asked, pulling at a bedraggled curl which could only be described as 'mousy-brown'.

'Na, not blonde,' said my flame-haired friend.

'What about my bum?'

'What, dye it blonde?'

'No you idiot, is it too fat? Has it volumised over Christmas?'

'Not really.'

'Not really! That's just what he said. What's that supposed to mean?'

'He who?'

'Jack.'

'Ah howay. Dain't listen to a word that plonker tells you. He's a pig, Jen, and he isny fit to do up the buckle on yer sandals.'

Maz grabbed another packet of crisps and fiddled with the remote control. In fact, my friend was rarely to be seen without some sort of food, drink or fag in her mouth. Despite that fact, Maz remained irritatingly thin. I put it down to her having more space to spread the calories out in, being 5'10". I was much more 'compressed', shall we say, being an average 5'5", size 12 and completely tone-free. Let's face it, mine didn't even deserve the title 'body'. Elle 'the Body' Macpherson. Jennifer 'the Blimp' Summer. Average, average, average.

'The problem with you, Jen,' Maz said between mouthfuls, 'is your low self-esteem.'

(Oh here we go again.)

'You reckon you need a man to make you feel confident so when he gives you the elbow you fall apart. You feel shite.'

'Says who?'

'Trisha.'

'What, she said 'shite' on TV?'

'No, I'm improvisin', like. If you've got low self-esteem, pet, a man just meks it canny worse, I tell you. You've gotta start lovin' yerself furst, Jen.'

Miss Talk-Show Host was in full swing. I knew she was right but I pretended not to listen and just nodded sarcastically. Maz knew all the phrases from all the shows. *Trisha, Ricki Lake, Jenny Jones,* they were all Maz's sources of inspiration. Even the tough-nut regulars in the pub were forced to endure three hours of talk shows most afternoons as Maz soaked up the gossip. Mind you, none of them dared to complain, Maz didn't take any nonsense.

Maz's unorthodox upbringing had prepared her for most eventualities and probably gave her a good basis for solving problems. Maz had been there, done it, nicked the T-shirt. After her mother died, Maz had been left to care for a family that became completely dysfunctional. Her dad didn't have the slightest interest in his three children. At school, some of us had thought it would be pretty cool to have a father who would let you do whatever you wanted but, for Maz, the reality was far from idyllic. All through school, she had juggled her studies and part-time jobs to try to keep the family afloat. Her dad would disappear for weeks at a time and, when he was home, he was like a distant stranger. The combination of no love and no money took its toll. Maz had failed her exams, gone to work in a pub and built up her tough exterior. Her eldest brother Dave had got involved in petty crime and finally took up residence in Durham jail. James, the middle child, had headed for the London drug and club scene and was never heard from again.

★ ★ ★

'Let's dae a makeover,' Maz yelled, suddenly leaping up from the sofa.

'What? This isn't the Richard and Judy show you know.'

'Howay man, it'll be a laff.'

'I don't need a makeover, Maz, I need Jack.'

The mention of his name made me feel instantly depressed.

'Jack bollocks,' Maz groaned. 'Look, Miss Summer, you're an intelligent lass with a lush

23

job, a geet nice flat and bags of opportunities but you can be reet stupid sometimes. Jack is a poncey twat who's messed you aboot for the last ten months and given you nowt but trouble. Now get over it, Jen, and stop bein' such a miserable cow.'

She grabbed my arm and pulled me to my feet.

'Get off yer backside and let's cheer worselves up!'

Ten minutes into the 'Copper Charm' hair dye activation period, the telephone rang.

'Hello Jennifer, it's Mother.'

'Hi Mum. Can I call you back? I'm in the middle of — '

'I just called to wish you Happy New Year seeing as you hadn't bothered to call.'

I could feel a lecture coming on from the dragon lady of the Summer family.

'Daddy is doing the crossword and I am terribly bored. I expected you to be here for dinner, darling. It is a New Year after all, or are you too busy with your own little friends to bother with your family any more?'

My mother had a very annoying habit of talking to me as if I was still in my first training bra. Whenever she called, I knew I was in for one of her guilt trips.

'Sorry, Mum, but I've had a bad day. I . . . '

'At least your sister keeps in touch on these occasions . . . '

(Bloody Susie.)

' . . . Susie is wonderful, darling. She appreciates us you know. If you had bothered to call, I would have invited you to dinner and Daddy would love to show you the new fencing he put up in the garden.'

Oooh, exciting. My poor, downtrodden father. He had obviously spent a long New Year's Day outside, trying to avoid the nagging of his tyrannical wife. Hogmanay would have been spent alcohol- and vice-free, not by choice of course. If Dad so much as sneezed or breathed too heavily, Mum would chase him with the hand-held Hoover and totally disinfect the surrounding area. Her house was so much like a show home, it amazed me how any normal human being could reside there without going completely insane.

I realised my mother was still talking at me. Out of the corner of my eye, I could also see Maz jumping up and down wildly and pointing at my hair.

'Bring your young man.'

'Where?'

'To dinner, Jennifer. I said bring James.'

'Jack.'

'That's right. I'll get the beds ready.'

25

Beds. Noticeably plural. There was no chance of scoring a bit of horizontal lambada at Mum's house. How I was ever procreated is one of life's little mysteries.

'Jack and I aren't together any more, Mum. He — '

'Oh Jennifer. What did you do this time?'

'Me? Why do you automatically assume it was my fault? I didn't do anything . . . '

'Oh Jennifer, I despair, really I do. Honestly dahling.'

Dahling. Ever since moving up North, my mother had become increasingly southern. Only areas south of Northampton were regarded as acceptable by her and her stuck-up friends.

I was beginning to tire of the voice droning on in my ear and I was aware of the need to rinse my hair.

'Look Mum, I really must go . . . '

' . . . Susie and her husband are so fantastic together . . . '

'Yeah look, I'll call you later . . . '

' . . . Why you can't be more like her I'll never know . . . '

Because I'd probably have to kill myself. 'OK, bye Mum.'

' . . . Sebastian is such a nice chap . . . '

'Mum, please . . . '

' . . . Were you drinking?'

'Mum, I . . . '

' . . . I don't know where I went wrong with you . . . '

'MUM!'

'Yes dahling?'

'BYE!'

'Oh . . . yes . . . goodb — '

I slammed the phone down and ran to the bathroom. Maz was about to shove my head in the basin when the phone rang for a second time.

'Aye, what d'ya want? . . . Who? . . . Aye, a'reet.'

'Jen!' Maz hollered. 'It's some posh git from gusset and jockstrap!'

Glisset & Jacksop. My law firm. My boss!

'Hello.'

'Miss Summer? This is Peregrine Bottomley-Glisset here. I'm so glad I caught you on New Year's Day. Are you busy, Miss Summer?'

'Hmmm, no, no not at all Mr Bottomley-Glisset.'

I rubbed the red dye out of my stinging eyes. 'Copper Charm' had now had about thirty-five minutes to activate.

'I am in the office, Miss Summer, and I see you have a holiday booked for tomorrow.'

'Yes, yes that's right.'

'Anything nice planned?'

'Ummm, yes. Well no, nothing special actually, just relaxing you know. I've been feeling a little under the weather and I — '

'Good. Cancel it.'

'Pardon me?'

'Cancel it, Miss Summer.'

'Certainly Mr Bottomley-Glisset.' (He can't do this to me!)

'I want you in the office at seven-thirty sharp.'

(Yeah right, as if.) 'Of course. Seven thirty. I'll be there.'

'Excellent. Goodnight, Miss Summer.'

'Goodnight. Happy New Year.'

He had already rung off.

'Bastard!' I screamed and ran to the bathroom.

Maz forced my head into the freezing cold water, which turned a hideous shade of orange in an instant. I decided at that point that this wasn't the best cure for an apocalyptic hangover. I came up for air just as the telephone rang for a third time.

'Leave it!' Maz shouted, almost drowning me as she pushed my head into the basin.

I heard the answering machine click into action.

Glug, glug, gasp.

' . . . Jack here . . . '

I struggled to get free but Maz was

28

determined to rinse my hair.

Glug, glug, glug.

' . . . to see you if possible . . . '

Glug, gasp.

' . . . I want it . . . '

Glug, glug.

' . . . a date and . . . '

Glug.

' . . . don't mind . . . '

Gasp.

' . . . love . . . '

At last I wriggled free and ran to the phone in the hallway. My hand reached the receiver just as I heard a click from the other end.

'Damn!' I yelled. 'Maz did you hear that? He wants to go on a date with me.'

I felt as excited as I had done on receiving my first Valentine card. Oh life was so simple then.

'He loves me, Maz. I knew he'd want me back.'

'Um, Jen, hang on a minute, pet.'

I was too hormonal to listen. My self-esteem had just rocketed to new, dizzy heights.

'He loves me. I'm sexy. I'm gorgeous. I'm a couple again.'

I grabbed the receiver and took a deep breath. This was not the time to play hard to get.

'Wait up, pet,' said Maz, trying to peel my fingers from the phone. 'You're like a dog on heat, man. Just calm doon and listen will you.'

'Let go, Maz! I know you don't like him but he's my boyfriend . . . '

'Yer 'regular date' you mean.'

'Yes, well whatever. I love him and I'll call him if I bloody well like.'

My raging hormones were making me completely unreasonable. I dived for the telephone buttons just as the doorbell rang.

'It's Jack!' I screamed hysterically.

'You're canny mental,' Maz replied.

I flung the door open with a huge, beaming grin and came face to face with my neighbour Mrs Diasio. She was the wife of the local pizzeria owner and not-so-secret mistress of my hideous landlord, Mr Brown. In fact, Maz said she was like a doorknob, everybody got a turn. She was an infuriating woman who stuck her nose into everyone's business and thought herself to be well above her station.

'Good heavens!' Mrs Diasio exclaimed. She looked at me with a peculiar gaze.

'Yes, what?' I replied impolitely.

'The thingy outaside.' She pointed towards the stairs. 'That poor excuso for a motor car.'

'Aye, that's my car,' Maz butted in.

'Moove it a'now.'

30

'Why?'

'It looks a'terrible. Ita devalue my property.'

'Bollocks!' we said in chorus.

'It'sa in my space so mooove it eh? Otherwise, I get a'someone to moove ita for you.'

'Oooooh big deal,' Maz shouted, stretching to her full height above the little Italian. 'Who are you gonna get, the Godfather?'

I didn't like to cause a fracas with the neighbours, as I had been lucky to get such a good flat in the first place. It was situated in the newly developed quayside area of Newcastle and was brilliantly close to work. Mrs Diasio was a particular threat due to her undoubted connection with the landlord. She had also never been particularly fond of me. I guessed it had something to do with the time Maz had come over for an especially raucous girls' night in and had puked on Mrs Diasio's white Persian cat. The poor, hairy thing had never looked quite the same since.

'We're actually busy at the moment, Mrs Diasio,' I said politely, trying to calm the situation.

'Beezy, huh! Doin'a what? Dressing up as clowns?'

I didn't quite grasp her intended insult so I brushed it aside.

'I'm sorry but I have to make an important phone call,' I replied.

'Mooove it!' she screamed.

'Ah piss off ya mad cow,' Maz interjected.

At that, my neighbour flew into a Latino rage. Knowing the average length of such outbursts, I went for gold, there was no time to waste.

'See ya,' I said and slammed the door in her face.

Maz and I took one look at each other and burst out laughing. We paused momentarily then I made a dash for the telephone. Before I could dial Jack's number, Maz pressed the play button on the answering machine.

Beep . . . 'Hello there, Jenny, it's Jack here. Everything fine I hope? A little less hysterical now perhaps? I wanted . . . um . . . to come over and see you, if possible. It's just, I . . . er . . . think I left a rather nice new shirt at your flat and I want it for this week. Um . . . well . . . Vicky and I are going on a date and I need something to wear, to impress, you know. I hope you don't mind but . . . um . . . I'd love to have it for the night. Yes, well, I guess I'll see you in the office, Jenny. Happy New Year by the way. Bye.' Beep.

I stared open mouthed at the machine as if it was lying to me. My feet were stuck to the floor and my whole body was weak. In the space of thirty seconds, I felt as if my heart had been ripped out and trampled on by a herd of stampeding rhinos. How could he? Jack, my Jack, was going on a date with Vicky, my secretary. My Jack who, less than twenty-four hours ago, had told me he needed space, that he didn't want the commitment right now. I wanted to deny it but it was there in front of me on tape. The same man had broken my heart twice in the space of one day.

I felt an arm on my shoulder and glanced up to see Maz looking down at me sympathetically.

'I tried to tell you, Jen,' she whispered, 'but you went all hyper on us.'

'I'm so stupid,' I moaned, as tears began to trickle down my red-stained face.

'Shush now, pet, you're not stupid. He isny worth it. He's just an arrogant tosser. Howay, let's sit doon.'

Maz kept a protective arm around my shoulder and guided me back towards the living room.

'I hate this year already,' I moaned.

'I know,' Maz replied, 'but it cannat get any worse eh?'

I forced a smile just as we passed the mirror in the hallway. I happened to look up and caught a glimpse of my reflection. I stopped dead and stared in horror.

'My hair!' I screamed. 'What's happened to my hair?'

'Oh,' Maz stuttered. 'Um, it isny that bad.'

'Not bad!' I shrieked. 'Oh my God, Maz, it's luminous orange!'

Things had just got worse.

3

2nd January, 8:15 a.m.

His hand brushed mine as he reached across the desk for the brief. He glanced up, his dark eyes penetrating my own with breathtaking intensity. I gasped and looked away coyly, sensing his gaze as my hair cascaded sexily over my pronounced cheekbone. After a short silence he spoke.

'We must win this case, Jennifer, for the sake of the firm and for our incredibly wealthy clients.'

'Yes.' I blushed and nervously shuffled the papers on the table in front of me. Tom, the beautifully toned, highly intelligent and stunningly rich hotshot American attorney on this case, fiddled with a baseball bat (found randomly in a corner of the room) and stared fixedly at our complicated flow chart of the facts.

'Gee, I know we're missing something,' he said pensively, 'but I'm darned if I know what it is.'

We were running out of time. The lives of our clients hung in the balance yet the answer eluded us. If only I could find the missing link. We would be victorious, I would be the sultry heroine and surely Tom would find me completely irresistible. Suddenly, my mind cleared and an idea sprang forth like an apparition. That was it, the missing link!

'Tom,' I purred passionately.

He turned provocatively to face me. We were all alone in the meeting room and I could feel the chemistry between us. We were powerless to stop it. I took a deep breath, opened my mouth to speak the words, the music building to an alarming crescendo, and —

RING, RING!

'Shit.'

I woke up with a start as the noise almost perforated my eardrum. I always got interrupted just as I reached the good bit. Blimey, I couldn't even get satisfaction in my dreams.

'Can't a girl get any sleep around here?' I muttered, reaching for the phone. 'Jennifer Summer speaking,' I yawned.

'Peregrine Bottomley-Glisset,' bawled a voice at the other end. 'Just checking to see how the documents are coming along.'

I woke up instantly and replied in my best alert/interested voice.

'Oh perfectly, almost done, absolutely no problems at all.'

Jesus, I'm surprised I didn't end the sentence with 'old chap'. I could get an ex-pat part in *Dad's Army* with that voice.

'Excellent. Now be sure to check every page from top to bottom won't you? This is a very important matter and the meeting is this morning. Any problems and I'll be on the golf course.'

There was no time for pleasantries as my boss rang off and, no doubt, headed for the nineteenth hole.

'Oh, the life of a trainee solicitor,' I sighed to myself.

I grabbed the next document in the seemingly bottomless pile.

★　★　★

I had wanted to be a lawyer since career week in the fourth year at school. The gorgeous, almost edible older brother of one of my classmates had come in to give us a talk on life as a solicitor in Newcastle. From that moment on, most of the girls set their hearts on legal careers, for all the wrong reasons of course. (The boys seemed to go for the nursing option. It could have had something to do with the young nurse's rather minimalist uniform.)

The fantasy had stayed with me all through

GCSEs and A-levels then on to university. I had visions of living my life in the fast lane of a John Grisham movie set. The reality, of course, was a far cry from that Hollywood ideal. I was still waiting for 'Tom' to walk into my office and ask me to get on his case. We didn't sit around in trendy bars 'bouncing' ideas off each other or indulge in convoluted brainstorming sessions as we sweated sexily in the gym. You could say that was obvious but I couldn't help it if my mind chose to live in a dream world while my body trudged around in grim reality.

Over the twenty-three months that I had spent with the firm, I had learned to think like my colleagues: to live my life in the future, looking forward to the day I made Partner and got the rich pickings. That would not be for at least seven years, if at all, but everyone in our hierarchical, grey little world seemed to find that sufficient motivation.

At this point, though, I was nothing more than a female trainee. In a profession existing in its own bizarrely archaic world, I was the lowest of the low, valued less than the cappuccino machine. No job was too tedious, no hour too sacred. I could proofread with one eye, photocopy like a demon and make a cup of tea that Earl Grey would be proud of. I was kept going by the fact that my training was almost complete. In just four weeks, I would qualify as a fully fledged solicitor and, if Glisset & Jacksop agreed to keep me on, I would step up a rung on that career ladder.

★   ★   ★

I read the same paragraph about four times as I tried to assimilate the facts and make any relevant changes.

5.5: All products referred to in Annex 3 hereof shall remain the property of the aforementioned television company, hereinafter referred to as 'The Vendor' . . . blah, blah . . . forthwith shall be delivered . . . rhubarb, rhubarb . . . shall be returned in their original condition . . . waffle, blah, blah . . . as referred to in clause 3.6 hereof . . . the purchaser . . . yawn, waffle . . . as referred to . . . Jack, waffle, sigh.

Damn. I had the concentration span of a retarded goldfish. I couldn't get Jack out of my mind, and having to read incredibly dull documents wasn't helping at all. The words were beginning to float on the page and they didn't seem to make any sense whatsoever. Of course, I couldn't possibly blame my poor brain capacity on the outstanding amounts of junk food and alcohol I had consumed over the past two days. I decided I must be coming down with something.

Thinking back to the disastrous start to my year, I realised how glad I had been of Maz's company. If it hadn't been for her surgically removing me from underneath my duvet and kicking me into the shower, I definitely would not have made it to work this morning. I would probably still be snuggled up in twenty-four togs with my mind wandering along a distant, romantic beach. I didn't know whether to love her or hate her.

Food. I needed calories to get me through this. Maz had brought over a batch of homemade muffins from one of the regulars at the pub, which I had skilfully removed from the flat as I left for work. I grabbed one and began extracting the blueberries before shoving the entire sumptuous mass in my mouth. Only 8:45 a.m. and I had already reached number four on the cake count. Seeing as they were a present, I felt obliged to eat my way to muffin-induced obesity. I like to support the view that food cures most ills, including stress. I wasn't exactly feeling stressed, though, more like totally spaced out, away with the fairies, out there on a planet with Anthea Turner.

★　★　★

'Cute headscarf, babe,' whispered the voice in my ear. 'Auditioning for *The Sound of Music*, are we?'

'Piss off,' I muttered, glancing up to see Matt, the other trainee in my department, looking at me with some amusement.

'If you're going for the innocent, virginal look, darling, don't bother,' he giggled effeminately. 'We all saw you in action at the Chrimbo party.'

'What do you mean?' I asked, trying to think back to my last day in the office before the festive break. With the events of the past two days preoccupying my mind, I had completely forgotten about any previous misdemeanours.

'Oh come on, Jennifer,' Matt laughed. 'You were pissed as a fart.'

(Uh-oh.)

'I think the bar had a lower alcohol content than you had.'

(Not good.)

'Jacksop nearly had a heart attack, the doddery old fool.'

(Help!)

I grabbed Matt's arm, pulled him into the nearest empty office, and quickly shut the door.

'OK, talk!' I yelled and braced myself for the gory details.

41

I was always slightly uncomfortable at office-dos. I never seemed to know quite how to behave in a social manner towards people whom I would never *choose* to associate with, but on whom I relied for my monthly pay packet. Faced with a room full of ancient Partners and aspiring bright-young-things, I turned from one of the latter into a bumbling, brainless, curly-topped bimbo, apparently incapable of engaging in any form of intellectual conversation. Unfortunately, I was also a great believer in the virtues of Dutch courage and, hence, usually formed an intimate relationship with the free bar. I wasn't totally surprised, therefore, by Matt's report on my recent festive behaviour.

Bit by bit, the night's events came flooding back as my bemused colleague recounted the tale.

Me, telling everyone that Jack and I would soon be husband and wife.

Jack spending most of the party engaged in deep conversation with the lovely Vicky.

Me, debating alternative childbirth methods with the Senior Partner and discussing suitable colours for a nursery.

Jack seeking refuge behind the eight-foot tall ice sculpture . . . with the lovely Vicky.

Me, trying to catch Jack's attention by dancing seductively in the centre of the room

. . . with the Senior Partner.

Jack trying to drag me outside for air . . . with the help of the lovely Vicky.

Me, choosing to audition for work as a table dancer, slipping on the artichoke salad and landing head down, M&S knickers up, in the lap of Mr Jacksop . . . the Senior Partner.

I was mortified. The night Jack had dumped me, he had mentioned my 'periodic outbursts of outrageous and completely unacceptable behaviour'. I had thought he was totally unjustified and put it down to a spur of the moment insult, but now I was beginning to see his point.

I looked at Matt, who was clutching his stomach and laughing hysterically. He appeared to be slightly out of focus but I thought that was probably just a symptom of the shock I was suffering.

'Oh no, it's true,' I groaned. 'I am a total disaster area. No wonder he doesn't want me, I don't deserve someone like Jack. I do have 'outbursts of outrageous and completely unacceptable behaviour'.'

'Hey don't worry, darling.' Matt put a well-manicured hand on my shoulder and shook his head sympathetically. 'You're great, Jenny, and you gave the rest of us a good laugh.'

He laughed loudly and made for the door.

'I'd just steer clear of Jacksop for a while, hon, you wouldn't want to kill the poor man off.'

He clapped his hands together and wiggled out of the door, leaving me standing alone and feeling foolish.

'Oh great,' I said aloud, 'I'm totally outrageous and a right 'laugh'. Hardly the tough, professional, lawyer-like manner I was aiming for.'

I suddenly felt rather light-headed and needed to sit down. My mind was racing and I felt queasy. I blamed it on hunger and headed for the muffins.

★ ★ ★

'My office, Miss Summer,' boomed the voice. 'Two minutes, and bring the documents.'

Peregrine Bottomley-Glisset stormed past my desk, sending papers flying in all directions as his portly rear tried to squeeze into the relatively small space. As a result of his unmistakable presence, secretaries, trainees and less-senior solicitors rushed around frantically trying to look busy. Personal calls instantly metamorphosed into serious business matters and all idle banter drew to a hasty conclusion.

'Sure thing, Perry,' I said dreamily into thin

44

air, lolling back in my seat and slapping my feet on the desk in front of me. I began to gaze at my computer monitor.

'Wow, that screen saver's cool,' I said after a while.

I stared at the monitor and was transfixed by the computer-generated images of fish that swam around the screen. The blue angel fish wiggled in and out of focus while the orange piranha's repetitive movements made me feel slightly seasick. I slowly came out of the daze and shouted to Matt across the corridor partition.

'Matt, hey, yo!'

'Yes Jen,' he replied hurriedly, looking up from behind a huge mound of work.

'These fish are really cool!' I shouted.

'What?'

'Fish. I said fish. Aren't they cool? They just swim about all day with not a care in the world. What a life, eh? Don't you reckon, Matt? Matt?'

'Um, yeah. Yeah, sure, Jenny hon, whatever.'

He looked over at me and shrugged his shoulders then returned to his work.

After a pause I shouted, 'Great colours. Really vibrant. I love bright colours, don't you, Matt?'

No reply.

'Oh well, suit yerself.'

My mind was racing and I had a bursting urge to talk and laugh. I still felt slightly sick but was also experiencing a strange calmness. I returned my gaze to the monitor and tried to focus on the images. Wowza, the colours were brilliant.

Suddenly, a large red fish swam to the front of the picture and wiggled his fins. I say 'his' because, as he did so, he winked at me provocatively. As I stared dumbfounded at the screen, the fish's lips appeared to move and I heard a muffled voice say, 'Hello, Miss Summer.' I jumped backwards, knocking the documents off my desk with my feet. They scattered across the floor, surrounding my desk with a papery moat.

'Wow!' I shouted. 'It spoke to me. I heard it speak.'

'Miss Summer!' I heard again, this time a little louder.

I stared open-mouthed at the screen and tried to focus. I felt like I was losing track of reality. This was all just too bizarre.

'MISS SUMMER!'

The voice boomed in my ear, only this time, I could feel the hot breath that went with it sliding down the back of my neck. I spun around in my chair to see the burning red face of Peregrine Bottomley-Glisset dangerously close to mine.

'TRAINEE!' he yelled. 'What the blazes are you doing?'

I couldn't think clearly. I didn't know what to say.

'I called you into my office twenty minutes ago. Twenty! I do not expect to be kept waiting! Are you stupid or just completely mad?'

I shrugged my shoulders.

'Where are the DOCUMENTS?'

He was perilously close to boiling point. I pointed to the papers underneath his feet.

'Good God woman!' he shouted. 'This is not good enough.'

He brought his face closer to mine. I could feel the heat radiating from him and could see the veins popping out of his thick neck. I could almost count each pulse as it hit the surface. I held his gaze as we faced each other in silence and I brought my feet slowly to the floor. It struck me how comical he looked, a huge mass of bubbling anger. I opened my mouth to speak but suddenly felt an irrepressible urge to laugh. I tried to suppress it but it seemed to come from nowhere. I started to giggle, then to laugh. I wanted to stop but I was out of control. My boss's face took on a look of astonishment. He straightened up to leave but I whacked him on the back.

'Hey, chill out, Perry. You'll give yourself a bloody heart attack, man!'

★ ★ ★

I couldn't believe what had just happened. The world had seemed to move in slow motion as every eye in the room had turned towards me in disbelief. I had run from the room and headed straight for the ladies' loo. I splashed cold water on my face and took a few deep breaths of stale toilet air.

'You are out of control, missy,' I said to my reflection.

The room was swaying gently and stars twinkled in front of my eyes.

'I must be sick,' I said aloud. 'This is a total nightmare and now I'm talking to myself.'

After my display of lunacy, Peregrine had been rushed to the safety of his office by his ever-capable secretary, who had, no doubt, been ordered to locate my P45. Fortunately for me, he had been unable to deal with the matter immediately as our clients had arrived for the scheduled meeting. I knew I was in trouble. In my profession, Partners are revered by all those who scurry beneath them. They had put in their years of hard slog and expected to be treated with the utmost respect. Some took it too far, of course, refusing to even acknowledge the existence of a mere trainee in their presence. Compliments, polite 'hellos' and severe butt-licking were all well received. I thought it was safe to assume that my recent actions had over-stepped the mark on the trainee/Partner relationship scale. All I could do now was try to be inconspicuous and hope that my morning's work had attained an unprecedented level of perfection.

*   *   *

'Let us commence, ladies and gentlemen,' growled the female Partner who was chairing the meeting.

The atmosphere in the conference room turned decidedly wealthy as one of the firm's major clients, the owner and President of Paradise TV, was led through the door by none other than my beloved Jack.

This was a very important day for all those working on the Paradise TV account. Many hours of work had gone into the subject of today's meeting, the takeover by Paradise of a leading competitor. The takeover, when finalised, would make Paradise the largest and most influential television network in the North-East. Jack, as the leading Assistant

Solicitor on the matter, would benefit greatly from the smooth running of the deal as far as his reputation within the firm was concerned. The name of the firm would also become even more widely known and the Partners' holiday-homes-in-Barbados fund would be bumped up quite nicely. Because of the obvious benefits, these meetings always involved a large amount of sucking up, which was lapped up by the clients, and a certain amount of rushing around and showing off.

I tried to look as inconspicuous as possible in a dark corner of the large room. I was happy to notice that Mr Jacksop had chosen not to join us, probably for fear of being subjected to another table dance experience. As silence descended on the gathered crowd, I noticed an irate-looking Peregrine glaring at me across the table. I sank into my seat and began to furiously take notes about absolutely nothing. As all the eyes in the room turned towards yours truly, I could feel my cheeks begin to glow. The more I thought about not blushing, the redder I seemed to become, until my face felt like a chaffed orang-utan's bum. The silence felt more painful than being forced to watch end-to-end episodes of *Noel's House Party* with no means of escape. Finally, I looked up and smiled pitifully at the room full of suits.

'Miss Summer,' Peregrine growled, 'you are not in the farmyard now. Please remove that ridiculous headscarf.'

Despite not wanting to reveal my Toyah-esque hair-do with its overdose of 'Copper Charm', I knew better than to argue with my boss in this frame of mind. Slowly, I untied the knot beneath my chin and watched the faces around me change as the bright orange curls revealed their true glory. The whole room gasped loudly and I sat there, feeling like the ginger Thompson Twin after a radioactive fallout incident.

'GOOD LORD!' Peregrine screeched. 'Whatever next?'

'Nice one, babe,' Matt whispered.

'Sod off,' I muttered, catching the look of sheer disgust in Jack's wide eyes.

At that point, the girl from catering reached my corner of the room with the coffeepot.

'Nice hair, lass,' she chirped loudly. 'That rocks!'

'Black with five sugars,' I hissed, and hurriedly began to pass the documents around the room.

The meeting got under way and my obscure hair colouring was momentarily forgotten. The conference room was warm and, as I sipped my sweet coffee, I began to feel sleepy. My eyes were starting to feel heavy and I could feel myself slipping into my own hazy little world. I began to dream of the last time that Jack and I had been together.

He lay next to me on the sofa, transfixed by a fascinating article on financial markets in *The Times*. We had just finished watching *A Question of Sport* and were waiting for a documentary Jack wanted to watch on the Stock Market and international trade. OK, I'll admit it doesn't sound like the most riveting of evenings but I convinced myself I just enjoyed his company. Anyway, I knew there would be more to look forward to later. We did actually wait until the end of *Stock Market Focus* to get it on, but that had given me a full forty-five minutes to warm up mentally. Jack was not a great one for foreplay so I usually took it upon myself to think about the act far enough in advance to ensure I got the most out of it.

His clothes were folded neatly on the chair with his Burlington socks rolled carefully inside his loafers. I stared at his body. Wow, it was fit. For a man who spent the majority of his life in an office, he was extremely toned and chocolate brown. The tan was from a bottle, of course, but it was amazingly effective. He went to a salon to have it done because, he said, it was more professional that way. Everything had to be so perfect with Jack. Lying back on the bed, with my skin against his, I looked as if I had spent my last few holidays in the Arctic Circle. After having spent the winter in the North-East, and too lazy to bother with fake tan, I looked almost transparent. Golden brown met albumen white, with a hint of pink.

He smiled down at me, emphasising the square shape of his jaw. Matt had said, 'Never trust a man who looks like he swallowed a table mat.' I didn't care. His jaw line made him look strong, serious and wonderfully masculine. I looked into his dark, almost black eyes and melted in his arms. Jack always liked Missionary best. I guessed it was because, from that position, he could see his own reflection in my dressing-table mirror, but I didn't like to pry. Anyway, who wouldn't want to look at a body like his? He was perfect.

I started to tremble as I felt his hips moving above me. I could feel the pleasure and sense the anticipation between us. Usually, Jack liked us to be the silent type, but this time I couldn't contain myself.

'Mmmmm Jack,' I groaned, licking my lips. 'Jack, oh yes Jack.'

He moved faster and I caught the glint in his eye. I wanted to explode.

'Jack,' I murmured. 'Oh yes Jack, JACK!'

'For God's sake, SHUT UP YOU IDIOT!'

A familiar voice bellowed very close to my eardrum. Reality came zooming back and I opened my eyes to see a conference room full of people staring at me incredulously. All I could see were wide open mouths and pair upon pair of huge, staring eyes.

'You stupid, mad fool,' said Jack in a loud whisper beside me. 'What has got into you? Have you forgotten what an important meeting this is? You sounded like you were having an orgasm.'

'First time for everything,' I beamed, tossing my hair dramatically.

Sniggers and splutters flew around the room but were soon silenced when an equally irritable Peregrine piped up, 'I don't know what has got into you, Miss Summer.'

'Jack, from the sounds of it,' added one brave voice.

'You are acting like a lunatic,' my boss continued, 'and as for these so-called documents you prepared, they are complete and utter gobbledegook.'

I reached for the papers and skim-read the first few paragraphs. He was right, it was total nonsense.

'Oops!' was all I could muster as a response.

'GET OUT!' yelled Peregrine. 'Get out of my sight!'

His temperature was rising quicker than a middle-aged woman's at a Cliff Richard concert. I guessed it was time to make a hasty retreat.

★ ★ ★

'Shish kebab!' I exclaimed as I ran for my ringing telephone. 'This is not a good day. I think I've totally lost it . . . Hello, Jennifer Summer here.'

'Jen, man, it's me lass,' rambled a very excited Maz at the other end of the line. 'Are you OK, pet?'

'OK?' I repeated. 'I am far from OK, Maz. I think I've gone completely mental. I'm rambling, hallucinating, making terrible mistakes . . . '

'I've tried to call four times.'

' . . . laughing at my boss, seeing talking fish on my computer screen . . . '

'Ah shite, it's all my fault.'

' . . . messing up the most important meeting of the year . . . '

'Damn, the bloody muffins.'

' . . . orgasming in public.'

I stopped for a breath and slowly rewound the conversation. Something Maz had said was resounding in my brain.

'Maz, what did you mean by 'damn the bloody muffins'?'

I could hear my friend coughing nervously. It was very unlike Maz to be stuck for words.

'Maz?'

'The ... um ... the muffins,' she stuttered. 'They're from the pub. This woman brought them in for us and I thought they looked nice, like. I didny kna.'

'Kna, I mean *know* what exactly?'

'I ... um ... I didny kna they were hash muffins. Well, not really.'

'WHAT?' I shouted. 'What did you say?'

'You kna, lass, hash muffins. You weren't supposed to tek them all, Jen.'

'HASH,' I shouted. 'HASH. WHAT DO YOU MEAN, HASH?'

'Hash. Like marijuana, dope, pot, tack, hash!' Maz shouted back. 'Jesus, you can be reet dim sometimes.'

I cleared my throat. I didn't know what to say. My mouth felt dry and my head was spinning.

'I've had six,' I groaned. 'Six hash muffins in one morning. No wonder I feel completely wacko. Lovely girl, wrong planet. Bloody hell, Maz, I'm a lawyer for goodness sake.'

I sat on the edge of my desk and shook my head.

'I'm on drugs at work, during one of the most important meetings of my career so far. I'm totally stoned!'

I waited for some earth-shattering advice but Maz didn't have time to answer before I heard a loud cough behind me. I turned slowly to see an army of Partners, staff and clients, fronted by Peregrine, gathered directly behind me and well within hearing distance. A stunned silence hung in the air. The silence felt louder and more profound than the usual noise that filled the office. All I could hear was the hum of my computer and the loud tick of the clock that hung on the wall next to my desk. The clock counted down to the final explosion.

'Get out of this firm NOW!' Peregrine yelled. 'Get OUT.'

I tried to offer an explanation but it fell on deaf ears.

'GET OUT, YOU HOOLIGAN! GET OUT OF MY SIGHT!'

I stared at my colleagues. I begged my brain to think of a clever, lawyer-style answer but nothing happened. My mind felt fried.

'I should have you arrested for this,' Peregrine continued.

I could see he meant business. I slowly replaced the receiver and shakily reached for my bag at the side of the desk.

'Get out NOW,' he boomed, 'and don't you

dare ask me for a reference. You're finished in this business.'

I stared at him as reality dawned. This was bad, very bad. Over Peregrine's shoulder, I saw Jack's face. He was the only member of the crowd who was smiling broadly. I realised that he was enjoying this immensely. I couldn't quite believe what was happening to me. My eyes began to fill up with tears of sadness and embarrassment as I sidled past the onlookers and walked unsteadily towards the door.

'Leave NOW, Miss Summer,' Peregrine hissed. 'You're fired!'

4

3rd January, 9:00 a.m.

'Well, yer best bet looks like an easy mornin' with Richard and Judy. Says here they're makin' over some bride-to-be, poor cow, and discussin' signs of an early menopause. Bloody hell, that Richard knows more about fannies than I do! Then you've got three cookery programmes, *Can't Cook, Won't Cook*, can't be arsed to cook, and get the f'kin lass ta cook, probably. Then a cookery chat show, cookery question time and a quiz hosted by a celebrity cook. That'll make you hungry fer lunch, which'll be followed by a two-hour run of Australian soaps with mix-'n'-match wardrobes and actors. Then, pet, the highlight of the day, four problem talk shows end to end. Jerry Springer, Sally Jessy Raphael, Jenny Jones and Ricki 'Go Ricki' Lake. Now lass, if *that* isny a day to envy, I deen't kna what is.'

Maz put the TV guide to one side and gazed curiously at the mound of crumpled duvet that I had moulded into my den of wretchedness. Enough room only for myself, five dozen man-sized tissues, enough calorie-laden food to not only feed the five thousand but give them a weight problem too, and a huge helping of self-pity.

'Jen,' Maz sighed, 'you should come to the pub with me, pet. You can sit there an' chat to us while I pull pints.'

I grunted and reached for the chocolate Hobnobs. Maz had been great, I realised, staying another night, absorbing my tales of woe and plying me with pizza to slowly ease my post-sacking depression.

'I'm *useless.*'

'No you're *not*, Jen.'

'I'm no use to anyone.'

'Aye you are, Jen.'

'I may as well die right now.'

'Have another slice of Hawaiian first.'

'OK then.'

Still, I was in pure, unadulterated self-pitying mode so I had no other choice but to make her feel guilty for leaving me in my hour of need to go off and earn a crust. Rub salt in my fresh, gaping wounds why don't you? I sighed. 'Yesterday an up-and-coming city solicitor, today a full-time member of the daytime TV club. A life of gardening tips, recipes and women's problems. Wow. What a difference a day makes.'

'Howay, at least it's not Saturday,' Maz

replied. 'Then you'd only have Des Lynam, a few pocket-sized jockeys, and a bunch of up-their-own-backsides cricketers for entertainment. That'd be enough to make anyone slit their wrists!'

'At least if Des was on there would be someone in this room with worse hair than mine.'

'Ooh I deen't kna like, I quite like his white flick.'

'Cheers. So now not only am I single, unemployable and suspected of heading a Colombian drugs cartel, I'm also less sexy than a sixty-year-old TV presenter. Thanks very much.'

Maz shifted the remains of the previous night's Super Supreme and perched on the arm of the sofa.

'Come on now, lass,' she said softly, 'there's no way you're unemployable. You're clever in that intellectual/qualification way, you're above average lookin' and you've got a great personality. So your hair's a bit dodgy but, bollocks, if you're unemployable then I'm about as welcome on the job market as a dyslexic amoeba.'

Ignoring the 'dodgy hair' comment, I felt a sudden pang of guilt. In truth, Maz's life had been a constant struggle against misfortune yet she had always fought to bring out the positive side of any situation. She was one of those people who would say, 'Well, the plants needed watering,' on a bleak, rainy day. I, on the other hand, was an 'Oh shite, it's pissing down again' kind of girl. My world would almost come to an end if Pizza Hut ran out of deep pan dough or if the scales showed nine stone four *and a half* pounds instead of nine stone four *exactly*. I could always be relied on to turn one of life's little blips into a full-blown crisis which Kate Adie would be drafted in to cover. Not altogether ideal qualities for such a highly stressful profession as corporate law. Mind you, at least I was consistent.

'I'm sorry, Maz,' I whimpered. 'Forgive me?'

She jumped up, her left foot landing on a cold garlic bread. 'Sorry for what? Don't get all soppy on me now, woman. Forgive ya. Howay, it's *my* fault you got the red card over them bloody muffins. It's me who should be apologising. We'll get through it though, Jen. Treat it as a holiday till you decide what to do, like. I mean, you could always pull pints at the pub with me.'

I started to laugh as I envisaged myself behind the bar of the Scrap Inn, dishing out endless 'broon ales' to Maz's crazy regulars.

Not a chance, my brain said firmly. 'All

right, bugger off to work and leave me alone,' I grinned.

Maz gave me a wave and retrieved a clammy slice of pizza from the soggy box on the floor. She left the room, loudly as always, sucking the congealed cheese out of the crust. Seconds later I heard the front door to my flat slam shut. It sounded remarkably like the cell door on the opening titles of *Prisoner Cell Block H*. Shite, she'd gone. She had actually gone. I felt suddenly alone, and tearful. Time to take a one-way ticket to self-pity city.

★　★　★

It's funny the things you can learn when you spend a weekday at home. From the TV alone, I discovered how to *feng shui* my flat, apply party make-up while preparing a gourmet meal, upholster a *chaise longue* with recycled bin-liners and lose four pounds by living in a state of prolonged happiness. Of course, Richard said that would be easy for Judy to do, they were so happy together. *Tosser.* I also became well versed in Australian after watching the lunchtime run of soaps, so I walked around the flat saying 'you dag', 'g'day', and 'fair dinkum' to various pieces of furniture.

I stared out of the window at the street below and watched the world go by its business. The postman came and went twice, not even pausing to consider my mailbox. Delivery men plied the neighbours' flats with furniture, carpets and catalogues, and the milkman delivered to the two couples in the block who were still adamant about maintaining a crumbling British tradition. I couldn't help but notice that the latter spent an inordinate amount of time at number 20, without doubt the home of another dissatisfied housewife. Cars whizzed by invariably, I noticed, with one person in each. Totally out of character, I found myself cursing the human race's lack of environmental awareness. Through the gap in the blocks of flats across the street I could see a constant stream of ships moving up and down the River Tyne. Presumably taking our non-beef produce out to sea. I thought about packing up a red-and-white-dotted hankie with sandwiches, fruit cake and a spare pair of knickers and stowing away, but I couldn't decide where I'd like to go. Thoughts that had never previously crossed my mind began to fill my aching head. I thought of anything just to suppress the feelings I knew were lurking inside me. I wanted to shout out of the window, to stop all the activity that was carrying on outside my four walls. I was alone, single and unemployed. Yet, from my solitary prison (I was back on the *Cell Block H* metaphor) I could see that the world carried on regardless. Nothing changes in the big picture just because one person feels bad. I was pissed off at being so insignificant that my problems didn't bring the whole planet to a sudden halt.

I moved from the window and slumped back in front of the TV to play couch commando with the remote control. A studio of incredibly vocal Californians were discussing the topic 'Teenage moms pregnant at 13'. I listened to the sob stories for a while then changed channel. 'She's too fat to wear Lycra' was the theme on this show. 'Hey girlfriend,' screamed one voluptuous guest at a member of the audience, 'I love my body and I ain't gonna have no jumped-up stick like you tellin' me I ain't no good, ya hear! I am the *bomb*!'

'Girlfriend' screamed back and the audience erupted. An army of 20-stone 'ladies' (to use the term very lightly) decked out in neon cycling shorts, crop tops and knee-high boots stormed around the stage, shouting obscenities at the audience. I was surprised there wasn't an earthquake warning with the amount of weight shifting around in a concentrated area.

Momentarily I forgot about my own worries as I watched the run of chat shows. 'I am an alien from outer space' followed 'Make this slob a real man' and 'My boyfriend slept with my sister'. I couldn't quite believe the things people were willing to admit on national television. The guests screamed at each other, the crowds went wild and the presenters totally lost control.

By the end of the afternoon I could almost understand Maz's obsession with these programmes. Before I knew it, I had been glued to the screen for three hours in sheer amazement. I almost felt cheered up until *Ricki Lake* ended and I realised all that lay ahead of me was a meal for one and yet more television.

'Right, Summer,' I shouted at myself, 'get off your fat backside and do something.' I looked at my watch. Four forty-five p.m. Probably an appropriate time to get out of my thermal pyjamas and get dressed.

★ ★ ★

Just as I was about to embark on my makeover, the buzzer sounded for the main front door to the block.

'Afternoon missus. British Telecom. I gotta

check yer phone line, a' reet?' I buzzed him up and opened the door to a six-foot, black-haired, rough-and-ready-looking phone engineer. 'Sorry to bother you like, but we're checkin' the lines. I hope ya dinny mind the intrusion, pet.'

You can intrude as much as you like, pet, my mind gushed, as all thoughts of Jack faded in the twinkle of a BT identification card.

'Ooh no, come in please *do*,' I drooled sexily. One day at home on a weekday and I had already metamorphosed into the bored, sex-starved housewife from number 20.

I showed 'Kyle' to the phone. I briefly considered leading him to the bedroom extension but stopped myself in time. Play hard to get, I told myself. I ruffled my hair and reclined against the wall as Kyle bent down and took out his toolbox. He looked up at me and smiled, revealing a set of perfectly white teeth.

'Cup of tea?' I purred.

'Na, I don't wanna put ya to any trouble in yer condition, pet.' He smiled and turned back to the phone socket.

'Excuse me?'

'When yer ill, pet, I dinny wanna tire you oot.'

I stared at Kyle, puzzled. My sex kitten image was slowly beginning to fade.

'Flu, is it?' he continued. 'It must be a bad one, you look canny *awful*.'

Sex kitten became fat, stray tabby. 'I'm not . . . I don't ha . . . Oh, piss off!' I yelled. I turned on my heel and stomped dramatically out of the flat, still in my teddy bear thermals, muttering as many obscenities about men as I could muster.

★ ★ ★

I passed the payphone in the main hallway and realised I hadn't called my mother to apologise for missing dinner the previous night. Although I didn't relish the thought, when compared with a trip to the shops in my PJs or an awkward conversation with my phone engineer, mother's undoubted lecture seemed strangely appealing.

'Oh Jennifer, you *finally* decided to call. To what do we owe the honour?'

Damn. She was in. I would actually have to talk to her now.

'Reversed charges, too. How sweet of you.'

As I'd thought, this idea had been a momentary lapse of sanity. Without waiting for me to speak, mother launched into a description of her heartbreak when I had failed to show up for her lamb casserole.

'I made your *favourite* dinner, Jennifer.'

68

'I hate lamb, Mother.'

'Don't be so ridiculous child. Of course you don't.'

'Lamb is Susie's favourite, Mum.' I immediately kicked myself for having mentioned the dreaded 'S' word.

'Yes, well, *Susie* would have called. She is *so* reliable, Jennifer. Always calls, always here on time.'

(Here we go again.) 'Yes Mum.'

'Her children are immaculate, her husband is a *darling*. She is *so* busy yet she is *so* dependable.'

'Yes Mum, but . . . '

'I don't know where I went wrong with you, Jennifer. Honestly . . . '

I allowed the lecture to continue in my ear as I concentrated on a fly that was sitting on the top of the phone. Infinitely more interesting than listening to my mother. It's funny how, in a time of need, I still think calling my parents will make things better. Invariably I wind up totally depressed with blood pressure that could raise the *Titanic*. My mother drones on so relentlessly (usually about my perfect sister) that I've often considered harnessing her hot air as a new form of energy.

'Susie says you think you are above us all, with that job and this new independent lifestyle,' she continued.

Susie, Susie, Susie. How could my only sister, whom I hardly ever saw, cause me so much aggravation? Susie was the eldest — 29 going on 40. Her ambition in life had been to have a mortgage and a rich husband before any of her precocious friends. All she needed to be happy was enough money to have her manicures, pedicures and whatever-cures at least four times a week, and to never have to work a full day in her life. I suspected that that had been my mother's goal before she had somehow married my father. In her eyes he had never been good enough for her. Susie, at 21, had married Sebastian, a banker (no prizes for guessing my title for him), and had two boys — Edmund and Nathaniel. Brats, the pair of them. With amazing ease she had settled into a life of nannies, shopping and dinner parties. I had no real qualms about Susie's choice of lifestyle (although I would have taken the hubbie and kids back for a full refund) but she had since become completely incapable of relating to anyone outside her social circle. Anyone like yours truly, who was not *au fait* with the latest Montessori teaching practice, Dior's newest iridescent eye shades or Prada's most recent handbag design, was not worth the effort. As children, I had been the tomboy, always scruffy, covered in mud and hanging out with the boys. (If only that was true now.) Susie had been Barbie's best friend and the apple of Mum's eye. I was a definite Daddy's girl. Over the years we had gone from being like chalk and cheese, to fire and ice, to Margate and Monte Carlo. It was when Susie finally 'found herself' in pearls, twin-sets and a dyed blonde bob that I realised our sisterly ties would always be hanging by a thread.

Mother was still droning on, slowly drilling a painful hole in my eardrum.

'Are we not good enough for you now, dahling, or are you taking drugs?'

Bloody hell, here goes. I quickly resolved not to try and explain how I had lost my job. Any attempt at a reasonable discussion would be futile.

At that point Mrs Diasio burst through the front door. She glared at me with a look of disdain. Her gaze moved slowly over my choice of day-wear, down to my furry cat slippers, and back up to my luminous orange hair. She raised her Roman nose and scurried past, muttering in Italian. I figured it wasn't an attempt at friendly conversation.

'Stupid old hag,' I said, perhaps a little too loudly as she disappeared into the lift.

As my ear began to turn numb, I gave up on politeness and patience and yelled,

71

'Mother, will you shut up!'

Mother Summer came up for air. Suddenly I had the silence I had wanted but I didn't know what I was going to say. I tended to beat around the bush at the best of times, but now my mouth was beginning to dry up. How could I tell my parents that I had thrown away the only thing that had ever caused my mother to be slightly proud of me? However, I could feel my mum winding up for a second assault so I had no choice but to go for it. 'I . . . um . . . I lost my job,' I said quickly. A never-before-heard silence boomed from the other end of the line.

I cleared my throat. 'Mum, did you *hear* me?' I asked. 'I lost my job.'

Again no response. I awaited the explosion and was surprised when I heard, 'Oh petal, you poor, poor thing. How terrible.'

I decided that she must have misheard. My mother never gave me sympathy.

'I'm so sorry,' she stuttered. 'Please, dahling, come and see Daddy and me. We'll make it better.'

'I can't believe you're taking it like this.' I smiled and relaxed a little. 'I thought you'd go mental when I told you.'

'Of course not, Jennifer. It's simply a disaster for you.'

Perhaps I had underestimated her. 'Thank

you,' I replied. 'It's comforting to know you're there for me, even though I got fired.'

'*What?*' The yell resounded through my ears. 'Fired!' she screamed. 'What the *hell* for?'

Mother never said 'hell'. This was bad.

'Jennifer?' she enquired loudly. 'Speak to me you stupid girl.'

'Mum, what's wrong?' In the background I could hear my father trying to take control of the situation. Fat chance of that.

'I thought you were made redundant, you silly idiot.'

Oh.

'The Summer family does *not* get *fired*! What happened?'

Shopping in my pyjamas was becoming a more attractive option by the minute. My mother's voice, sounding strangely high-pitched and strangled, was ringing in my ears.

'I despair of you, Jennifer. When will you *ever* grow up? Why can't you be like your sister?'

'STUFF bloody Susie,' I yelled, ignoring the sounds of shock from my mother. 'I'm not *her*, OK? I'm me, Jennifer, and I'm not that bad, you know.' My brain was picking up speed. 'Yes, I'm single, *yes*, I've been fired, but I'm *not* a bad person, Mother. There's only one person on this line who needs to wake up, and it's not me.'

I slammed the phone down and felt my body shake with fury and shock. Bloody woman. My father was great but his support was always in the background, overshadowed by the strange ways of my mother. I suddenly felt a wave of hopelessness sweep over me. Even my own family thought I was a failure. Through the haze of self-pity I heard a cough and turned to see the lift doors closing, with Mrs Diasio inside. I was puzzled as I thought she had already gone. It seemed Mrs Diasio had added eavesdropping to her list of neighbourly traits. Tired and depressed, I began to trudge my fluffy cats up the stairs.

★   ★   ★

I was woken at about 8:00 p.m. by a sharp rap on the door. The day had already felt like an eternity and it still wasn't over. I groaned from the effort of getting up from the sofa and tramped to the door. I was surprised to see my landlord, a lanky, greasy excuse for a man, marching up and down the corridor impatiently. Mr Brown (an apt name for a man whose wardrobe consisted only of brown jumpers, brown slacks and the odd tank-top) only ever appeared on the scene to moan, collect money or 'romance' my neighbour. I presumed the former was today's mission.

'Mr Brown,' I said as politely as possible, 'how can I help you?'

'Miss Summer.' I shivered at the sound of his gruff voice. This man perspired sleaze. 'I dinny wanna pry, like' (a likely story) 'but I been hearing stuff about ya.'

'*Stuff?* Any stuff in particular?'

'Aye, like I heard you're wurkin' for the DSS now, lass.'

'Um, I'm not sure I . . . '

'Worra said was, yur signin' on like.'

My brain clocked in for its evening shift and I began to understand his bush-beating drivel.

'Well, news travels fast in this block, doesn't it?' My thoughts instinctively turned to Demon Diasio.

'So I'm reet then am I?' he continued.

'Yes, Mr Brown, you're right. I lost my job.'

'Well lass, I'm sorry.'

I was momentarily taken aback. My brown-jumpered rent collector was one of the last people I expected sympathy from but I figured that my choice of shoulders to cry on was rapidly dwindling, so I'd take anything I could get.

I smiled. 'Well thanks, Mr Brown, I really appreciate it. I was feeling a bit down, actually, so it really helps to — '

75

'Na lass,' he interrupted, 'that isny what I meant. I mean I'm sorry but I've come to tell't you that ye've gorra gan.'

'Gan, I mean *go*, where?'

'Gan, like leave. These flats are for professional business people like and I cannat risk you not payin' yer rent.'

'But I'll pay. I've only been out of work *one* day. I've got rights.'

'Na pet. I mek yer rights and I can tek them away. That's how it works, see. I can dae what I bleedin' well like and I couldny give a monkeys what the bloody law says.'

I couldn't believe what I was hearing. First Jack, then my job. Surely I wasn't going to lose my flat as well. I considered that it could be a practical joke but realised that Mr Brown wouldn't know humour if it jumped up and bit him on the tank-top. I tried for the pathetic, helpless look.

'*Please* Mr Brown,' I pleaded. 'I'm going to get another job. Just give me a few days. I'll even give you an advance on my rent.' It would mean a painful trip to the bank manager or, failing that, my dad, but anything was preferable to being homeless.

He stared at me then smiled, revealing a set of rotten yellow chipped teeth. My stomach churned but I held his eye. He moved closer, enveloping me in *eau de* BO.

'Well maybe there is a way like,' he said strangely.

'Please, *anything*,' I replied, holding my breath.

'Well that nice Italian woman . . . '

'*Nice* . . . ? Oh, Mrs Diasio?'

'Aye. She tell't us that you havny got any men around much. Jest mentioned it like.'

Oh I bet she did, the nosy old bint. I was beginning to lose track of the conversation.

'And well ye kna if yer desperate and alone like . . . ' He winked and exposed his teeth again. He obviously thought they were one of his strong points, well actually, no others sprang to mind. ' . . . I was thinkin' maybe we could come to some . . . uh . . . some *arrangement*, pet.'

Arrangement? Surely he didn't mean . . . ? My stomach threatened to empty its contents over Mr Brown's slacks as he moved even closer and clasped his hands on my waist.

'Get off me, you freak,' I yelled, pushing his hands away and taking a step back.

'Howay now,' he shouted, 'dain't be gettin' like that, pet.'

'I'm not your pet and I can't believe you'd even suggest such a thing! Wouldn't a weasel be more your type, you perverted little rat?'

'Tek it easy, woman. You better watch what you're sayin' like.'

'Just because that oversexed Italian tart is desperate enough to touch you, that definitely does not mean you're irresistible.'

Any form of diplomacy escaped me as I continued to hurl abuse at my landlord. Of course, he did deserve it but subtlety would probably have been a more appropriate way of keeping a roof, this roof in particular, over my head. Nevertheless, I ploughed on, driven by an urge to put the male species in their place. ('I'd rather snog Roy Hattersley than get within a mile of you . . . You're about as attractive as a lizard with herpes . . . The day you and I get together will be the day Satan goes snowboarding . . . ' That sort of thing.) I stopped only when a brown-jumpered arm was raised in the air, revealing a tightly clenched fist. I thought back to third year self-defence class but all I could remember was to spray your attacker with an aerosol or stab them with a nail file, neither of which I kept in my pyjamas. I closed my eyes and waited for the punch.

'Ach yer not worth it, ya sad auld tramp,' I heard him say. 'I can see why you're not gettin' any.'

Bastard.

'GET OUT OF MY FLAT,' I yelled. 'I've had it with men like you.'

He started to laugh. 'Na lass, you can get

oot o' my flat, reet now. Yer lease has expired.'

No, no, no. That wasn't meant to happen. Great negotiation skills, Jennifer. I wanted to plead, I wanted to beg, but I was too enraged. The events of the previous days had culminated in unadulterated female fury.

'With pleasure,' I yelled. 'I'd rather live in a cell in Alcatraz than pay rent to you.'

'Aye, well, ask if they've got a padded one. Give me yer key before you leave.' He turned on his slip-on leather-look heels and left me standing at the door dumbfounded.

'Shit, shit, shit.' I stamped my foot and hit my head on the door frame. 'Shit, shit, shit, shit, shit.'

Across the corridor a door opened. I looked up to see a bemused Mrs Diasio looking my way. She waved, then laughed. '*Arrivaderci*,' she chuckled and slammed the door.

5

8th January, 12:30 p.m.

'Gis a packet o' tabs an' two pickle't eggs,' he shouted. He threw his empty chicken pie wrapper at me, I gathered as a sign of affection.

'Aye, an' a pint of Exhibition,' yelled his missus, from the opposite end of the bar. This sparked a heated response.

'Howay woman, get yer own chuffin' pint. I'm not ganna pay fer you to get fatter than you are.'

'Piss off, ya bleedin' scruff.'

'I'll smack ya if yer startin' on us like.'

I turned away and busied myself with fishing the putrid-smelling eggs out of the jar that stood on the counter behind the bar. Another typical lunchtime shift at the Scrap Inn, especially when Denise and Derek were present. I glanced at the clock above me — 12:32 p.m. Maz probably wouldn't be back for at least another two hours. I was starting to feel tense. This was my first time going solo behind the bar and I would admit to being absolutely terrified. Maz had finally decided to go for her first talk-show host audition and, in a moment of madness, I had agreed to do the shift alone. 'Yeah, sure Maz, no problem. It'll be good experience for me.' Good experience, my arse. Having my teeth forcibly extracted without anaesthetic would have been more enjoyable. My original bravado was starting to dwindle.

The eggs and cigarettes had just changed hands when the pub door burst open, smashed against the wall and sent the recently hung 'No smoking section' sign crashing to the floor.

'F'kin' na smokin' section. What a load o' shite,' shouted 'Auld Vinny', the pub's eldest regular, as he stumbled through the door and kicked the sign across the floor. He tripped down the stairs and wobbled towards me, as I hurriedly uncapped his bottle of 'broon'. Auld Vinny was not one to be kept waiting.

'What f'kin' time d'ya call this to open eh?' he yelled, waggling an ancient finger vaguely in my direction. 'I was ootside at eleven o'clock and ya wasny open. I cannot believe it disny open at eleven. I'm ganna call the f'kin' brewery, man!'

I decided against explaining the intricacies of licensing laws and instead smiled inanely as my third customer attempted to climb onto the bar stool which was nailed to the floor. Auld Vinny definitely had an individual style. He wore a dirty brown jacket, black trousers tied with string, white socks, and lime-green deck shoes. His house key hung on a string around his thick neck. As always, the ensemble was finished off with a neon orange cap bearing the logo 'The Ultimate International Sex Machine'.

'A bottle o' broon an' a pint of arsenic,' yelled Vinny. 'I'm sick as shite.'

'Here you go, Vinny.' I put the bottle in front of him and watched his bunch of ring-clad, tattooed fingers shakily clasp the bottle.

'Chuffin' hell,' Auld Vinny exclaimed, spitting a mouthful of beer all over the bar, 'what the hell d'ya call that, man?'

'Umm,' I stuttered. 'Umm.' I pointed nervously at the label.

Vinny lifted the bottle and held it close to my face. 'Serve cool,' he said seriously. 'That's what it says on the bleedin' label woman. *Cool*, not friggin' arctic.'

'S . . . sorry,' I began, grabbing another bottle that hadn't come straight from the store room. 'S . . . sorry.'

'Aye, well.' Vinny eyed me cagily. 'Aye, well you'll learn.'

I tried to smile pleasantly while I racked my brain for some form of conversation.

I can't do it, my brain stressed. *I can't relate to these people.*

'What'r ya smilin' like a bleedin' loony for, woman?' Auld Vinny finished his half-bottle swig and stared sternly at me with his dark grey eyes.

'There isny much ta friggin' smile aboot today, woman, I tell't ya.'

I smiled meekly then forced a frown in a vain attempt to fit in. Fearing for my health, I looked away and hurriedly began cleaning the bar for the fourth time that morning.

From the outside looking in, this job had always seemed so easy. Pull a few pints, say, 'What can I get you, darlin'?' and show a bit of cleavage. How hard could it possibly be? Harder than eating rice with chopsticks, I had since discovered. I couldn't even serve a decent beer from a ready to drink bottle.

Maz was so good at the banter. She gave as good as she got, if not better. I, on the other hand, always seemed to be stuck for words so I spent most of the day smiling like a mental patient (post-lobotomy) and making agreeable noises. The regulars were all hardened Geordies, fully qualified in alcoholism, fighting or swearing or even a mixture of all three. I was assured by Maz they were harmless yet I still feared for my life at least a dozen times a day, usually from the women.

83

Maz had promised me that I would find it easier and more enjoyable given time, but I wasn't convinced.

Mind you, time was the one thing I definitely did have. Over the previous five days, I had received my P45, said goodbye to any hopes of a job in the legal profession, been unceremoniously removed from my flat, and moved in with Maz. It was a strange role reversal, having to rely financially as well as emotionally on my best friend. I had convinced myself it was temporary but as the days had passed I had realised that Maz's offer of some shifts in the Scrap Inn was my only option. There was no space for pride in the equation.

'Are ya listenin' ta me, wuman?' yelled Auld Vinny. I stopped cleaning and quickly uncapped another bottle of Brown Ale.

'What was that you were saying, Vinny?' I asked shakily.

'Jesus. Does naybody listen these days? I said me father went doonstairs like.'

'Downstairs? What for?'

'Aye. Doonstairs, ye kna. He cannat have gan to heaven the auld bastard.'

Auld Vinny was definitely one for random conversation. If one could do a degree in irrelevant banter this guy would have a PhD.

'Auld bastard I tell't ya me father,' he

continued. 'I was happy as piggin' shite when I see him get dead. Happy as chuffin' Larry when the auld twat died. I tell't ya there al' the same, fathers.'

'Actually, my dad's really nice. I — '

'Auld git. I'd say hello to the blowk and I'd be on the deck, man. Wham, just fer lookin' at him like.'

'Oh dear.' (Zero out of ten for inspirational responses.)

Vinny continued. 'And mention God in the house, man. He'd deck ya. 'Never mention that bloody word in this house again.' Floor ya, he would, the auld git.'

He paused, took a swig of beer and redeemed the half-eaten meat pie that had been festering among the fluff in his jacket pocket. I looked anywhere but directly at him, to avoid the open-mouthed chewing display. It was like watching a trifle in a washing machine. When the horse-like chewing noise became less deafening, I made a further attempt at conversation.

'So how are you feeling today, Vinny?' (OK, so it was boring but it was a start.)

'Terrible man,' he growled. 'I went to the bloody doctor this mornin' like before I came to the pub which was fuc — '

'Not open yet.'

'Aye. A bloody wuman the doctor was that

85

I saw. Anyway, I meybe auld but I'm not sexualist ye kna. I divny give a monkey's what the bastard is as long as they kna what to do when they get us like.'

I nodded enthusiastically as his eyes held mine.

'D'ye kna what she tell't us?'

'No Vinny, what was that?' I cleared my throat and tried to relax.

'She says, 'Vinny, you're as fit as a lion.' I says, 'Piss off man, woman, man, I'm fit to drop.''

I laughed nervously.

'Straits that's what I tell't her. Aye they're ganna make me suffer before I go I tell't ya.'

At this point, Denise and Derek finished another argument and decided to join us. We made a peculiar foursome. Auld Vinny, a wrinkled old seaman, with skin like a crocodile handbag, Denise, whose 'wide load' frame was squeezed into stilettos and ski-pants, Derek her husband, whose idea of heaven was three pints before breakfast and daily re-runs of *Auf Wiedersehen Pet*, and me. I listened to them talking, tried to nod and laugh at appropriate moments, but rarely added anything myself. I felt as out of place as an over-sized tunic in Anneka Rice's wardrobe, totally surrounded by jumpsuits and unable to relate to a single one of them. I was sure they were hardly aware of my existence, unlike Maz who held court when she was on duty. The whole scenario was light years away from my none-too-distant previous life and I wasn't sure how to adjust. I must admit, though, I was beginning to find them strangely entertaining.

'How much d'ya get a week, Vinny?' asked Derek through a mouthful of pork scratchings. The conversation had somehow jumped from coronary thrombosis, haemorrhoids and bed baths to economics.

'Aye Vinny tell't us how much ya get,' shouted Denise, hitching up her knickers above her ski pants.

'I get sixty-seven pount a week al done.'

'Howay man, Vinny,' Denise interjected, 'you should be well off, man. I get aboot thirty-five pount a week and that's my lot. You should be livin' in a f'kin' palace, Vinny man.'

Vinny did reply but my attention was diverted by the sound of 'The Shoe' pulling up outside. 'Thank you God.' Maz was back. I glanced at the clock — 1:30 p.m. I heard the back gate open and close and waited with bated breath for my friend to appear. I had survived.

'Where the *bollocks* have you been?' Vinny shouted as Maz strode up to the bar from the back entrance. 'Left us with a bleedin' southerner you did.'

'Howay y'auld git. She's my best friend so shut yer flippin' mouth.' She laughed loudly and knocked Vinny's hat off.

Everyone laughed and I felt a twinge of jealousy. *Like me too. Like me too.* I almost started to sulk but then I remembered Maz's audition. As she gabbled away with her regulars, keeping them in hysterics, I thought I detected a slight watery look in her eyes but I couldn't be certain. Anyway, Maz never cried, it wasn't her style. She was 'tough as auld boots', as she herself often said.

'Aye Vinny man. It's yer birthday tomorra, isn't it?' said Maz as she opened a bag of scampi fries and shoveled half of them into her mouth.

'Aye it is, bloody birthdays. I'm sick of the swine, they shouldn't be allowed.'

'Well, Jen here and I thought we'd give you a party.' (First I'd heard but I nodded agreeably.)

'Jesus chuffin' Christ. I hope I don't even *see* me bloody birthday me! They're a waste of bloody time. I've never had one good day in me life so what would I wanna gan celebratin' aboot eh?'

'Oh come on, Vinny.' We all joined in, sensing Maz's enjoyment.

'Piss off. I divny wanna birthday.'

Maz grinned, 'Well we're havin' a party anyhow, you miserable sod, and if you dain't come we'll be celebratin' without you. So pack it in and get another pint doon yer neck.'

★ ★ ★

The next couple of hours continued along the same lines. It was only when our regulars left for a short break before their night shift that I finally had a chance to talk to my friend.

'So come on then,' I said, jumping up to sit on the bar. 'How did it go?'

'How d'you think?'

'Well I don't know. Did you get an audition? Tell me.'

'Aye I got an audition alreet.'

'Great!'

'Na, shite. I got to say aboot three sentences before they interrupted us.'

'What did they say?'

'Exactly? Well the blowk in charge of production said nothin' but his little gobshite of an assistant had plenty to say.'

Maz broke into her best posh voice: ''I'm awfully sorry, sweetie, but that will be all for now. You aren't raylay what we're looking for.''

'Well what were they looking for?' I asked. I could tell that Maz was upset.

She said, 'Um, you know, somebody a little less . . . *regional*.'

'*Regional?* What the hell is *that* supposed to mean?'

'Exactly, bleedin' cheek. In other words, I was too flippin' Geordie to host the show. Well what do they expect if they do the bloody auditions in Newcastle? It's a load of crap man!'

'That can't be it. They can't possibly use that as a justification. What's wrong with having an accent? Not every person on TV has to sound like Sue Lawley for us to understand them. That's *shocking*.'

'Aye. Well I went canny mental but she didn't budge. She said I didn't have the right *experience*.'

'But you know those shows inside out.'

'I kna. I tell't her that. Jen, I know I'd be good at it. I've been through so many of the sorts of things that people need to discuss on these shows. Except, maybe, transgendering, sleeping with aliens or reincarnation, but anyhow, I'd be good. I know I would.'

I could see how hurt Maz was feeling. She'd opened herself up to rejection and hated feeling the pride that had taken so long to build up be bashed away by a mid-twenties media bitch with little grasp of everyday life in the real world.

90

'Don't worry, mate.' I put my arm around Maz's shoulders and gave her a wink. 'I like you common.'

She smiled and punched me in the arm.

'F'kin' southerner,' she laughed.

We hugged then sat in silence for a minute. Maz gazed up at the framed autographed photo of Ricki Lake that hung above the last orders bell. She had sent off for it from the official fan club and it hung as a shrine to her ultimate goal.

Finally I broke the silence. 'So who did they pick in the end?'

'Ah some auld tramp who looked like Judith bloody Chalmers on steroids. Apparently she had the experience but I reckon it was the accent she had. She spoke as if she had a gobful of royal plums. 'Aybsobloodylootly Bloomin' Marvellous Actuarly.' She was a reet cow, looked down her nose at us the whole time. Bitch.'

I laughed at Maz's Queen Mum voice and cracked open two beers. A medicinal Bud (or several) was required.

'I might as well give up,' Maz sighed after a couple of mouthfuls.

'Shut up,' I replied. 'You don't give up. What was it you told me last week? 'If you give up on your ambition you aren't going to go anywhere but down.' Well, you're not going down and you're certainly not going to go through life like a sad cow wondering 'What if?' I'll see to that, so pack it in and get that beer down your neck!'

'Ooh, look out girlfriend,' Maz chuckled in a mock-Texan accent. 'Wooee, she's got spunk. Lordee, that afternoon in the pub did her some good, she's back to her old self again!'

We laughed till we felt sick. It was a rare moment to savour. At that point we both realised that we were relying on each other to keep our ambitions alive. To be honest, things couldn't get much worse, so what did we possibly have to fear?

6

Auld Vinny's birthday party was really just an excuse for Maz to reduce the draughts to 90p a pint and get the punters in the door. Over the previous two months, the pub had been partially revamped by the brewery to resemble an olde worlde inn. The idea was to target families who would come for a quiet Sunday shandy and a scampi basket meal. The pool table, pinball and fruit machines had been removed and replaced with a no-smoking section, sepia photographs, and low lighting. Maz had tried to tell the powers-that-be that no amount of interior design and classical music could possibly change the make-up of the Scrap Inn. Mr and Mrs White-collar, their two-point-four children and golden retriever would not dream of parking their Audi family saloon within hiking distance of the pub for fear of returning to find out the parts had been auctioned by the local kids, piece by piece, to the scrap metal yard across the street.

Maz had been offended that her regulars

were not considered worthy enough to drink the brewery's beer, paid for with their hard-earned cash or social. Inevitably her words of wisdom had passed unheeded. The plans for reform had been implemented almost entirely before someone in a high place suddenly woke up to reality and withdrew the budget. The madcap scheme had done nothing more than create a pub with bizarrely conflicting decor and alienate the rough and ready characters who had brought in the profits.

The official manager, Gordon, a quietly confident businessman from Edinburgh, was rarely to be seen inside the pub. He preferred, he said, to manage at a distance, usually of around 200 miles. He never confessed to being scared of the customers but he nearly had a hernia every time he walked through the door. Rumour had it that the brewery planned to sell if profits stayed low, so Maz's plan was an attempt to rejuvenate sales and get the pub back to normal. I had started to feel of some use as we had collaborated to find ways of increasing the Scrap Inn's popularity. Keeping my mind occupied was the best medicine, I had decided, and better for my figure, as troughing obscene quantities of anything fattening was the only other option.

'Where's the bloody pool table gone man?' yelled a yellow-puffer-jacketed skinhead from across the bar.

'It got taken away, I'm afraid,' I replied, smiling as widely as possible in a 'please don't punch me' kind of way.

'What a load of bloody shite,' came the reply, 'gis us a pint then woman.' (Polite as ever.)

The pub was beginning to fill up as rumours of the 90p pints spread like wildfire through the nearby estates. Auld Vinny was also a popular character with the locals, who liked to listen to his ramblings. The tales usually involved his days at sea, his sexual conquests (even at the age of 73), the state of the government or whatever else took his fancy. A lot of people had come, allegedly to help celebrate Vinny's birthday, but when he failed to show up, they seemed happy to settle for the cheap pints and bowls of scampi fries. Hardly surprising really.

'Having fun, Jen?' Maz shouted as she clomped past me to serve another of the loud-mouthed puffer-jacket people encamped at the far end of the bar. There seemed to be an unwritten rule of puffer-jacket hierarchy, I had decided, dictating who bought the rounds, who got to sit on a bar stool and who got to talk the loudest. I had so far deduced that tango orange came before neon yellow but both were surpassed by faux-aluminium foil reflective silver.

'Magic,' I answered sarcastically, frantically shaking my head. 'This is bloody hard work. Perhaps we shouldn't try and attract all these people.'

'Aye, I'm sweating like a pig,' said Maz, flapping her hands under her armpits and pulling dramatically at her top.

As usual, Maz had opted for the simple-yet-sexy look. Blue men's Levis that hung off her slim hips and showed off her ridiculously long legs, Nike trainers and a crop top T-shirt with 'Babe' scrawled across the chest. I had wanted one myself but decided the writing would have to be minute to fit 'Fat Miserable Heffer' across the front. I had opted, instead, for a black velour catsuit which was up there with pleated culottes and pop socks in the chart of desperately unflattering women's fashions. The jumpsuit demons had also encouraged me to apply eight layers of red lipstick and to diffuse my hair to within an inch of its orange life. All I needed was a pair of Christmas-tree decoration earrings and a cigarette holder and I would have been in the running for landlady at the Rover's Return. For some reason, the disasters in my life had made me lose any iota of style and decorum that I may have previously possessed. In an attempt to 'wash that man right out of my hair' I had achieved an alteration of image which left me looking and feeling ridiculous and which made me sink even deeper into depression. As I'd learned while staying with Maz, the talk shows always blamed it on 'low self-esteem'. I preferred to blame everything on Jack.

★ ★ ★

Maz and I had spent the whole morning in Newcastle undergoing an intensive session of retail therapy. My aim had been to find a young, dynamic, foxy, with-a-hint-of-sporty wardrobe to get myself back on track. Maz's goal had simply been to spend until she had more carrier bags than Tescos and to inflict grievous bodily harm on her bank balance.

Personally, I hate trying on clothes in shops. If I am already feeling hassled by the crowds, communal changing rooms only serve to heighten my anxiety levels. They must have been invented by a man with a fetish for groups of semi-naked women, sweating together in a horribly confined space. Of course, that would cover about two-thirds of the male population (the remaining third prefer open spaces). Not only must we endure the wall-to-wall mirrors, the smell of sweaty feet and the dangerously low oxygen levels, but we are also forced to bare every lump, bump, stretchmark and orange peel plantation in the name of recreational shopping. More often than not, it's always the day that I choose to wear the slightly faded, holey granny pants that pull up to just below my boobs (which are, of course, covered with the grey, ill-fitting ten-year-old bra).

At the fifth communal hell-hole of the day, I had finally put my foot down and refused to 'submit to this hideous torture any longer'. I had sat gloomily in one corner while Maz tried on (and suited) all two-dozen of her 'three items only please.' I had watched with amusement and disgust as endless Kate Moss and All Saints wannabees strutted their stuff in front of the mirrors while the latest boy-band love song CD (on repeat) ate into my brain.

'Be honest, Stacey, does this make me look fat?' asked one beanpole loudly of her equally emaciated friend. I'd seen more meat on a butcher's pencil. Such words as 'stick insect', 'toothpick' and 'bitch' had instantly sprung to mind.

'Na Tracey, it looks cool lass. Like really sexy.'

Eugh, even their names rhymed. I half

expected them to break into song and start doing backflips across the room, although there would have been a real danger of structural damage to the trowelled-on make-up. Anything more stressful than pouting was a definite no-no. Stacey and Tracey had eventually opted for matching pink and white PVC hot pant and jacket ensembles. Their next port of call had probably been to pick up their fake IDs and acid tabs. They had soon been replaced by what seemed like a hundred more Spicy clones. Leopard skin, combat trousers and Lycra tops that would hardly clothe a small bee had flashed before my eyes from all angles. It seemed bodies were being stopped from developing beyond the age of 15, while eyelashes, shoe heels and attitudes were on the increase. Finally I could take it no longer and had plucked Maz from the madness. I had grabbed the first item of clothing, thrown the rest into the manicured hands of a completely uninterested shop assistant, and had headed for the nearest bakery to drown my sorrows in two extra large cream dough-nuts (commonly referred to by Maz and I as cellulitees, for obvious reasons). Hence, my extremely unflattering and inappropriate choice of outfit for the evening's pub bash.

★ ★ ★

'Hiya gorgeous,' growled a balding fat man through his wispy ginger goatee. I could hear the static from his black and orange shell suit as he leaned over the bar, bringing his chubby red face to within punching distance. 'Ten pints for the lads in the corner and mek sure ya give us good head.'

Oh yes, that's a good one, ha ha, mmm, very good. I forced a smile as his tribe of equally gross friends erupted in what could only be described as 'guffaws'.

I concentrated on pulling the pints and prepared myself for the next line. Sure enough . . .

'Ooh pet, you pull that long wooden handle like a true professional. Fancy getting yer hands round somethin' even bigger?' (More guffaws.)

Ho, ho, ho, oh stop, you're splitting my sides. It was like watching Jimmy Tarbuck without the aid of canned laughter. The ten pints were poured and delivered amid a barrage of similarly hilarious puns. Just when I thought I'd escaped, my cue-ball-headed admirer, armed with a pint of Dutch courage, returned for the second act.

'So darlin', what's a southerner like you doin' in a place like this eh?' He'd obviously got to number one of 101 chatup lines for sad people. Perhaps by the fourth pint we'd be on, 'Aren't you tired cos you've been running around in my dreams all night.'

My plastic smile returned and I forced myself to answer. 'Just working to earn some pennies. Maz is my best friend so we help each other out.'

'Well me and the lads think yer canny. Fancy a date?'

I struggled to find a suitably negative answer, while steering around the truth that I found him completely repulsive.

'Er, sorry . . . I'm really busy at the moment.' (Fantastic. Nothing like a witty put-down to put him off the scent.)

'Howay. Not reet now. After yer shift like.' (He was persistent anyway, worse luck.)

'Hmm, well sorry but I . . . I've actually g . . . got a . . . a boyfriend. Big man, very active. Yes . . . six foot four actually, and wide. Very wide. Gets possessive.'

'Where is he then?'

'Karate. He teaches self-defence . . . um . . . extremely intelligent though. Hmm . . . speaks ooh at least four languages. Watches *Countdown*. Does the number puzzle in half the time. You know . . . the clever type . . . Not a Himbo.' (Not that I'm one to overdo my answers.)

For some reason, I find it physically impossible to say, 'No, piss off, in your dreams mate,' even to someone whom I find completely loathsome. Even if there is a zero per cent chance of me ever crossing paths with that person again, I still can't bring myself to be cutting. I suppose I just don't want to hurt their feelings when they've gone to the trouble of chatting me up. Pathetic really.

'Sorry . . . I'm really flattered, thanks.' I waffled on, hoping he'd get the message.

'Howay, I only wanted a good shag love.' Ginger burped loudly and headed back to his cave. 'I just like lasses with big bums,' he yelled over his shoulder. 'Ya need something ta hold on to, ye kna. A whole lotta woman.'

OK, so he'd definitely got the message. The Neanderthals guffawed loudly. Bastard. Pig-ugly lard bucket.

'Give me a match and I'll light your shell suit,' I muttered under my breath.

Even Gazza's fatter, ginger brother didn't fancy me. What chance did I possibly have of finding everlasting love? Zero, nada, zilch, rien. I clenched my bum cheeks and growled 'Whaddywant?' at the next customer.

★ ★ ★

Maz was stoked to see the pub so full for a change. She breezed around the bar with a

102

constant smile on her face, laughing and joking with everyone she met. They all loved her. I felt like the shorter, fatter, miserable friend who would be overlooked by all the boys and picked last for games. With so many different characters within the four walls of the Scrap Inn, though, I did notice a buzz in the air. In the rare moments when I forgot to feel sorry for myself, I found the atmosphere strangely intoxicating, not to mention intoxicated.

Auld Vinny arrived half an hour before last orders and proudly introduced us to his dozen new-found female friends, the local lesbian darts team. Bold, buxom and boisterous, they were twelve good men and true. Maz immediately signed them up for her newly invented fortnightly league. Auld Vinny quizzed them incessantly about how they 'did it'. I rapidly concluded that, judging by this lot, if I ever developed lesbian tendencies, I'd have to shave my head, spoon myself into black drainpipe jeans and maroon DM boots, and change my name to Conny Lingers. If my love life didn't improve rapidly, it wouldn't be long before I got the clippers out.

After a few too many offers of 'and one for yerself, pet', I began to feel a bit worse for wear. Too little blood in my alcohol stream, I concluded. At such moments I find there is a very fine line between giggling hysteria and manic depression. I inadvertently settled for the latter.

'Why is my love life so continuously crap?' I moaned, as Maz and I ducked to avoid the pickled eggs and beer mats that had been selected as ammunition for an impromptu pub war.

'It's not that bad,' she replied as an egg whizzed past and exploded all over a framed photograph of 'Gordon, your Manager'. A definite improvement. 'You're just at a low point, Jen, it'll pick up.'

'Low point. Any lower and I'll be scouting for a date with an Australian bush pig. We're talking nun-status here.'

'Ah bollocks,' Maz laughed, narrowly avoiding an eggy missile, 'I've seen people flirtin' with you all neet. You've got loads of blowks lookin' at you.'

'Yeah great. Three lesbians, a ginger slaphead who gets his fashion inspiration from Jimmy Saville, and a 60-year-old whose chat-up line was, 'If I tek oot me falseys I can suck the fillin' oot a meat pie in four seconds, straits!' Meanwhile you leave a trail of drooling men in your wake who at least all pass the subhuman standard. It's not fair.'

I considered stamping my feet and

throwing a tantrum, but at that moment a jet-propelled egg flew overhead and came into contact with Maz's shrine to Ricki Lake. Sacrilege!

'A'reet, ya bunch of wankers!' Maz roared. 'Fun's over.'

She jumped up and aimed a blow at the egg bomber's face. He stumbled backwards, holding his nose. Maz turned on the crowd. 'Howay that's enough. Sit doon or I'll twat the lotta yas.'

No fear, that was my friend.

'Why-aye Maz,' they cheered. 'We love it when ya get mad!'

Maz quickly brought them under control and I proceeded to pick up the debris, wishing I could be as brave.

'Jen,' Maz whispered over her shoulder, 'how aboot the fella over there? He's been watchin' you fer ages.'

I glanced over towards the far end of the bar and saw a blond-haired athletic-looking man staring at me through the chaos with piercing, almost black eyes.

'Leave that shite,' Maz ordered, 'and get yerself over there.'

I stood up slowly, wiping the egg off my velour catsuit as best I could. He was still staring intensely in my direction with a stern yet appealing expression on his rugged face.

He had the demeanour of the star of a trendy beer advert but with the hands of a mechanic. *Perhaps this is what I need*, I wondered. *To be ravaged by a real man, one who can fix a leaky pipe, service my car, drink six pints and get active in the sack all in an afternoon.* I tingled at the thought and walked seductively towards him.

'Your boyfriend is a lucky man,' he growled sexily. 'I bet he wakes up every day with a smile on his face.'

I leaned on the bar and tried to smile, but with the effort of holding my stomach in, sticking my boobs out and tucking my bum under, it was more of a teeth-baring grimace.

'Oh, I don't have a boyfriend,' I purred. 'I'm single and available.' (Tattooing 'desperate and gagging' on my forehead would perhaps have been a little less obvious.)

'Really?' he replied. 'I heard he was some sort of karate expert, as well as being the intelligent type, of course.'

'Oh him.' Damn, I'd been exposed as a liar already and we'd only been acquainted for 20 seconds. 'Well, he's a . . . um . . . he's . . . '

'Hey, you don't have to explain yourself to me.' He laughed and took a sip of Guinness, then slowly licked the milky froth from his lips.

'Let me do that.' (Oops, didn't mean to say that out loud.)

'What?'

'Nothing. So . . . um, do you come here . . . much?' On a one-to-ten scale of unimaginative I was pushing 18.

He laughed again. 'Chip,' he said and held out a rugged hand.

'Salt and vinegar?'

'No, Chip, that's — '

'Just chips? I'll see what I can do.'

'My name. Chip is my name.'

I blushed. 'Oops, sorry, of course it is. Chip.' I could feel myself getting flustered. We were building up to a conversation and already I could think of absolutely nothing to say. 'Chip,' I repeated. 'That's very American. Like Chuck, Charlie, Frankie, Hank, and Lance, only . . . not.' (Lunatic.)

He looked at me blankly then smiled again but made no response. Hardly surprising really.

'I'm Jennifer,' I quickly continued. 'Jennifer Summer. I work here.'

'No kidding. I wondered why you were standing behind that bar. Well, hello Jennifer Summer. I'm delighted to meet you.'

I was even more delighted. Since Jack, Chip was the first man, worthy of that description, who had taken an interest in me. Somewhere in a rarely visited region below my waist, I could hear champagne corks popping.

We carried on chatting about nothing in

particular. Chip was witty, flirtatious, sexy and fascinating. There was something about him that made me inquisitive. I felt as if he was holding something back but I couldn't put my finger on it. Anyway, I wasn't thinking too deeply. I was simply enjoying a much-needed dose of flirting.

'Have you always worked here?' Chip asked after a while.

'No, not at all. I used to have a job on the quayside.' I wanted to impress him.

'The bars there are really posh, aren't they? Quite a few have appeared since I was here last. Bit poncey for me, though. Were you a waitress or a barmaid?'

'Neither' — my stupid pride was now doing the talking — 'I was a lawyer actually.'

Expecting gasps of impressed amazement, I was surprised to see his face change from a happy healthy Chip to a withered McDonald's French fry. The smile faded and his eyes narrowed to a look that sent a shiver down my catsuit. I instantly sensed that the chemistry between us had become more of a fourth-year science experiment than a Chernobylstyle explosion.

'So . . . um . . . What about you?' I asked shiftily, after a heavily pregnant pause.

'I just got back from Durham.' His voice was monotone.

'Oh, it's a lovely place, Durham. Was it nice?'

'Yeah, bloody great. Especially when you're doin' ten years for GBH because your bleedin' lawyer cocked up.'

Oops. I guess an ex-lawyer/ex-con romance was out of the question then? If there was ever a conversation-stopper, that was it.

Suddenly, and fortunately for my health, my attention was diverted by a figure standing at the door directly behind Chip. The figure was dressed in a dark blue blazer, a crisp, expensive-looking shirt and beige moleskin trousers. His dark hair was slicked back perfectly, not a single one out of place. In the commotion of the Scrap Inn, he stuck out like an Eskimo in a sauna. I was speechless and unable to move as the figure walked towards me. I thought I was dreaming as I realised it was Jack.

A vision flashed through my mind of this slick, gorgeous man lifting me gently over the bar, kissing me passionately on my trembling lips and whisking me out into the night. Not dissimilar to the final scene in *An Officer and a Gentleman*, except he wasn't wearing a white uniform and I wasn't working in a factory. Had he realised his mistake and come back to say he was sorry? My eyes searched his person for chocolates and flowers. I'd expect a good few bunches after all this palaver.

'How did you find me?' I asked, trembling as he reached the bar. He was as irresistible to me as ever.

'A little bird told me,' he replied, looking around the pub in bewilderment. He seemed to be taking in every detail. I decided that he felt guilty about getting me in this predicament (totally his fault, of course) and couldn't look me in the eye.

'So how are you?' I asked softly. (Please just kiss me now and get it over with.)

'Fine, fine.' Still he looked away.

'I miss you Jack.' The words were out before I knew it but this was no time for playing games. 'I'm glad you came.'

'Oh, so am I.' At last he looked at me. 'So am I.' There was a twinkle in his eye which I couldn't quite understand. Then he started to laugh. He laughed loudly, not pausing for breath, clutching his sides and throwing his head back. The pub fell silent as Jack roared louder, banging the bar with his fist and wiping tears from his eyes.

I felt Maz close behind me. 'What's that tosser doin' here?' she whispered.

'This is great!' Jack chortled. 'What a dump!'

I heard Maz's teeth grind.

'Look at it,' he carried on, 'and look at you, Jenny. What do you look like! Lawyer come barmaid, oh fantastic. Haven't you done well?'

I could feel my eyes filling up with tears but I couldn't speak. My heart was breaking into tiny pieces . . . again.

He calmed down a little, until he could breathe at least. 'We, the firm, are acting for the people who might be selling this place. When Matt said you were living here, of course I offered to do a recce. I couldn't wait to see what you were up to but I never expected this. Ha, it's the best laugh I've had in ages.'

'Apart from when you last looked at your todger, you prick,' Maz seethed.

By now the tears were rolling down my face. My mascara was in danger of becoming floor polish but Jack didn't care. He was in his element and continued regardless.

'Maybe I should get Vicky out of the Beemer. She would find this absolutely hilarious I'm sure.

My heart sank. Vicky. Bloody Vicky. I had hoped she had caught some rare, tropical disease and died a slow, painful death. No such luck. Before I could say anything Maz leapt over the bar and grabbed Jack by the collar of his shirt.

'Right, you little pile of shite,' she yelled. 'That's enough! Get oot of my pub before I bloody well throw you oot, piece by piece!'

Jack's face was turning red but he continued to smile and struggled to get free.

'But it's hilarious,' he spluttered. 'I mean, look at these people!'

That was it. A lawyer in the Scrap Inn exuding wealth was bad, but a cocky lawyer publicly degrading the locals was as good as dead.

'Get him!' roared the crowd.

'Ya f'kin' poncey bastard.'

Tables and chairs flew as Maz let Jack loose and the charge began. The dogs were after the hare with their teeth bared. Howls, growls and screams filled the smoky air.

In a flash he was gone, pursued by my new friends. I couldn't see his loafers for dust. I don't usually condone violence but after that verbal assault I felt peculiarly happy to see him run. He really knew how to trample on a girl's feelings. Before long, the roar faded and the pub was empty except for Auld Vinny snoring in the corner. I let out a deep breath. Maz locked the front door.

'He'll let himself out.' She nodded at the birthday boy and led me to the door of the flat like a lost child. I still hadn't uttered a word.

Maz lifted a bottle of vodka from the shelf as we passed the bar.

'Come on, let's get pissed,' she said, smiling at me knowingly. 'A toast to that tosser,' she said, raising the bottle above her head. 'And God help his shiny shoes when they catch him!'

7

10th February, 7:00 p.m.

The next four weeks passed by monotonously. Everything that had been new to me became the norm as my previous life turned into a distant memory. Maz and I worked hard at the pub, managing to increase the number of customers with cheap deals, gimmicks and partially cloaked bribes, in an attempt to convince the brewery not to sell.

Auld Vinny and Co were a constant source of entertainment, and I soon found myself becoming acquainted with people whom I wouldn't even have considered talking to a few weeks before. Many would not have been regarded as 'appropriate' friends for a city lawyer, especially those who had often sat on the other side of the legal divide.

Unsurprisingly, I hadn't heard from Jack since the day of the fight. Rumour had it that he had surpassed himself in his athletic attempt to escape the pursuing crowd. To my selfish delight, he had omitted to stop for the lovely Vicky and his BMW.

For the first three weeks I was more

celibate than Cliff Richard. Much longer and I would have been dangerously close to taking a train to Wimbledon to sing 'Living Doll' in the rain with Sue Barker.

When I wasn't working, my nights were spent in front of the TV with a depressing movie, a bottle of wine, four tons of chocolate and a roll of super-absorbent toilet paper. My a-ha tape was on constant play, blaring out melancholic Norwegian ballads at all hours. It was only when I turned to my 1982 Greatest Love compilation album that Maz threw in the towel and made it her mission to rectify the situation, much to my annoyance.

★   ★   ★

My first organised date therapy was with Pete, a motorbike enthusiast from Byker. After having promised Maz that I would put some effort into her new venture, I had gone to the expense of a manicure, a hair-do, and a new outfit. I looked about two feet taller with my hair piled high — what the hairdresser called 'renaissance style' — and my feet shoved into a pair of high-heeled mules. I had to hand it to bar work, though — all those hours on my feet seemed to have done wonders for my legs. What had previously been well-cultivated fat had now been upgraded to relaxed muscle and, in my opinion, worthy of a mini skirt. I felt like a slapper, but it would keep Maz happy and I wasn't looking for a meaningful relationship anyway.

Pete was rugged, with a slight quiff and far too long sideburns. I had to admit that some girls would find him attractive if they had ever had a thing for Fonzy or Alvin Stardust. He was friendly, though, and chatted constantly as we sat in the pub getting to know each other.

It was only when I had a black-and-red-flamed helmet shoved on my £12 hair-do and a leather jacket emblazoned with 'Pete's Chick' forced over my velvet basque that Maz and I finally realised our mistake.

Three hours later I managed to dislodge myself from the back of Pete's super-bike and peel my legs away from his leather trousers. Of course, this was only after I had been given a full description and practical demonstration of the effects of G-force at 120 miles per hour. Conversation had been nearly impossible at that speed, but Pete had tried his damnedest to shout over the roaring engine for fear that I'd overlook some glorious feature of his grown-up toy.

'Hey, doesn't this baby zoom. Woo-hoo yeah, feel that acceleration! I'm moving up model next month, double muffler and eighteen hundred cc . . . Yeah, baby, let's rock!'

Feeling like I'd been on a date with ZZ Top, I was finally deposited back at the pub, much to the shrieking delight of our regulars. I declined the invitation to see Pete's ten-year collection of *Motorcycle Monthly* and strongly resisted a private viewing of his newest tattoo, a naked 'babe' riding his 'throbbing machine'.

Naively I believed Maz when she assured me the next date would be much better. How could it possibly be any worse? So along came Stuart, later known to Maz and I as 'Nervous Stu'. Date number two was a friend of Gordon's, the manager. A computer programmer from Jesmond, he was wealthy, intellectual, and in need of an escort to his company's February bash. 'He can be a little nervous,' Gordon had said on a rare visit to the pub, 'and he's not too confident with women, so be nice.'

Nervous! Bloody hell, this guy was the epitome of a blubbering wreck. Being a friend of Gordon's, I should have known. The trouble was, I had always been attracted to the idea of a wealthy, intellectual type. Surely there was one who wasn't a geek? Apparently not. Nervous Stu arrived in a chauffeur-driven limo, already suffering from the effects of having quickly consumed a bottle of bubbly.

After smashing several glasses in the pub, poking his bony, shaky finger in my eye when he tried to kiss me, and calling me every name except my own, Nervous Stu proceeded to throw up in my lap as I took my first ever ride in a limo.

'Oh . . . I'm sorry, I'm . . . I'm j . . . j . . . just a bit nervous with women and you're . . . you're . . . beautiful.'

Torn between a choice of mothering him, even though he was old enough to be my father, and calling him a stupid twat, I decided on the latter. I then felt pathetically guilty when he appeared to be about to burst into tears. Against my better judgement, I decided not to throw myself immediately in front of the nearest bus home and agreed to go on to the party (after stopping the limo at a roadside McDonald's to sponge the puke off my skirt).

The party was a swanky affair packed with computer whizz-kids and their compu-literate partners. I smiled dumbly while my dinner companions bounced around the latest computer language and discussed websites, packages and megabytes. I tried to join in the conversation but, being about as computer-literate as a Masai Mara farmer, I could add little of value. All my computer work at Glisset & Jacksop had been done by my secretary. That made me realise that Vicky knew far more about computers than I did, which only served to make me more depressed and sealed my decision to drink myself into oblivion.

Nervous Stu, I noticed, was also downing the free drink with great enthusiasm. As his bravado increased, every now and then he would gingerly attempt to touch my bum or stroke my breasts. On the third such occasion, I threatened to shove his megabytes where technology wouldn't reach them. At this point, my date dropped profiteroles down my cleavage, vomited all over his boss's wife, and wet himself, before passing out on the dessert trolley.

Nervous Stu was followed by John. John was, like many men, a passionate football fan and did little or nothing to hide his religious adoration of anything remotely connected to St James' Park. He pledged his allegiance to Bobby Robson every morning and lived his life in black and white stripes. We spent our date behind the goal at a Cup match, shouting obscenities at the Liverpool fans and cheering on Shearer and 'the lads'. I learned several Newcastle team songs, which made Gary Barlow's creations sound promising.

Mind you, having to chant 'Toon, Toon, Black and White Army' in return for watching twenty-two fit pairs of legs chase a ball around a pitch seemed to be an ideal way to pass an afternoon. It was just unfortunate that John so strongly disagreed with the linesman's offside ruling in the fifty-ninth minute. Storming the pitch, punching the official and flashing to the crowd had not been well received by the ground's security force. I had been picked up as an accomplice and we had spent the remaining thirty-one minutes plus extra time locked in the cells. We had then been reprimanded, fined, and forcefully removed from the ground and told never to return. My first and, apparently last, live football match and I didn't even get to see them exchange jerseys at the final whistle.

After experiencing Liam, the wannabee pop star, Gio, the wannabee actor and Pierre, who had a penchant for porn, I considered signing up for the lesbian darts team. Perhaps they had the right idea after all.

'Howay Jen, just one more date,' Maz groaned, stomping around the flat behind me.

'Maz, I may look desperate but I'm not a registered charity. Give me a break!'

'He's geet nice,' she persisted.

'Yeah, that's what you said about the other

bunch of cavemen you sent me.'

'And he's rich.'

'So he says. Maz, you may be my best friend but I think I give your choices of date the red card.'

I started to run a bath and slopped handfuls of 'Magic Mud' on my face. After my recent spate of apocalyptically bad dates, I was looking forward to a night in with my good friends, self-pity and self-indulgence. Their team-mates, alcohol and kilocalorie would be popping in at a later stage.

'Please, Jen.' Maz burst in through the bathroom door. 'Aaagh, your face!'

'Aaagh, yours too!'

I climbed in the bath and grabbed my tacky magazine. 'Rock his world — a sexy how-to guide', 'The British male and his desires', 'Great loving in ten days'.

'What is this female magazine preoccupation with men?' I shouted. 'I should have bought *Combat Weekly*.'

'Jen!' Maz roared. 'Please go on the date.'

I glanced at my friend. She was pacing nervously up and down the length of the room, fiddling with her watch and biting her nails.

'Maz, what is it?'

'Nothing.' More nail biting.

'Right. Good. I've said no and I mean no,

121

so piss off and leave me in peace, you mad woman. You're making me nervous.'

Frantic fiddling with hair and lip-gnawing.

'Maz, your body language is not looking good to me. You're practically strangling your watch.'

Twisting of ring and humming.

'Oh shite,' she said finally. 'The thing is, he'll be here in five minutes.'

'Who will?'

'Troy.'

'Troy who? Who's Troy?'

'Troy, your date. I met him in the pub earlier. He seems canny, Jen, and the thing is he'll be here in . . . ' Drrring. ' . . . about now.'

A deathly silence.

'Oh damn, he's here!'

I jumped out of the bath screaming, 'You cow, I hate you, you interfering old tart!'

I frantically began scrubbing Magic Mud off my face. I soon discovered the magic was in its abnormal powers of bonding with human flesh. I had a choice between emerging from the bathroom closely resembling a female mud wrestler, or simultaneously scraping off the mud and three layers of skin. I must admit it certainly unblocked the pores.

Troy, for God's sake. Which reject of the human race had she dug up for me this time?

Just by the name, I envisaged a second-rate gladiator in a white Lycra thong. All pecs and no performance.

'This is the last time, Maz,' I muttered to my reflection in the mirror.

White thong, if only. This man was a peach. Ripe, luscious and good enough to eat. Whilst being introduced, I was speechless, in the taxi I was drooling like a rabid dog and by dinner I was positively gagging, legs akimbo with two large glasses of wine stirring in my loins.

'So Troy, tell me about yourself.'

I stared at this perfect specimen through the plastic tulips on the table. His wide blue eyes glistened against the tanned skin of his smiling face. His blond hair was cut close to his perfectly sized head, and two rows of sparkling white teeth reflected the glow of my over-exfoliated skin.

'OK, uh, I'm twenty-nine, I'm from California but I have a house in Hawaii.'

'Hawaii!' I squealed, almost choking on my garlic bread. Visions of white beaches, palm trees and me in a grass skirt flashed through my mind. Lose the 'me in a grass skirt' bit and it was almost perfect.

'Hawaii,' I repeated. 'How lovely.' (Lame I know but I was trying to play it cool.)

'Yeah,' he drawled, 'it's paradise for sure but I'm considering a move to England.'

'Good God, man, you must be mad.'

'No I like it. It's really historical, everything's so old. And the pubs, wow man, the pubs are just so cool.'

I smiled inanely, trying to think of something to say, but his sparkling smile was so distracting. I opted for another slice of garlic bread instead.

'So Jennifer. Can I call you Jenny?'

(You can call me Frank if you like. I'll still answer.)

'Yes sure, Jenny's fine.'

'So Jenny, do you enjoy working in the pub?'

I loved the way he said my name. 'Jaynee', it made me feel like a movie star. Damn, I really must concentrate. My conversational skills appeared to have slipped somewhere below my waist. I fiddled with the garlic bread. What was the question again? Oh yes.

'The pub? Yes, it's great, it's fun. Great people and lots of fun.'

'It's fun then?' he laughed.

I blushed.

'I bet you're a fantastic barmaid,' he smiled. 'Not that I've seen you in action yet.'

What are we waiting for? Action stations, I'm ready when you are. God, this was getting desperate.

'I'm fairly new actually,' I replied. 'I used to solicit but . . . '

'Excuse me?'

'Solicit . . . solicitor, solicitor. I mean I was a solicitor, ha ha.' My laugh erupted like Lulu on acid. 'I was a lawyer but I got fi — I left. Yes, over a drug problem. Not *my* drug problem, I don't have one of course. Ha ha. I know they say denial is the first sign of addiction but I really don't. Big misunderstanding.'

Shut up, Jennifer.

'Silly really,' I added.

Blimey, a fly on the wall next to our table would have been marvelling at the social incompetence of the human race by this stage. I'm supposed to be an intelligent woman, for God's sake. Why, when I'm trying to impress, do I lose all ability to string more than two words together? I saw Troy's brow wrinkle in an 'oh no, she's a complete lunatic' kind of way, so I opted for silence and reached for the last slice of garlic bread. Except that there wasn't one. I'd eaten it all, his portion and mine. Fat trollop.

'So what are your hobbies, Troy?' I asked, making an attempt at sensible conversation.

He grinned. 'Shopping. I just love shopping.'

'Shopping? But you're a man. Men loathe

shopping. Any man I've ever tried to take shopping loses all ability to stand when he gets within a mile of a clothes shop. That's why they have sofas in stores these days.'

He laughed raucously. 'Man, you're so funny.'

'I bet you that was the whole reason behind the Internet,' I continued. 'That way, men can shop without moving out of earshot of the football.'

'Not me. I love the whole shopping thing,' he winked. 'Especially the changing rooms, if you know what I mean.'

I have absolutely no idea but whatever you say.

'You're weird,' I laughed, sitting back to let the waiter place a huge bowl of pasta in front of me.

'Thanks,' he smiled, also sitting back and giving the waiter an obvious wink.

Must be an American thing, I thought, tucking into my dinner. Thank God I'd had the sense not to order spaghetti.

'English people are so different,' Troy said dreamily, turning his head slowly from the direction of our retreating waiter. 'I thought you'd all be really stiff upper lip.'

'And live in castles?' I added.

'Yeah and read Shakespeare.'

'And have tea with the Queen.'

'Exactly! Man, you are so funny, Jenny. You're all so friendly. Everyone's cool. The guys . . . and the chicks of course.'

I felt the blood surge to my cheeks.

'I've never been called a chick before,' I giggled.

In one smooth sentence, Troy had propelled my fantasies from part-time barmaid in the Rover's Return to red-swimming-cozzie-clad silicone beach babe on *Baywatch*. I was Pamela Anderson and Troy was my David Hasselhoff. Only, Troy was better looking, about twenty years younger and without the dodgy hair-do.

'Of course you're a chick. You're a great chick and I'm glad I met you.'

'So am I.' I rested my chin on my left hand and gazed into his blue eyes. Blue and tranquil like unpolluted oceans.

'And I hope we can be great friends.'

'Yes, me too.'

Friends? Stuff the friends part, lover boy, I'm going to marry you. Marry you, move to Hawaii and hula till the coconuts come home. OK, I'll admit, I was one hundred per cent swayed by his looks. I hardly knew the man and there was something about him that I wasn't sure about, but my hormones were all aboard the rocket, blasting off for planet pleasure. My mind had gone fluffy and I had to concentrate far too hard on making decent conversation to worry about niggling little doubts. I gazed at his tan. We just don't make men like that in England.

'You've got a great tan,' I grinned. 'Is it real?'

'Sure it's real,' he replied. 'I've built it up slowly and deeply.'

'Slowly and deeply,' I repeated. I shifted uncomfortably in my seat. 'I like that.'

'Me too,' Troy said dreamily, his blue eyes following our slim Italian waiter as he squeezed past our table. Far too much bum wiggling for my liking. Damn, I was losing his attention.

'Oh, you haven't even told me what you do yet, Troy.'

'Huh?' he replied distractedly.

Somewhere in the back of my head, an over-enthusiastic bell ringer was sounding the alarm, but I chose to ignore it.

'Your work, Troy, what is it that you do?'

He suddenly looked animated. OK, we were back at first base.

'I work in the airlines, Jenny.'

Holy guacamole! Kelly McGillis eat your heart out, Top Gun's in town. Second base here I come.

'I fly a lot, usually Hawaii-Japan so I get to see the sun all over the world. It's just fantastic.'

'Wow,' I drooled. 'Take My Breath Away' played loudly in my head. 'Are you a pilot?' Hello third base.

'Huh, I wish. No, I'm a flight attendant.'

'A what?'

My home run faltered slightly.

'Flight attendant. Oh sorry, man, you guys call it a host.'

'A host? Ooh, an air hostess.' (OK so there were negatives.) I laughed loudly, 'So you're an air hostess. Ha ha, are you gay?'

He looked at me blankly. Fourth base faded into the distance as I began to wake up to reality. I stopped laughing. Troy stared at me intently then began to roar with laughter.

'Ha ha man, you English.' He banged the table with his hand. 'You're just so crazy.'

Yes, well I don't think I'm the only crazy one around here.

'It's the sarcasm, I get caught out every time.'

'Ha ha,' I tried. Please God, strike me with lightening.

'I thought you were serious, *Jaynee*,' he howled.

'Oh right, ho ho.' Just one life-ending bolt.

Troy clutched his side and tried to catch his breath. 'Am I gay?' he chuckled. 'Nice one.'

Now God, give it your best shot, just don't miss.

He sat back in his seat, puffed out his chest and threw his arms wide open. 'Of course I am, Jenny. Of course I'm gay. Gay, homo, bent as a fiddler's elbow. G-A-Y and proud, that's me.'

Somewhere inside my body, the hormonal rocket veered off course, crashed and burned while the bell ringer shouted 'see I told you so' in my aching brain.

Troy beamed his glistening white smile and leaned across the table towards me. 'Now honey,' he whispered, winking conspiratorially, 'are you going to order a dessert because I want another close look at that waiter. Man, he's all that with sugar on top.'

★ ★ ★

'Howay man, he didn't say that,' said Maz, her mouth agape.

'I swear he did.'

'Piss off. He said, 'all that with sugar on top'?'

'Yep the very same.'

'Wi' sugar on top? Howay.'

'He did. And close your mouth, I can see your bacon sandwich.'

Maz shook her head in disbelief, wiped her

130

mouth with the back of her hand and plonked herself on the end of my bed.

'Shite, Jen man, bit of a nightmare.'

'That's an understatement. It was so embarrassing. I was like a dog on heat all through dinner but that little gem certainly doused the flames.'

'Aye I bet.' Maz sucked the ketchup out of a third bacon sandwich. 'I just thought he was canny. He seemed geet cute, ye kna, not that I talked to him much.'

'He was canny,' I groaned, 'and he was certainly cute. The only problem was that he thought our small-bummed waiter was cuter. How could I compete with buns like that?'

'Bummer.'

'Most probably.'

I groaned, collapsed back in my bed and covered my face with the pillow. How depressing. Admittedly, there had been signs, not least when he practically foamed at the mouth every time Little Bum walked within wiggling distance, but I'd been distracted. I thought we were on a date, not a platonic bonding session. That was the last time I let my hormones reach intergalactic proportions (until the next time). We sat in silence mulling over my total humiliation.

'Bacon sandwich?' Maz said at last, thrusting the plate of ketchup-soaked burnt offerings under my nose.

'Might as well,' I grumbled. 'I might as well eat a whole pig farm. No one would notice.'

Maz suppressed a laugh and gave me a look of mock sympathy.

'Three days till Valentine's Day and I've got bugger-all chance of getting a card now,' I continued, determined to stay miserable.

'Not necessarily pet,' chirped Maz. 'We've still got time.'

'Oh no. Absolutely no way are you setting up another date for me.'

'It'll be no problem. The next one will be lush, honest.'

'Noo, no, no,' I said, pulling the duvet protectively up to my neck. 'Thanks to you I've just had the shortest love affair in living history. My 'boyfriend' wanted a boyfriend, slight problem Maz.'

Maz shrugged her shoulders. That was the closest I was going to get to an apology.

'Now piss off and let me wallow in self-pity,' I grouched. 'I'm not getting up for at least a month.'

'Oh,' Maz began, 'I think you'll have to, pet.'

'Why?'

Maz jumped up far too quickly and headed for the door. 'I almost forgot,' she said over her shoulder.

'Forgot what?'

'You've got visitors. Down in the pub.'

'Visitors? Who are they?'

'Your parents, they're here to see you.'

The bacon sandwich in my stomach did a triple salco. I almost threw up. 'My parents, you're kidding.'

'Na man. Mummy and Daddy Summer in the flesh. Good morning eh?' She laughed loudly and stomped out of the room.

I must have done something terrible in a past life, I thought morosely. Oh God, give me strength.

8

'Eleven bloody players and not one o' them
was born in Newcastle, eh. Bloody foreigners,
the lot o' them. It's a load o' canny shite,
man, I tell't you.' Auld Vinny's voice rang out
through the midday crowd as I entered the
pub feeling only partially human. 'Aye you
gan to see a bloody football match and you
end up watchin' Ravioli, Gino Ginelli, flippin'
Julio what's 'is face. I mean, what happened
to the Geordies, man? I deen't give a
monkeys whether they're prettier than Peter
Beardsley. I tell't ya if they cannot play a bit
of real footie it's a load of shite. Divin' and
cryin'. Howay, bunch of bleedin' ponces.'

My father listened open-mouthed, trying
desperately to find the appropriate answers to
Vinny's soliloquy.

'Um . . . um . . . but . . . ' he stammered,
'what about Alan Shearer and Robert Lee,
they're good players?' My father looked
childishly pleased with himself.

'Jackie Milburn and bloody Kevin Keegan,'
Auld Vinny continued. 'Them were the real

134

days. Aye in them days you could walk doon the street withoot a care in the world.'

'True,' sighed my father.

'We worked hard, mind. Bloody worked us till we were fit to drop, man. I tell't you. Bloody twenty-six hours a day fer a couple o' poont. Aye these youngsters deen't kna when they've got it easy, man. Used to work on the ships me, you kna. Proper sailor. Aye, I had a lass in every port I did, when I were a nipper.' He tweaked his 'Ultimate International Sex Machine' cap and winked mischievously at my mother. She frowned.

'Aye, if I were ten years younger, woman, I'd show you.' He laughed.

My mother turned a shade of green and looked away, making her usual 'tsk' noises. I felt obliged to rescue them from Auld Vinny's onslaught but I was getting far too much enjoyment from the scene.

'At least in our day we had some decent music, mind. You could neck wi' a lass to our sort of stuff. Not all this bleedin' jumpin' up 'n' doon, and screamin' at each other. Load o' shite man. That bleedin' Prodi-wotsit fella with the green hair and bloody bolts up 'is nose. Bloody loony man. What's that all aboot then?'

'Mmm, I don't know them really . . . ' my father stammered.

'All the rest are jest as bad I tell't you. F'kin' Brit pop they call it. More like shit pop. I mean all the swearin' at photographers and shite. Should be bloody locked up, man, they're mental I reckon.'

'Do you like dance music, Vinny?' my father asked politely.

'Aye. Give us a good wuman and I'll show 'er how to dance. Used to call us Vinny the Gyrator. Straits! Just cos o' the way I gyrated me body. Aye the lasses loved us man. They'd come to chez Vinny to see us move! Can't really do it now, mind. Meks me bladder weak, all that bloody jigglin'. I'd have to get up ten times a neet fer a piss.'

My mother tutted loudly and stomped away from the table with her nose in the air.

'Marilyn, tell that awful man to leave us alone.'

'Ah, he's harmless Mrs S,' Maz replied, suppressing her laughter. She signalled to Auld Vinny to keep it down.

'Why-aye Marilyn,' he shouted loudly from across the pub, before starting up a rendition of 'Diamonds are a Lass's Best Friend'.

'Hello Mother.' I leaned across the bar and kissed her on both cheeks. She liked the European greeting style. It made her feel somehow upper class. This was our first meeting of the New Year.

'Petal,' she said snootily, 'I've been rather upset with you, but Daddy says all this fighting is silly.'

'Fighting? Who's fighting. I'm just staying out of your way.'

She ignored me. 'Yes, Daddy persuaded me to come, so here I am. Though goodness only knows what possessed you to come and live in a place like this!'

'Hang on a minute,' Maz interrupted. 'Have a go at her, Mrs S . . . '

'Gee, thanks pal.'

' . . . but leave 'this place' and my home out of it, if you don't mind.' Maz furiously began to clean some already spotless glasses.

'Anyway Jennifer. Daddy and I have decided what you should do.'

'About what?'

'About this silly mess, of course.'

'What mess?'

'If you stop interrupting I may be able to tell you. Honestly dahling, where did you learn your manners? It certainly wasn't from me, that's for sure. Really. If only you were more like — '

'Oh get on with it, Mum.'

'You see what I mean? No manners at — '

'MUM! I've got work to do, so I don't mean to be rude but what do you want?'

'You call this work, do you? A barmaid in a

137

public house. This public house especially.'

She ran her hand along the bar, checking for dirt, and shook her head disapprovingly.

'No, no, no, Jennifer,' she tutted loudly, 'this just won't do.'

'Mum, it's fine, it is great. At least we have fun and it's not as bad as you think.' I suddenly felt very protective of my new abode.

As if on cue, Auld Vinny stumbled to the bar and slung a tattooed arm around my mother's cashmere-clad shoulder. She grimaced as he smiled and reached into his pocket. He pulled out a dirty piece of food, held it to my mother's face, burped loudly and said, 'Pickled egg, lass?'

'Get away from me, you disgusting human being. Good gracious, Jennifer, do you see what I mean?' She was shaking with disgust and frantically rubbing the sleeve of her sweater as if she thought she would catch a nasty disease. 'I will not have any daughter of mine come to this.'

'Come to this? Bloody hell, Mum, I'm not a prostitute.'

'Oh, swearing as well, now. Aren't we clever?'

'Jesus Mum . . . '

'And blaspheming. What would my friends say? That's it, dahling, you're coming home with us.'

'What?'

'It's all arranged. Susie's husband has kindly offered to find work for you at the bank, an offer he may live to regret.'

'But — '

'You will have your old room at the house, work with Sebastian and try to bring some respectability back to this family.'

'Mother, I — '

'Now get your things, stop all this nonsense and let's leave. In time we may be able to put all this silliness behind us.'

'Wait just a minute, Mother.' I felt as if I had been whisked back to my childhood. Mother and I had never really seen eye to eye. I seemed to get the blame for everything, ranging from the washing machine breaking down to mother burning the roast. She was an awful cook. Until I was ten, I thought most animals descended from the charcoal family. I think I was the only kid at school to beg for seconds of school dinners.

'I am almost twenty-seven years old. You can't order me around like this any more, Mother,' I said forcefully.

'Dahling, don't be silly now.'

'Aagh! You're driving me crazy. I live here, I work here, I earn money and, personally, I couldn't give a toss what your poncey twin-set friends think. As for working for

Sebastian, I'd rather impale myself on a sharp implement than work for a stuck-up, materialistic, arsewipe like him. This isn't the Victorian era, you know. I may not be keeping up with the Joneses, Mother, but I'm happy and if you don't like it you can just . . . well . . . it'll give you something to discuss at your ludicrously overpriced therapy sessions, won't it?'

We glared at each other, both seething with rage. The pub fell silent. It was handbags at dawn. In the far corner, I noticed my father cowering behind a pint of shandy. I supposed it would be too much to hope for him to stand up to my mother. The once strong, funny man had learned only too well over the years who was to wear the proverbial trousers in their relationship.

'I hope I'm not interrupting anythin', you guys.' An American accent broke the silence. Troy. I smiled nervously at the perfect tanned face. What a waste.

'Oh not at all,' replied my mother huffily. 'We were just leaving.'

My dad looked up at the sound of the royal 'we'.

'Come on, Daddy, I need you to drive me home.'

There was an uneasy moment as my father looked anxiously from my mother to me and then to Troy. I realised he was blushing.

'Daddy,' my mother ordered, 'finish that shandy and take me home now.'

'Shandy! Howay man woman man,' Auld Vinny retorted, 'this man isny drinkin' bleedin' shandy in my pub. He's drinkin' beer an' nothing else. Jen, gis a bottle o' broon for wur new mate and you better get 'im a whisky to wash it doon with.'

I obliged. Daddy reddened further. Mother stared at Vinny, dumbfounded.

'Daddy, come now.' She repeated the order.

'Howay woman, leave the man be. It's a bloody sad old world when a man cannot drink his ale withoot his wifey shoutin' in his bleedin' ear.'

'Served cool, as you like it.' I grinned at Vinny, handing him the two bottles of Brown Ale and the whisky chasers.

'Aye, that's right pet,' Vinny replied, and turning to my father added, 'She's a reet good barmaid your lass.'

I beamed at the old sailor's compliment. Praise from Vinny was praise indeed.

'WILLIAM SUMMER!' my mother yelled, ignoring Vinny's comment. 'I'm waiting.'

Vinny was undoubtedly of the old school of masculinity but at this precise moment I liked his methods.

'William. Canny lush name man. That's me middle name, reet solid. Now, drink yer pint.'

My father lifted the glass to his lips and began to drink. Slowly at first, but without pausing for breath. Mother huffed. He drank faster. She stamped her foot. He threw it back. She yelled. He sculled the whisky.

'Aye man,' Auld Vinny smiled. 'That's what you needed. A man's gotta have some pleasures in life eh? Dain't be lettin' people stamp you doon, man.'

'William . . . ' Mother had reached the door.

My father looked at me and winked. He smiled broadly for the first time in years. 'Well Jenny,' he said. I sensed a new strength in his voice. 'Let's see how good a barmaid you are. A pint for me, and one for my new friend Vinny.' He paused. 'Hey, make that two each, I'd like to stay for a while.'

★ ★ ★

'Why do men have nipples anyway?' I pondered aloud while reclining on the sofa in the lounge. Well, I think in a past life it had been a sofa. Now it was simply a hideous mass of brown velour threadbare cushions.

'I deen't kna,' Maz replied, 'but they'd look pretty daft without them.' She slugged her half-full plastic bottle of very cheap red wine.

'Not if they all didn't have any. They don't really have a purpose do they? Our nipples nourish and nurture an entire population. What do theirs do? Sweet FA if you ask me. Make their bodies look symmetrical, big wow.'

'Aye. Do nothin' except get hairy and get hard sometimes.'

'Is that just nipples you're talking about, or men in general?'

'Ha ha.' We laughed loudly, slugged more wine and threw popcorn at Troy in a show of girl power. He just giggled and said, 'Oh you guys,' playfully, as he had been doing all night. Americans are just so . . . American, aren't they?

'I've got one,' he said suddenly from his cross-legged position on the floor. 'How come you always get loads of unpopped corn in the bottom of a bucket of popcorn?'

'Well, it's heavier. Dur.' Maz giggled.

'Yeah, sure, but I mean you can cook the stuff till you're blue in the face, burn the pan to buggery and you'll still have half of it unpopped to break your teeth on. It really does my head in, man!'

'A dentist's dream,' I added. 'Good question, Troy. Maz, you're next.'

She frowned, deep in thought.

'You kna that Boy George song?'

'Which one?'

'That karma, karma, karma, karma one.'

'Yeah,' we said together.

'Did anyone have a clue what the bleedin' hell that man was singin' about?'

I pondered the question. 'Reptiles wasn't it?'

'No, sex,' Troy said firmly. 'He was great, man.'

'Sex? How come?' Maz asked.

'That's what all songs are about, little lady.' His eyes twinkled.

''Jingle Bells' isn't,' I piped up.

'Well, obviously not, but — '

'Or *The Sound of Music* — 'How do you solve a problem like Maria?''

'OK, true, but — '

'Or 'Somewhere over the Rainbow'.'

'No . . . '

'Or 'Chitty Chitty Bang Bang' . . . although, come to think of it, it could be.'

'OK, OK! There are exceptions.' He looked flustered.

'Anyway, Maz,' I continued, 'that was the eighties so nothing made sense. That's what the eighties were all about. Nonsense. Karma, karma whatsit, Frankie goes to Hollywood, Howard Jones' electric shock hair-dos, pink plastic bangles . . . um . . . '

'Spotty leggings,' Maz added excitedly.

'Definitely. I mean exactly who do they flatter on this planet? Big huge belts, ankle socks, neon, snogging boys wearing tie-dye Relax T-shirts at roller discos. See, none of it made sense.'

'What's wrong with Relax T-shirts?' Troy asked.

We stared at him blankly for a brief moment.

'Aye man,' Maz giggled, gathering her thoughts, 'I was hideous. Why I ever chose Madonna as a role model I deen't kna. Rara skirts and black lace fingerless gloves. Bloody hell, I'm surprised I wasn't locked up, like.'

Troy stopped flossing his teeth with a chocolate bar wrapper and joined in. 'Just think, you guys, we'll look back on these days in ten years' time and realise how horrible we look now.'

'Na man, this is it, we're cool now.'

'Yeah, but Maz we thought that in 1982. Troy's right. Our kids will look at us and die laughing.'

'How do you think we'll be when we're old?' Troy was becoming more philosophical with every swig of beer.

'I reckon I'll wake up one day and suddenly find fluffy hats, hand-knitted cardigans and Pac-a-macs totally irresistible. All old people seem to hit that purple rinse and beige phase at some point.'

'Eugh, howay, Jen.' Maz choked on her wine while trying to shove a third Mars bar in her mouth. She laughed loudly. 'D'you reckon we'll still dance to things like Cypress Hill and The Chemical Brothers? Ravin' grannies on E?'

'No, probably Neil Sedaka or Lionel Richie. They'll come at the headscarf and tartan shopping trolley on wheels stage.'

'Never!' Troy shouted.

'Kill me now!' Maz yelled.

'OK, maybe just Cliff Richard and Billy Ocean then.'

We all giggled then paused to choose more munchies from the pile in front of us. I started on the ice cream.

'You kna Cliff Richard?' Maz asked after a moment.

'Yup,' Troy replied.

I nodded with a mouthful of mint choc chip.

'D'yas reckon he really is the Messiah?'

'What?' We broke into hysterical laughter. 'Aagh, ice cream headache,' I screamed.

'Na, but listen reet. He cannot be livin' that pure life for nothin'. I mean he's a rock an' roll star, man. He cannot be here just to sing them crap songs and be al' holier than thou.

He must be gettin' somethin' at the end, like crucifixion or risin' from the dead, mustn't he?'

'Maz. He isn't the Messiah, though.'

'Why not then?'

'Well, I don't know . . . because . . . because . . . I don't know. That bloke Lloyd Webber is. You must admit, he works miracles with musicals.'

'Aye true. And you'd have to be a bloody saint to marry someone lookin' like Sarah Brightman. Scary woman or what?'

The night was rapidly degenerating into a post-work alcohol and junk food session. After the unsettling episode in the pub, I had needed de-stressing with calories. Maz was only too happy to oblige and Troy had tagged along for 'a new experience of you British folk'. I had somehow managed to swallow my pride and invite Troy to join us for a girlie night in. I admit it felt odd. Yesterday, boyfriend potential, today as off limits as a Black Forest gâteau in Jodie Kidd's fridge. To be honest, I don't think Troy even realised how close he'd come to being accosted by a rampant woman. In fact, Troy was so baffled by British humour, he didn't seem to understand what was going on at all half the time.

Such nights with Maz generally ended up with us playing games like 'count your stretch marks', 'who would you want to be in your next life?' or 'name all the people you've ever shagged, even the pig-ugly ones'. Tonight's game was 'mysterious questions of life'. OK, it wasn't too taxing, but in this state, we were the first to admit that Trivial Pursuit was a little out of our league. Answering impossible questions for plastic bits of pie . . . What's the point? I'd rather ponder over stupid questions and get real food. Much more satisfying.

While Maz and Troy discussed how it was possible for all the kids from *Fame* to know the same dance when they impulsively broke into song, I thought back to the afternoon's events.

★ ★ ★

My mother had left the pub alone, after my father's unprecedented rebellion. War had been declared on all those responsible for the family's so-called demise and I had been cursed for single-handedly ruining my mother's life.

'You were too much like me,' my father had said honestly. 'She can't stand the sight of me, so you were never going to have much of a chance. She blames you for everything. She even says she knew from the start. Apparently, she thinks her body stayed perfect after

148

Susie, then you came along and messed it all up.' Oh what a selfish, vindictive foetus I had been.

'You weren't planned, you see.' He was drunk and desperate to explain. 'She likes everything to be planned, Jennifer. It all has to be organised and perfect, so that people will see and be impressed. She only wanted one daughter. A perfect only child.'

Silly me for disappointing everyone. Perhaps the stork should just have dropped me off somewhere else.

'You were always my favourite.' He had become tearful. 'You were my little girl. You still are.'

My poor father. He had continued to talk and explain and cry as if to release all that had passed unspoken between us over the years. Why he had never stood up for me, why he had let her try to push me around. It was strange to hear and upsetting to see, but I felt as if a new honesty had come into our lives. Perhaps we could try again and support each other openly.

Father's morose stage had been brought to a conclusion by Auld Vinny demanding that his drinking partner 'Stop actin' like a ponce and play catch up'. The bizarre duo had occupied their own corner of the pub, gibbering away until after last orders. My father had always had a fascination with boats and listened intently to Vinny's wildly exaggerated tales of life at sea. It was so good to see a sparkle in his usually dull, saddened eyes. The man who had finally stumbled out of the door singing 'Sloop John B' was not the man who had traipsed in behind my mother several hours before. I had felt so proud. Proud of him, proud of myself, even proud of my new job. It had somehow changed things.

★ ★ ★

'Earth calling Jennifer.' Maz waved her arms in front of my glazed eyes. 'What do you reckon then?'

'To what?'

'Sex.'

I glanced quickly at Troy. 'Um, it's OK I suppose. It depends on . . .'

'Nah, you gobshite. You weren't listenin'. Why is it that when you're havin' sex, you suddenly start thinkin' about weird stuff?'

'How do you know? I do not . . .'

'Na, not just you, everyone. You kna like about shopping, or . . . or what's on tele, or what you have to do the next day.'

'Yeah,' I joined in. 'Like 'Ooh, I must tidy my knicker drawer and clean the oven'.'

'Or you remember the name of someone you've been tryin' to think of fer the last two weeks.'

We erupted in fits of laughter.

'Or the special offers on the meat counter at Tesco's.'

Troy laughed heartily. He didn't seem at all embarrassed. I put on a straight face and stopped giggling. 'Well, I don't know Marilyn, that's never happened to me in my life.'

'Bollocks!'

'Oh yeah.'

Remembering Troy's existence, I regained my composure. I glanced at him as he sat on the floor and tried to take in the view. The wide shoulders, the tan, the perfectly ironed, crisp clothes. He was almost too perfect. I sighed. Perhaps it was a blessing in disguise that he had only had eyes for our hip-wiggling waiter. Let's face it, new relationships are such hard work. You have to get to know him; he'll try to get to know you. You'll have a good time but pretend to be something you're not. You'll have fumbling kisses, then it'll get passionate. You'll hold hands in the street and he'll tell you you're beautiful. Then he'll ask you to move in perhaps. You'll spend more time together. You'll get to know his habits; he'll find out you really do burp, fart and occasionally pick your nose. He'll start wanting nights out with the lads, weekends alone. You won't hold hands any more. You'll stop going to movies and on dirty weekends and start going to Ikea and B&Q instead. Then you'll get bored. He'll stop telling you you're beautiful. You'll get paranoid, feel ugly and start eating more. He'll watch *A Question of Sport* and fall asleep without saying he loves you. You'll read all your horoscopes in every paper and get totally confused. Then, just as you convince yourself you're being stupid, he'll run off with a silicone, brain-dead secretary and break your heart. Aagh!

I stared at Troy as my imaginary future flashed before my eyes. He caught my psychotic expression and coughed nervously. Bloody hell, I'd had a lucky escape. I had saved myself months, perhaps years of emotional trauma. Thank God for gay men.

'Boy I'm beat,' said Troy, after a silent pause. He scrambled to his feet and smiled at us both. 'Goodnight girls.'

'Stay if you like, Troy. You're very welcome,' I beamed through my new inner peace.

'Gee, thanks, but Julio, the waiter . . . ' He tilted his head towards me for a sign of recognition. As if I could forget. ' . . . Julio knocks off at one.'

'And he'll be knocking you off shortly afterwards,' Maz howled.

'Maz!' I squeeled.

Troy blushed and gave us a knowing wink. I followed him to the door, kissed him on the cheek and watched as he bounded down the stairs with an 'I'm going to get lucky' spring in his step. I felt my inner peace start to crumble.

'Jammy sod,' I grumbled. 'At least somebody's getting some action around here.' I slammed the door, huffed exaggeratedly and trudged back to the sofa for another glass of cheap red wine.

9

13th February, 10:00 a.m.

People always say that your body is at its thinnest point first thing in the morning. This particular day I strongly opposed that theory as I awoke to find someone had cruelly switched my own body during the night with that of a beached ocean mammal. In a vain attempt to spoon myself into a pair of jeans which had fitted me — rather sexily I thought — in December, I had almost cut off the circulation in the lower half of my body and ripped both side seams at the hips. Considering that jeans were originally designed to withstand about 40 years of tough cowboy life, this was no mean feat. 'They've shrunk,' I moaned to myself, and started to gripe about 'shoddy workmanship'.

So as not to live in fat person's denial, I locked myself in the bathroom and forced a glance at my naked body in the full-length mirror. Lordy, lordy, I thought, staring at my hips. Who filled up the saddle bags?

Full-length mirrors are a cruel invention as far as the naked human body is concerned.

The combination of a full-length mirror and weighing scales comes close to sadism.

'How much? You're wrong!' I yelled, kicking the scales and fiddling with the adjustment knob. 'You just can't find an accurate pair of scales these days. Total crap.'

After forty minutes of trying to strangle the scales, staring at my reflection with only one eye, holding in my stomach until I could no longer breathe, and blaming the earth's gravitational pull, I finally had to admit the inevitable. My recent diet of alcohol, pork scratchings and chocolate, combined with a distinct lack of physical activity, other than working behind the bar, had taken its toll. The chance of my achieving supermodel status in the near future had seriously dwindled. Today, in my eyes, I was disgusting, obese, repulsive . . . depressed. I slumped on the turquoise woolly bath mat with my back to the mirror. My stomach rested on my thighs, exhausted from the effort of being held in for more than ten minutes. I needed a plan.

* * *

My first idea was swimming. I dug out my rarely used navy Speedo cossie, and smuggled it to the bathroom. No chance. My hips and thighs sprang out of the elasticated leg holes with amazing volume. No way was I going to reveal my white, dimpled body mass to any toned athletic lifeguard. Besides, I decided the chlorine was bad for the condition of my hair. A very important consideration.

Next came aerobics. That idea lasted all of thirty seconds. The thought of throwing my newly accumulated bulk around a huge mirrored room, surrounded by two dozen Lycra-thonged anorexic fitness freaks made me feel physically sick. I had never been very good at public displays of co-ordination and I envisaged having to pay the equivalent of two entrance fees to cover the amount of space I took up in the studio compared to everyone else. I was exaggerating, of course, but it was one of those days.

A personal daily exercise routine was my next bright idea. Exercise confined to the boundaries of the flat involving neither Lycra nor leg-warmers. Perhaps eventually, when I was closer to presentable, I could hire a strapping male personal trainer, preferably black, six foot, and called Leroy, to take me through my paces. After this spurt of initial enthusiasm, I managed three partial sit-ups before collapsing in a heap with severe indigestion. So much for Leroy.

I finally decided on the simple option of

jogging. Every day I saw people of all shapes and sizes ploughing the streets, Walkman in one hand, sweatband on the other. It did have a public aspect but I figured that with a cunning sporty disguise I could perhaps pass unnoticed. It would be worth it in the long run. I had to at least reach the outer limits of toned. I mean, how hard could it possibly be?

★   ★   ★

'Help me, I'm dying,' I wheezed, falling through the front door of the flat and collapsing at Maz's feet. 'Water . . . food . . . Ambulance.'

'Bloody hell, lass, what have you been doing?' Maz was laughing hysterically at the crumpled sweaty mass on the floor.

'Dying . . . I can't take the pain . . . Water,' I spluttered. 'Must kill . . . Mr Motivator.'

Maz continued to laugh as I rolled onto my back, arms outstretched, with 'Wake Me Up Before You Go Go' still blaring in my ears.

'Maz, my head's boiling up.' I took a few deep breaths. 'I can't feel my legs. Help!'

My trainers, or rather £9.99 plimsolls, felt like shackles on my feet. I couldn't move my body, and my sweat-soaked T-shirt clung with gay abandon to every spare tyre. Sweat dripped from my bedraggled curls, stinging my already red eyes. I could feel the pink 'Dance Crazee' headband slowly compressing my throbbing head. Wow, jogging a mile was harder than I thought.

I was suddenly roused from my post-exercise stupor by the sound of an unfamiliar male voice. 'Flippin' 'eck, it's Mad Lizzy! You've let yersel' go a bit, haven't you, pet?'

I jumped to my feet with sudden ease as I saw a tall, muscular, huge man standing over me with a stupid grin on his big face. 'I thought headbands went oot years ago,' he roared, clutching his sides. 'You're the funniest thing I've seen fer ages.'

'Charmed I'm sure.' I scowled at what I assumed was another of Maz's one-night stands. 'Yeah, and I suppose you're fashion personified, I don't think,' I growled.

The stranger laughed again and held out a large, strong hand. 'Jen, I'm Dave.'

'My brother,' Maz added, 'recently released from Her Majesty's Hotel, Durham.'

*   *   *

Maz and Dave — not to be confused with a famous cockney singing duo — spent the next few hours catching up on four years' worth of sibling banter.

I quickly returned to my usual fitness-free

self and settled down to hear 'Tales from the Inside' à la Dave. Each story seemed to consist of 'dirty screws', incredibly inventive smuggling of contraband and wildly elaborate escape attempts by Dave's fellow 'residents'. The details were obviously greatly exaggerated but Dave was a professional yarn-spinner and Maz was in her element in his company.

Dave's last four-year stint had been the result of a bizarrely pathetic attempt by himself and his gang of mates to rob the local ten-pin bowling alley. More stoned than St Stephen, and in search of financial backing for a late-night curry binge, the four friends had broken into Ten Pin City — Fast Family Fun. Closed-circuit-TV tapes later revealed the clearly identifiable troop staggering round the building, using 50p pieces from the safe to win cuddly toys from the clamping machine and each carefully selecting a suitable pair of Happy-Days-style bowling shoes.

Although the safe had been successfully cracked and bags of paper money extracted, Dave and the boys had never received any financial gain from their crime. Stig, the least intelligent and most stoned member of the group, had fallen asleep while guarding the money as the other three had attempted to

159

ice-skate down the bowling lanes. A joint had fallen from his mouth and onto the surrounding bags of notes. It was estimated that £10,000 was destroyed in the resulting fire. Dave was picked up by the fire brigade, still sporting a pair of red and blue shoes with '11' painted on the back, and delivered to Whitley Bay police. The group had become known as 'Smokey and the Bowling Bandits', and Dave had returned to jail for a third time.

'Aye wor Maz, you've done well fer yerself, pet. Pub, flat an' al' this. I'm glad, you didny turn oot like us.' Dave rolled a big joint and lay back on the sofa. His massive frame dwarfed the room. 'Aye, you've got it sorted, lass, well done.'

Maz was quieter than I'd ever seen her. She just smiled at her brother and puffed on a cigarette. Dave hadn't let her visit him in prison. He didn't want her to be embarrassed by her own brother. From the look on Maz's face, she thought Dave was fantastic.

Dave turned to me. I felt sheepish next to this big man. In his enormous presence, I actually felt petite. Something made me want to talk like one of the Kray Twins, but I quickly banished the thought from my mind.

'So you're Jen,' he asked loudly. 'Funny 'ow we've never met, eh?'

'Yes, funny, hmmm.'

'I thought you'd be reet posh. Big house and geet swanky job and al' that.'

'No, not at all, A'im not porsh.' How Now Brown Cow. Oh God, I didn't know what to say to a . . . a criminal. Thoughts of knee-cappings flashed through my ridiculously vivid imagination.

'What do you do, Jen?'

'I work for Maz. I used to . . . ' I suddenly thought back to my brief encounter with ex-con Chip. Although my career in corporate law was a far cry from the lawyers Dave would have met, I felt the intricacies of legal practice would be lost on him. ' . . . to um . . . not work here, but now . . . I do, see,' I stammered.

'Uh, right, aye.' He stared at me blankly. 'Well, I need a piss,' he said, and left the room.

I breathed for the first time in about half an hour. I could be so daft. He was Maz's slightly clueless brother and here I was treating him like a serial killer, making the poor guy feel completely uncomfortable. Luckily Maz didn't seem to notice.

'He's lush isn't he?' she sighed after a while, lighting another fag. 'He learned tons of stuff in jail you kna. Speaks French an' everythin'.'

It seemed Dave had entered prison as a

poorly schooled amateur criminal, but had emerged, four years later, educated in French, carpentry, hot-wiring, ram-raiding and drug-dealing. He had enough contacts in the criminal underworld to start up his own branch of the North-East Mafia.

'Oui, juz parles france-ay,' said Dave in a strong Geordie accent as he re-entered the room. 'Ave-hey voose le fer?'

'What does that mean?' I laughed.

'Ave yuz got a light? Wait, I kna better stuff than that.'

'Ya posh git . . . '

'Hang on, sis, I'm thinkin'. Aye, voolez-voose couchez avec moise. J'ai un trayse grand sex?'

'What did that last bit mean?' I was beginning to relax. 'Will you come to bed with me . . . '

'I've got a geet big — '

'Hi guys!' Troy suddenly appeared in the room. 'The apartment door was open so I kinda let myself in. Howzit goin', guys?'

'Great, Troy.' I jumped up and grabbed the arm of his crease-proof shirt and kissed his smooth cheek. I instantly wished I'd put on more make-up, or had a full body transplant. Gay or not, being in the presence of such carefully groomed and toned physical perfection made me feel like Cilla Black on HRT.

162

'Troy, this is Dave, Maz's brother.'

'Hiya Dave, great to meet ya.' Troy smiled broadly and patted Dave on the back, almost hugging him in the process. 'Great name, Dave. Kinda manly,' he joked.

'Aye right.' Dave looked puzzled and ignored Troy's offer of a handshake.

Troy continued unabashed. 'So Dave, what's up? You've got a really great body, man, d'you work out? What d'you press?'

Great, Troy, why not just ask him his favourite position and be done with it? The barrage of questions remained unanswered as Maz and I looked on, intrigued. Dave stared blankly at the sparkling, enthusiastic American. He was totally lost for words, which, I imagined, was not a regular occurrence for Dave. Of course, compared to the people Dave had spent the last few years with, Troy was as alien as a great musical talent in the Top Ten.

Dave took a long, slow drag on a tab as Troy questioned him about where he liked to buy his clothes, what aftershave he wore and which cocktails he preferred. Maz and I tried not to laugh. Eventually, frowning, Dave stood up, blocking the light as he did so. 'I'm gan fer a piss,' he growled, and left the room.

★ ★ ★

Troy and I walked out past the scrapyard and down the steep incline towards the river. He swung my arm playfully as I attempted banal conversation. Fearing Dave would stamp on Troy's head if he heard 'you've got a great body, man' one more time, I had offered to take Troy out for a bit of cold, fresh air under the guise of showing him the sights. As to which sights, I was still trying to think of some, although four generations of one family wearing matching radioactively orange shellsuits had provided a moment of special interest.

The sky was bleak and a strong north wind played havoc with the collection of anti-frizz products that I had cemented to my hair. As we reached the derelict pub halfway down the hill, I heard muffled laughter, followed by a loud explosion. A rocket landed at Troy's feet and set fire to the laces of his incredibly shiny boots. Bangers exploded all around us as Troy danced about in an attempt to extinguish the flames. I suppressed my giggles at the sight of Troy doing a very good impression of Riverdance, and pulled him away from the war zone.

'A'reet ya chava!' shrieked the gang of small boys from the top of the crumbling wall. 'Ya dance like a bleedin' lass, man.' They laughed loudly.

'Damn kids,' Troy growled. 'They can be so cruel.' I was surprised to see tears welling up in his eyes.

'Howay man, come 'n' get us! Gis a kiss, auld wuman.'

Worried that my delicate friend might start sobbing hysterically, I guided him down the hill, feet still smoking from his close encounter.

A small ginger-haired boy of about thirteen strutted past with a car stereo under his arm. He stared menacingly up at Troy and began to approach us. As he reached into the immense folds of material in his jeans, searching for a pocket, I felt Troy flinch. Ginger kid pulled out a half-smoked cigar. 'Got a light, mate?' he asked. Troy stared blankly and hurried past.

'Fuck ya then, ya ponce!' came the reply.

Bravery, I decided, was not Troy's strong point, but everyone has their weaknesses. He hadn't kept such a perfect set of teeth from being a fighter. I squeezed his arm reassuringly.

'Troy, are you finding it hard to adjust to living here?' We sat quietly on a bench by the river. I glanced down the road in the direction of my old flat.

'Oh, not really,' he stuttered. Troy fiddled with the toggles on his coat and stared down at his slightly charred boots. I attempted conversation.

'So, Troy, as it's Valentine's Day tomorrow . . . ' (Not that I believe in all that sentimental tripe of course) ' . . . will you and Julio be doing something special together?'

Troy continued to fiddle with his toggles and avoided my gaze.

'Do you have any plans at all? Have you bought him a card?'

No answer was the loud reply.

'Earth calling Troy.' I waved my hand in front of his eyes. He turned towards me. 'It's a miracle, he's alive!' I joked.

'S . . . sorry, Jenny, I . . . um.'

'Did your satellite move out of range for a while?'

'I'm s-s-sorry, Jenny . . . '

'Stop saying s-s-sorry. What's wrong?'

A guaranteed zero-response question to ask a man.

'Nothing.'

'Are you upset about your shoes?'

'No.'

'Did someone die?'

'Jenny.'

'Oh, don't you celebrate Valentine's Day in America?'

Suddenly Troy took my hand and held it tightly to his chest. I stared at his tear-stained face. He was positively blubbering. I was all for the new man as far as doing menial chores and leaving the best jobs for us was concerned, but this seemed a little excessive. I suddenly felt like Troy's mother. I had an urge to either throw up or laugh, but I controlled myself and patted his shaking hands.

'What is it, Troy?'

'He dumped me,' Troy cried, squeezing my hand even tighter. 'Dumped, chucked, tossed away. Tossed like one of his mixed salads.'

Mmm, nice analogy. 'Oh, oh dear,' I stuttered.

Troy tightened his grip. 'I feel so used.'

The exertion of my morning jog had clearly taken its toll on my brain. I could think of absolutely nothing of any help or relevance to say.

'Um, Troy,' I began hesitantly.

He sniffed and stared at me with tear-filled, puppy dog eyes. Oh God.

'Y . . . yes,' he whispered.

'Um, do you think you could let go of my hand? I think you're cutting off the circulation.'

He sighed exaggeratedly and pulled his hands away. Help, I had no training in these man-dumps-man scenarios, I didn't know the rules. Following my recent experience of the man-dumps-woman scenario, it was hardly my favourite topic of conversation either. Come on, Jen, I said to myself, don't be selfish. He's hurting, he needs advice. How different can it be from man-dumps-woman?

'What a bastard,' I said strongly. 'He's a bastard, forget him.'

Troy wailed loudly. 'He's not a bastard, he's lovely.'

Ok, so it was different.

Troy shook his head, sending more than one globule of snot flying through the air. 'He's gorgeous, he's fit, he's Italian . . . '

Good point.

'I love his clothes, I love the way he walks, I love the way he wiggles his neat little butt.'

Right, I get it.

'I love the way he kisses me. I love his smooth, tanned skin.'

Yeah, yeah, I really do get it now.

'I love the way he's so tender in bed. I love his . . . '

OK, too much information coming up. 'Oh dear, oh dear, oh dear,' I interrupted loudly. (Give me a break, it's all I could think of.)

'I love it all, Jenny,' Troy sobbed. 'I love him.'

Oh come on man, you've only known the bloke two bloody days. What are you, an emotional leech?

'I understand, Troy, you poor thing,' I said aloud.

I put a reassuring arm around his shoulder and listened as he poured out his sorry tale, nodding and making comforting noises in all the right places. Blimey, this was heavy stuff for a forty-eight-hour relationship. I mean, we're all entitled to the grief, the self-pity and the lashings of attention but I was quietly thankful that he hadn't turned out to be boyfriend material. Troy carried more baggage than a 747. Dumping a man like him would not be a pleasant experience. Not that I'd dumped many boyfriends in my life, unless you count James Harvey. He was nine, I was just ten and we had been going out since first break (approximately three hours). I wrote a note on his times-tables book along the lines of 'you're not my boyfriend any more, boys smell'. Short but to the point, I thought.

'Well, if you're at a loose end,' I began, trying desperately to change the subject, 'we could spend Valentine's Day together.' (It's not like I'll be particularly busy.)

Troy stared at me blankly.

'Let me see, we could watch a film,' I smiled.

Not a hint of enthusiasm.

'Or a meal . . . '

He brushed away a tear.

'Whitley Bay, drinks . . . '

He attempted a smile but said nothing.

'Bingo, knitting club, mass suicide, a Julio Iglesias concert . . . '

He burst into tears. Shit, I had to say 'Julio' didn't I.

'Sorry, bad choice of words.' I scrabbled in my pockets for a tissue as tears seemed to erupt from every pore on Troy's face. You'll look back on this and laugh, I wanted to say, there's plenty more fish in the sea, he's not worth it. I was teetering on the outskirts of cliché city. If we had been at home, I would have put the kettle on and baked a cake. Luckily, I opted for silence.

'Jenny,' Troy managed during a lull in the emotional overload. He reached into his pocket and pulled out an envelope. Flippin' heck, please don't be a suicide note.

'My cousin runs a television company,' he continued, handing me the envelope 'Well, him and my uncle actually, they run it together now.'

I smiled a confused smile.

'I know how much Maz loves talk shows and I thought you'd both enjoy seeing one.' He wiped his eyes.

'Thanks, Troy, what a kind thought, Maz will love it. Are you coming with us?'

Troy shook his head and let out a faint sob.

'I'm going back home for a while, Jenny. I think it's for the best.'

I nodded sympathetically. Lucky sod — given a choice between a tropical beach in Hawaii and a minuscule Italian waiter I had known for all of five minutes, I had no doubt about which one I would choose.

'Enjoy the show,' Troy said through a watery smile, 'I hope it makes you happy.'

10

14th February, 9:05 a.m.

'It is just a normal day. Do not check the post.' I made the same vow for the fifth time in as many minutes as grim reality dawned. The one totally depressing day that instills dread and pitifully false hopes in the minds of most single people had trundled around again. Blimey, a year just flies by doesn't it?

At 26 and, in my opinion, rapidly going downhill to meet my sagging backside, I still awoke early with the thought, *Perhaps this will be the year*. The year in which unidentified truckloads of roses and cuddly bears hugging lacy cushions emblazoned with 'I heart U 4 eva' are delivered to my door. Disgustingly shiny padded cards bearing pictures of skipping bunnies, the EC chocolate mountain, red-and-black racy knickers, heart-shaped helium balloons and gifts in equally poor taste flood to my door and necessitate the hiring of extra staff by the postal service.

'That Jennifer Summer,' marvel the crowd of onlookers, 'she always gets the most cards

on Valentine's Day. I wish I could be like her.'
(Swoon, swoon.)

Of course, on any other day of the year, any
semi-sane person with an ounce of good taste
would puke at the sight of the majority of
these gifts. Let's face it, satin padded cards
really suck. Two-foot tall, pastel-coloured,
satin padded cards should burn in hell, along
with ski-pants, wheel clampers and techno
music. What sort of poor, disillusioned
creature designs those things? I'd like to see
their ideas on interior design. Satin padded
wallpaper probably, with matching strait-
jacket.

Why then, on February 14th, am I, along
with a large proportion of the population,
scanning the horizon for my two-foot tall
envelope? Praying to Saint Pat, the patron
saint of postmen, for my fair share of satin,
padding, pastel and skipping bunnies. Dying
to read those gold-embossed italic words, 'To
my girlfriend', and marvel at how the card
can stand up with just a thin sliver of cheap
cardboard on the back half. (They're only
ever padded on one side, you see. I suspect to
keep them below the highly-inflammable-
mattress rate of postage.) I feel ashamed but,
apparently, on February 14th anything goes.
I, along with the rest of the world, lose touch
with reality. Even a card from the 96-year-old

blind man from down the road would be better than no card at all.

Well, this year, I was determined to rebel against this evil force of our society. No satin for me. Not even a hint of red aluminium foil helium balloons. This year, February 14th was to be a day like any other. So far, my willpower had lasted a total of 6 minutes 45 seconds from waking up. Only about 14 hours, 53 minutes and 15 seconds to go.

★　★　★

By 10:00 a.m., I had checked the letterbox and surrounding area four times, under the pretence of expecting an important bank statement. By 11:00 a.m. I had rummaged through Maz's gigantic pile of cards, mostly unopened, in a vain attempt to find one of mine incorrectly filed. By 11:30, I had re-checked the letterbox numerous times, telephoned Royal Mail to ask whether there was an industrial strike and consumed an entire 500g box of Milk Tray, which I promised to replace later in Maz's pile when my own eventually arrived. Things were not looking altogether bright and breezy.

Eventually, after being told to 'p*** off you sad cow and stop phoning!' (quite rude, I thought, for one of Her Majesty's postmen. It was only the fourth time I'd rung), I gave up hope. Feeling sick from stress (or perhaps too much chocolate), I finally resigned myself to a romance-free life on Single Street. I dragged myself up to my room to get ready for my lunchtime shift.

'Jen! Jen! I found this at the door. Someone must have delivered it!'

Maz burst into the room waving a pale yellow envelope above her head.

I sighed. 'Yeah right, Maz, nice try. Thanks for the kind thought but I haven't quite resorted to lesbianism yet.'

'Howay man, I didny send ya it. I'm not wastin' good beer money on shite cards for you like.'

She laughed and threw the envelope on my bed. It was definitely a card. Pastel colours were promising. Visions of Jack's lips lovingly licking the envelope flashed through my mind. After all, it was the day for romance. Even I deserved a declaration of undying love. I glanced over at Maz, bit my lip with nervous tension and slowly reached for the envelope.

Perhaps there is something worse than not getting any cards on Valentine's Day. The realisation at 26 that your only hope of a card is a sympathy vote from your dad can be deeply depressing. The thought crossed my mind that he could have opted for the unsigned version. That would at least have given me the chance to pretend it was from someone else. 'Luv Dad' was maybe a little obvious. I'd thank him later.

★ ★ ★

'I tellt you wuman man,' said Auld Vinny as he sucked the filling out of his lunchtime meat pie, 'it's jest another excuse fer the lasses to get presents oot o' their fella. Aye man, it's a load o' canny shite. A lass invented it, I bet ya.'

'Who's Valentine then?' Denise asked. She fiddled with the black bra strap that was escaping from underneath her white, chunky-knit tank top.

'He's Italian i'n he?' Derek replied.

'That's Valentino,' I offered. 'It was after Saint Valentine.'

'The singer? The one in the rocking chair wi' the dodgy cardies.' Denise looked pleased with herself.

'That's bloody Val Doonican, ya stupit wuman.' Derek tutted and gestured to me for another pint.

'Aye well, whoever it was,' Vinny continued, 'he must have been a bloody florist. They're lovin' it man. Better than bleedin' funerals fer

176

them it is. Straits, all the bunches of red flippin' roses at fifty poont a go. Bloody lasses.'

'Even the men get flowers these days, Vinny,' I smiled.

'You what?'

'Yeah sure, it's 'PC' for the men to get flowers as well as the women these days.'

'I'll give ya 'P flippin' C' like.' Vinny tutted and shook his head. 'Howay lass, dain't be stupid.'

'It's true Vinny. Some men love getting flowers. It's supposed to be romantic.'

He stared at me incredulously for a moment.

'Aye, well it's nay wonder the world's in such a canny mess.' He hung his head dramatically. 'The men are turnin' into bleedin' ponces. Jaysus man, the day I get flowers I hope they're on me bloody gravestone, I tell't ya.'

I laughed at Vinny's disgust and patted him supportively on the arm.

'Men even give each other flowers these days, Vinny,' I added for good measure.

'Howay! Now I know yer havin' us on. Give us another pint.'

I was glad to be working. At least it took my mind off my lack of admirers, secret or otherwise. My unrequited love for Jack and my recent spate of disastrous dates did not bode well for a day of unadulterated romance. In my honour, the pub had been declared a couple-free zone. No public displays of affection, no Bryan Adams songs within a one-mile radius and certainly no heart-shaped canapés or special celebratory lurve cocktails. Denise and Derek were the exception to the couple rule. They maintained their usual habit of shouting obscenities at each other from opposite ends of the bar. Very refreshing, I thought. I would forgive you for thinking I was a party-pooper, driven by the green-eyed monster, but that wasn't true at all. I saw my task as providing a much-needed public service. Carefully maintaining one haven of doom and gloom in this pink, fluffy, love-struck world.

★ ★ ★

How is it that a single period of twenty-four hours can drive a person totally insane? I was beginning to develop a nervous twitch from looking at my watch so many times while praying for the speedy arrival of February 15th. I hoped it would just sneak up on me but to no avail. I prayed to Saint Jude, the patron saint of hopeless cases (the one I seemed to use most often), but no response. I think Jude was probably tied up trying to sort out the rest of my life, which was bound to keep the poor sod busy. The minutes crawled by with the brain-numbing pace of the Queen's Christmas speech. Metallica, Dexy's Midnight Runners and various heavy thrash bands were playing on repeat in a wholly unromantic manner and I was slowly metamorphosing into Victor Meldrew's granddaughter. I would be lying if I said I had completely given up hope of a sudden rush by Interflora but it appeared my admirers were so secret that even they didn't know who they were.

By 11:00, I was more than happy to call last orders. A cold, lonely single bed seemed to be the only suitable conclusion to such a crap day. I sighed and rang the heavy bell at the end of the bar. Hearing the front door slam shut, I turned just in time to see two small boys creeping down the steps into the pub. The smallest had a drastic haircut which resembled a few pieces of velcro stapled to his head. He wore baggy green combat trousers and a reflective silver and orange jacket. Hardly the correct attire for a covert mission. His friend had straggly, long brown hair, a stained T-shirt adorned with images of marijuana leaves and a pair of jeans big enough to set up camp in. A heavy silver chain trailed from the front pocket of his jeans to the back. I wondered which pocket housed his pet Rottweiler. Both boys, I noticed, sported the latest look in trainer technology. Fabric that glowed with radioactive proportions and enough air pockets to keep a man alive in space for weeks.

Blissfully unaware of having been rumbled, the smallest boy led the way past the cigarette machine, underneath the tables that ran alongside the barred windows, towards the furthest corner of the pub where they would be out of sight of the bar. I headed them off at the dartboard and grabbed the warm, discarded pint of lager just as it reached the smallest boy's lips.

'Evening boys, nice of you to join us.'

The young drinker lifted his odd-shaped head and glared at me. What he lacked in height, he certainly made up for in bravado, unlike his friend who cowered behind his overgrown fringe.

'Ah howay man, wuman, man,' the boy growled, 'I jest want a sip, like. Wor da' lets us drink.'

'Maybe he does but not in my pub.'

'I'm eighteen, ye kna.'

(Eighteen months more like.)

The taller, skinny boy cast a quick, puzzled look at his friend. He nudged him and whispered, 'Give it to 'er.'

'Give me what? Or perhaps you'd like to give whatever it is to the police?'

I was slightly concerned about the prospect of being done over by two four-foot assailants but I managed to keep my headmistress-like cool.

'Ah bloody pigs, man,' the small boy grunted, 'locked wor Chad up they did, the bastards.'

He reached down into the depths of his knee-length pocket and pulled out a crumpled envelope.

'Posh git ootside tell't wur ta give ya this.'

'Aye, paid wuz an' all,' added his friend shyly.

'Aye, we didny wanna gan in yer poxy pub anyways, but he said ta give it ta the fat 'un wi' curly hair. Must be you, like.'

(Bastards.)

I stared at the envelope, immediately recognising the handwriting. During my time with Jack, I had received enough scribbled notes excusing him from one date or another to recognise his scrawl at twenty paces, the coward.

'Where is he?' I yelled at the boys, a little over-excitedly.

'Ootside!' they screeched simultaneously, pointing towards the door.

Without stopping to read the contents of the letter, I scrambled for the door and almost fell out onto the dark street. Playing hard to get was not my style.

'Sad cow,' I heard the young boys say as I left them behind.

The Shoe was the only car parked nearby, as Maz had taken the Metro to her latest hot date in town. Up the hill to the left, a group of lads kicked each other, and occasionally a football, around the road. A broken street light restricted my view down the hill. Straining my eyes, I could just make out an old couple walking slowly hand in hand and two large dogs doing unmentionable things against a lamppost. No sign of Jack or his midnight blue BMW (known affectionately in the area as a Break My Windows). Damn. A millisecond of expectation had got my hormones raging. Suddenly remembering my underage customers, I unwillingly dragged myself back into the pub, clutching the envelope in my sweaty palm.

★　★　★

Eventually, the pub cleared and the mouths of my two young friends were surgically removed from the spouts of the beer pumps. Through an amazing display of willpower, I had managed to keep the envelope sealed and in my pocket. My immediate reaction had been to rip the damn thing open, but I had decided that a Valentine's note from Jack was a moment to savour. Finally alone, I settled myself on a barstool and, shaking with anticipation, slowly opened the crumpled, ivory envelope and began to read its contents.

Dear Jennifer

I apologise for my lack of correspondence but I have been terribly busy with my career, a word I'm sure you recognise from your past. [Snobby git.] The account with Paradise TV is thriving and I am doing terribly well. Our last meeting was amusing if nothing else. Your 'punters' were quick to the chase but a little out of condition to outrun me. I must say, seeing you as a barmaid was a real eye-opener. You seem to have slipped into the role so easily. [Not sure if that's a compliment. Come on, get to the slushy bit, Jack.] Anyway Jennifer, I shall come to the point. [At last.] Further to my visit, I have decided to advise my client to sell the Scrap Inn as soon as possible. I have explained that the pub is not viable for future investment and would be better sold to a buyer outside the industry. The land

183

would be valuable as a quayside development prospect. In other words, Jennifer, the pub shall be no longer. I hope you appreciate my forewarning you as, of course, there will be no need for barmaids in the very near future.

Yours sincerely,

Jack.

P.S. I suppose I should wish you a Happy Valentine's Day as I'm sure you're pining for cards.

[Git, git, git, git, git!]

I stared at the letter for what seemed like hours, trying to absorb what I had just read. OK, there wasn't much scope for an incorrect interpretation, but I couldn't believe it. The tone was so cold and heartless. How could he be so spiteful? Blimey, I used to nibble this man's earlobes and lick squirty cream off his body and this is how he repays me. From the tone of the letter, I half expected Jack to appear in a flash of lightening and dry ice, wearing a long black cape and yelling 'Ha, Ha, Ha' in a deep blood-curdling voice.

Jack, my Jack, was pushing for the closure of the pub and, knowing him, he'd get it. I couldn't believe the vindictiveness of it all. Maz would be heartbroken and I would lose my second job in as many months. We'd both be homeless and broke. This wasn't supposed to happen. At that point, I should have been in the middle of a candlelit dinner with the man of my dreams, preparing myself for a night of passion, not sitting alone contemplating the prospect of living in an upturned skip and eating out of bins. Mind you, even skips are extortionate to hire these days. We'd be lucky to get a generous-sized shoebox.

It suddenly hit me how important the pub was to both Maz and me. Not to mention how big a role it played in the lives of the locals. Auld Vinny, Derek, Denise and the rest of my new, unlikely group of friends lived for their days of banter in the Scrap Inn. The lesbian darts team, where would they practise? Even my father loved the bizarre escapism the place provided.

I wanted to cry but I was too shocked. Did Jack really hate me that much or was the 'All Men Are Bastards' theory really so true? To Jack, work was everything. It seemed the pursuit of Partnership and wealth had clouded his vision. People obviously didn't matter any more.

Looking around the empty bar, a sudden rage built up inside me. Slightly dingy, rough and full of so-called no-hopers (including myself) the pub may be, but it was special. It had an atmosphere I had never experienced before in my life and it had a purpose. There was no way I was going to let Jack ruin this place just to hurt me and close another deal. Screwing the letter up in my clenched fist, I threw it across the bar in anger.

'You forget, Jack,' I seethed aloud. 'I was once a lawyer too, but I'm a real person. I won't let you push me around any more. If it's a fight you want, you've got it!'

11

23rd February, 8:00 a.m.

Maz, Dave and I sat around the green plastic garden table that half-filled the kitchen, drinking treacle-like coffee out of semi-mouldy mugs. Numerous beer cans littered the pink-painted work surfaces, and the stench of curry wafted around my nose from the remains of various kormas, biryanis and vindaloos. It was becoming apparent that Dave's presence in the flat did little for its aesthetic qualities.

'Dave man,' Maz sighed, 'you've gotta clean up after yerself.'

'Aye, I kna.' Dave sucked the life out of a fourth cigarette and began to roll a joint.

'And maybe limit these parties a bit,' Maz continued.

'Aye, I kna.'

I could see she wasn't getting very far.

'And stop smokin' so much like. How'r you gonna get work if yer bloody stoned all the time man?'

'I deen't kna. Aye whatever.'

Maz groaned and returned to the agenda

for the meeting. 'So, has anyone thought of a plan, like?'

It was over a week since the delivery of Jack's 'love letter' and we hadn't yet thought of a possible way to thwart his master plan. Although we had heard no more about the proposed sale, I knew better than to ignore Jack in this devious frame of mind. I had never seen Maz so upset as when I had revealed the contents of the letter to her later that night.

Dave's original suggestion had been knee-capping. It was horribly violent and totally out of the question but so far it was the only solution that had been offered. Hence the early morning war conference.

'There must be a way to stop him,' Maz said as she sipped the painfully thick coffee. 'He can't jest get rid of the pub that easy.'

'He's the lawyer though, Maz,' I replied. 'No one will even consider that he could possibly have ulterior motives.'

'Let's tell 'em then.'

'Yeah, and they're sure going to listen to me, aren't they? The supposed drug baron who was fired from the firm after turning our best client's meeting into a circus.'

She thought for a moment. 'Meybe the brewery won't listen to him. Aye, meybe they'll keep the pub anyhow.'

'I doubt it. Jack's got a good reputation as a corporate solicitor. If they've asked for his advice then basically what he says goes. He hates me. I embarrassed him at work and I suppose he's disgusted by the thought that people would connect him to a barmaid. If he's out to get us, he'll stop at nothing.'

Maz looked morose. She lit a tab.

'Aye well, we're fucked then.'

'Thanks Dave for that analysis of the situation. Perhaps you could come up with something a little more positive.'

'Howay, I did.'

'Knee-capping is not really a viable option.'

'Aye, but I . . . '

'Neither is kidnapping, nor death threats.'

Dave sat back sulkily and sparked up the joint. We all sat in silence, staring at the crumpled letter that lay in the middle of the table. The brain drain seemed to have dried up already.

'I wonder if this is how Maggie felt?' Maz pondered aloud.

'Maggie who?'

'Maggie bloody Thatcher.'

'When?'

'You kna when everyone decided to gang up on 'er and kick 'er oot.'

'Well, it's hardly the same, Maz.'

'Aye it is, kinda. Only difference is I didny

give a shite when it happened to her.'

'Aye,' Dave nodded approvingly. 'It's like a declaration o' war, man.'

I tried to retrieve the conversation from its bizarre tangent. 'Let's look at Jack's strong points.'

'None,' Maz chipped in.

'BM-bloody-W,' Dave added through a haze of smoke.

I groaned. This was pointless. Suddenly Dave sat forward and cleared his throat, before taking a long drag on the spliff.

'Howay, lasses, it's obvious man. The tosser's ganna tell't the brewery to sell cos the land's worth more to them than the pub, reet? Buyer comes in, canny loaded and doesny want a pub. Knocks doon the pub, reet, builds bloody swanky flats an' sells 'em for a packet. Howay, the whole quayside's gan that way. So, all wuz need to do is mek the land worth less an' put the buyer off when he comes round.'

We stared open-mouthed at the previously incoherent Dave. He was right, of course. The land was the attractive asset for a buyer. With all the new developments in the area, pubs like the Scrap Inn would soon be a thing of the past. If we could somehow devalue the land in the buyer's eyes we could perhaps thwart the sale. The only question was how.

'Blimey, Dave. I don't know what was in that joint you were smoking, but it must be good stuff.'

He laughed and got up in search of refreshments.

'More coffee, lasses?'

'No!' Maz and I replied in unison. All right, so he could come up with intricate analyses of situations, but his coffee really sucked.

We continued making plans until we had consumed a large packet of chocolate-chip cookies, five cold naan breads, and a litre of flat Coke. Well, they do say breakfast is the most important meal of the day and our brains desperately needed sustenance.

By 10:30 a.m. the fundamentals had been decided. I, 'Agent Summer', would contact Matt at Glisset & Jacksop in an attempt to discover the identity and visiting time of the proposed buyer. I would also vow never to think of Jack sexually again. Tough measures indeed. Maz, 'Agent Fagash', would discreetly rally the support of the punters and keep an eye out for suspicious characters. Dave 'Agent Hard-as-nails' would formulate a plan for land devaluation. Dave had 'friends', he said, who could be relied upon to help out in such a situation. To be honest, I wasn't exactly sure of Dave's intentions but, as land could not technically be knee-capped, and because we were getting desperate, I agreed to give him a fairly free rein.

'Dave! Phone!' Maz yelled from the lounge. 'Some blowky called Chip. Bloody stupid name.'

'My cellmate at Durham,' Dave said in my general direction as he stumbled out of the room.

'Really?' I gulped. 'Mmm, I think we've met.'

While Dave made plans with Chip for a fun-filled day of 'drinkin', smokin' and sharkin',' Maz and I began to get ready to leave. Today was the start of our talk-show adventure, courtesy of the now distant Troy. The show was to be filmed in Newcastle the following day. All guests and VIP audience members (which was us) were to be provided with overnight accommodation in a five-star riverside hotel. Of course, this extravagant service was for those who had travelled far and wide for their fifteen minutes of fame. Not to be denied a night in a posh hotel, and weighing our finances against those of Paradise TV Company Ltd, Maz and I simply 'omitted' to inform the company representative that we lived approximately seven minutes up the road. Well, needs must.

Gordon had unwillingly agreed to work in the pub for once, so Maz and I had two days to let loose, one hour of which would be on national television. All we had to do was travel into town, rendezvous with the Paradise rep at Central Station and be driven to the luxury of the welcoming champagne reception.

★   ★   ★

'You must be Marilyn and Jennifer,' beamed the bony blonde woman, holding out a thin manicured hand. Fearing it would snap if I shook it too hard, I gave her hand a feeble squeeze.

'Excellent, excellent, I'm Torica. Welcome to Newcaahstle, girls, marvellous.' We had pretended to disembark from an Intercity train at the station and headed straight for the woman who held up a large sign reading 'Welcome to Paradise'.

She bustled ahead of us towards the station exit, occasionally glancing over her shoulder to throw us a well-practised smile. Her tight-fitting red suit jacket and miniskirt turned most of the heads in the busy station. The pair of long, tanned legs slipped into four-inch-heeled navy court shoes turned the remaining few.

'So glad you could join us, girls,' she continued without looking at us. 'The other guests are already here, awfully nice bunch. Very good. First time in New*caah*stle? Jolly good.'

We didn't even attempt to interrupt the speech.

'Must dash, girls. Awfully tight schedule you know. Television, busy, busy, lots to do. Marvellous.'

'You're not from round here, then?' Maz mumbled sarcastically at Torica's back.

We reached a gleaming white minibus which was parked inconsiderately across several parking spaces. A group of about ten bewildered-looking folk stood, as if awaiting orders, in a line stretching from the minibus door.

'Not on the bus yet, dears? Chop chop. We must dash, awfully tight schedule.'

We were shepherded onto the bus like a herd of unruly cattle. Hardly the chauffeur-driven limo Maz and I had been expecting. We grabbed the back seat and settled down to a bus tour of the city.

Throughout the journey, the group remained painfully silent except for our host, who seemed to suffer from verbal diarrhoea, and Maz, who occasionally hooted out of the window at fit men on the street.

Occupying the two seats in front of me on the left-hand side of the bus were a woman and a girl of about fourteen, who looked suspiciously like an extra from *The Addams Family*. Daughter was totally dressed in black, complete with a black lace veil partially covering her whitened face and black lips. Her mother fitted the image of Marks & Spencer's number one customer. Her delicately pleated knee-length, Paisley-patterned skirt was teamed with an ivory blouse and a pale lilac cardigan. The ensemble and demi-waved greying hair wasn't exactly befitting of the mother of one of the Evil Dead. During the journey, 'Morticia' toyed with the three-inch black talons on the ends of her fingers while mother gazed out of the window, sighing occasionally.

In front of this odd pair sat a tired-looking single man, probably in his late forties or early fifties, who evidently had a thing for beige. Uninspired by Torica's factless description of the city, beige man was engrossed in a book entitled *A Marriage of Three*. He made no attempt at conversation but occasionally shot rather menacing glances at the couple who occupied the double seat across the aisle. She also looked on the far side of forty, dressed totally in fuchsia with a shock of dyed plum hair. She gazed longingly through her pink eyeshadow at her much younger companion. He held her protectively and occasionally kissed her forehead or whispered in her ear. I had a feeling we were witnessing her mid-life crisis and his one and only older-woman experience.

'Don't kid yourself woman,' I mumbled, 'it won't last.'

'Nearly there, people!' Torica boomed from her position at the front of the bus. 'Lots of traffic, I'm afraid. Absolutely awful. Tut, tut. Anyway, girls and boys, let's start with names, shall we?'

I threw a puzzled glance at Maz.

Torica grabbed the arm of the young man who sat at the front of the bus. 'Come on, honey, you start. Jolly good. Let's all get to know each other.'

The remainder of the trip was spent learning each other's names, nasty habits and deepest darkest secrets. After the name-badge distribution and 'team sing-song', Maz and I were relieved to reach the solace of our five-star hotel room.

'Lock the bloody door,' Maz shouted from somewhere inside the minibar. 'She's canny mental that woman! Flippin' name badges and stuff. Jesus, we're only here to watch the bleedin' show. I deen't kna if I can face it now.'

I laughed and ripped open the complimentary packet of chocolate shortbread. 'One more round of 'The Wheels on the Bus', and I would have had to put her under them.' I looked at my watch. 3:00 p.m. 'Two hours till the champagne do, Maz.'

'Oh shite,' she replied, 'I need a drink.'

★ ★ ★

Maz and I totally drained the minibar of alcohol, biscuits and chocolate before rolling into the Paradise TV champagne reception in the hotel lounge. I instantly spotted out ten bus-buddies, still bearing their name tags, huddled in a corner of the room. The rest of the party was made up of media types, media socialites and media hangers-on. A glamorous Torica held court in the centre of the room. 'Yah, yah, well, I told them I wasn't going to get out of bed for that much, you know. I mean, *puhlease*. I'm a professional woman . . . yah.'

Maz and I made a beeline for the champagne, doing our best to bypass Torica's verbal barrage.

'Yah, well, it's a new show, new format, new presenter. Yah, she's marvellous, an absolute dahling. We're very excited, totally. Can't fail with my PR skills really, ha, ha.'

We had almost reached the pyramid construction of champagne glasses when I felt a bony hand on my shoulder.

'Marilyn.'

'Jennifer.'

'Jennifer. Marvellous, excellent. Enjoying yourself?'

'I . . . uh.'

'Marvellous. Come and meet some wonderful people. Mingle, network, that's the way.'

Torica pulled me towards the centre of the room as Maz dived behind the table of nibbles.

'Peoples, meet Jackie, one of our lovely guests.' A small crowd of people formed a circle around me and stared intently. Torica continued.

'Phoebe, Amelia, Zoë, Melvin, Beth . . . ' The crowd nodded in unison and mumbled, 'Yah, ahbsolutely, yah.'

Torica wiggled off to mingle and I was left in the centre of my circle of new acquaintances. They remained silent and continued to stare. I began to feel suspiciously like a very small mouse in a very big cattery.

'Jackie, Beth,' piped up a tall, buxom woman. She had jet-black cropped hair and wore gold earrings that would have worked equally well as napkin rings.

'It's Jennifer actually,' I said apologetically.

'So, Jennifer, you're a guest.'

'Yes, I'm — '

'Great. That's super, isn't it people?'

'Yah, absolutely.'

'Awfully brave.'

I stared at Beth blankly. 'Brave? Why do you think that?'

'Well, raylay, I just think it is.'

'What's your pwoblem, dahling?' Phoebe added.

'Problem?' My problem right now was this circle of media freaks.

'Yah, you know, pwoblem. Alcoholic? Husband scarpered with the maid? *Do* tell, Julia.'

'It's *Jennifer*, and I don't have a pwoblem, I mean a problem. I — '

'Oh, we *all* have pwoblems hon, especially *you* people,' Phoebe oozed.

I stared at her blankly.

'Phoebe hon,' said Melvin in a peculiarly female voice, 'don't push the poor child, she obviously doesn't like to talk about it.'

'Yah, yah, ahbsolutely.'

'Look guys.' I felt the circle closing in around me as I tried to speak. 'I really don't know what . . . '

'Should be an excellent show,' Phoebe continued, oblivious to my unfinished sentence. '*Très* fantastic.'

'Oh totally, rahlay fab. She is just so down

to earth, you know. Should raylay get all the super gossip.' The girl introduced as Zoë waved her arms wildly as she spoke. I noticed how her long pink nails matched her Chanel suit perfectly.

Down to earth, I thought, perhaps you should all try it sometime.

'Yah, I've been working on her style, you know. We've got a fantastic look. You will love it, people. She can totally relate to these unfortunates.'

'Well, Zoë, we all know how *absolument formidable* you are at your styling thing.'

Zoë blushed on cue and tossed back her hazel-coloured mane of hair. I yawned and started to chew on a tatty thumb nail. The conversation dribbled on around me — each person insincerely complimenting the others and no one taking the slightest bit of interest in matters outside the circle.

'Zoë hon,' yelled Beth as she slapped her hand on my shoulder. 'You should give Jane here a makeover before tomorrow's show. That would be super fun.'

I glowered up at Buxom Beth.

'It's Jennifer,' I seethed.

She ignored me and threw her Liberty shawl around her immense shoulders, hitting me in the eye as she did so.

'Yah. Oh totally,' Phoebe added. 'Would

that be like *totallement super*, or *quoi*?'

'Yah, Zoë, and Lord knows she needs it. We can't let the poor gal go on national television looking like that, can we peoples?'

Ooh, heaven forbid, I look normal. Silly fat cow. Who does she think she is?

The crowd yah'd and tittered in approval of their great plan. I glanced round desperately for Maz to come and rescue me but I couldn't see past Melvin's frills and the silent Amelia's shoulder pads.

'What do you think, hon?' Beth asked, peering down at the 'unfortunate' below her.

'What do I think?' At last, I was no longer invisible.

'Yah, sweetie,' Melvin piped up. 'Great idea, isn't it dahling?'

I shrugged his clammy hand from my arm. 'First, I think I'm not your dahling, and if I was I'd have to seriously consider topping myself.'

Melvin stepped back with a loud gasp.

'Secondly, I think I wouldn't let Zoë here touch me with a barge-pole if it meant I'd end up looking as much of a subhumanoid as she does . . . ' More gasps. 'And lastly, I think none of you really cares what an unfortunate like me thinks cos you've all got your heads shoved too far up each other's arses to take any notice of the rest of the world!'

Stunned faces greeted my outburst and I noticed the circle gradually begin to disintegrate. I saw my chance for freedom and took it.

'*Au revoir*, peoples,' I chirped and made for the nearest alcoholic drink.

★ ★ ★

Armed with two glasses of bubbly and a mouthful of unidentified canapés, I found refuge behind a ten-foot cardboard poster advertising the new show: 'Real People, Real Problems, Real Solutions' exclaimed the poster.

'Real load of pricks,' I mumbled, spitting bits of cracker and caviar in all directions.

'Who are?'

I span around at the sound of the deep voice beside me. So much for my secret hiding place. He was about six feet tall with straight mousy-brown hair that flopped over one eye in a relaxed, unstyled fashion. He wasn't classically good looking — his nose was fairly large and his cheeks were rosy — but I couldn't help but notice his eyes. They twinkled like pale green glass in the sunlight and gave him an approachable, friendly manner. I felt like I knew him already.

'Who are?' he repeated.

'What?'

'Pricks?' He laughed an almost musical laugh.

'Everyone in this room.' I frowned. 'There's more pricks in here than at a thistle convention.'

'Charming. You don't even know me!'

'True. But that also means I can't exclude you because I don't know if you're a prick or not.'

'Oh I see.'

'Yep, so we better include you just in case.'

'Aye right.' His voice was lilting with a soft Geordie accent. He paused and shoved his left hand casually into his jacket pocket. He looked uncomfortable in the stiff black tuxedo.

'Are you?' he said finally.

'Am I what?'

'A prick?'

'Certainly not! I'm probably the most normal person here.' I said with mock seriousness and added sarcastically, 'Blimey, I don't think much of your manners.'

'Sorry, I'm just a prick.'

He threw me a quick glance and we smiled broadly at each other. I felt oddly relaxed in his company. Whether this was due to the free champagne or the pond life that formed the alternative, I wasn't sure.

He leaned back against the wall and looked down at the heavy black boots he wore. 'I take it you don't like these sort of dos then?'

'Oh I'd love them if you could just lose most of the people. The free food and drink is great. It's just the free doses of snobbery and insincerity I can't stand.'

'I agree,' he said. 'So what brings you here?'

'Do you mean, do I come here often?'

He laughed. 'No, I mean what's a lovely lady like you doing in a place like this?' He crossed his legs at the ankles and reclined against the wall, impersonating a nightclub sleaze. It didn't suit him.

'Hurgh!' I pretended to throw up.

He grinned.

'I'm just in the audience at this new show tomorrow,' I said eventually. 'To tell you the truth, my friend and I only live up the road but we got VIP passes. It's a long story but my ex-boyfriend of about an hour, who wasn't actually my boyfriend because he was gay, but not because of me . . . he was *actually* gay. Well, he got us the tickets. His cousin *owns* the station. I thought we'd use the offer of a free hotel.'

'Cheeky but cunning.' His eyes sparkled.

'Yeah, well, I'm sure Paradise TV won't go

broke because of it.'

'I'm sure it won't.'

'I hear they're absolutely loaded after the takeover so it's nothing to them if I grab a few freebies.'

'I admire your initiative.' He took a sip of champagne and fiddled with his starched white collar. Functions were obviously not his cup of tea. I looked at his hands. His fingers were long and thin as I would imagine a piano player's to be. He had strong square nails that were neatly cut. Obviously not a manual worker.

'What do you do?' I asked.

'When?'

'For a job, obviously.' I could tell he was being purposefully cagey.

'Oh, this and that.'

'This and that? Well, that's very informative, thanks. Is that 'this 'n' that' as in doctor, sportsman, nuclear physicist, or as in Colombian powder importer?'

He winked and tapped his nose. I felt intrigued. I wanted to know more about him.

'If I tells you, I vill have to kills you,' he said in a poor German accent.

'At least I'll die knowledgeable,' I added.

Finally, after much persuasion, he admitted he was doing work experience at the TV station.

'You're not still at school, are you?' I asked, quickly looking around for a satchel and pencil case.

'Na, I'm just trying to experience a few different projects at the station, first hand, and this talk show happens to be one of them.'

'Lucky you.'

'It's OK. The people aren't all that bad really.' He didn't sound very convincing. 'And I get to meet nor . . . um . . . '

'Normal people?'

'Yes.'

'Like me?'

He looked at his boots again and kicked his feet together. I wondered how he would choose to dress usually. Trousers and a checked shirt or jeans and a loose sweater? The latter seemed fitting but I decided a pair of neat-fitting boxer shorts and a generous covering of massage oil would be more appealing. The alcohol was kicking in. Little Miss Oestrogen was warming up.

I sat on the floor with my legs stretched out towards our cardboard screen. He smiled approvingly and settled down next to me. We stayed that way, oblivious to the frantic socialising and networking going on beyond the partition. We talked about everything from food to football, with none of the usual awkward silences. I wanted to say, 'I feel like I've known you for years.' It was true but it sounded too corny. He felt like a friend.

Suddenly we realised the party crowd was dwindling as the sound of idle chatter began to lessen. I peeked out from behind the poster just in time to see Maz striding out of the lounge door with a bottle of bubbly in one hand and a tray of food in the other. Supplies. She never was one to miss an opportunity. I laughed and crawled back to find him standing up, tucking in his slightly ruffled shirt.

'Better look neat,' he said.

'Just in case the boss catches you.'

'Er . . . yes.' He bent down and took my right hand in his left. I tried to stand up but stopped when he gave my hand a firm squeeze.

'Thanks for a good night,' he said.

'Well, it was one step up from behind the bike sheds.'

He laughed gently and let my hand drop. I didn't want him to leave. He was interesting and he made me laugh.

'Oh by the way,' I added.

He turned towards me and inadvertently flicked his hair.

'You're not a prick after all.'

'Glad to hear it,' he smiled. 'I value your opinion.'

He raised his arm and gave me a salute-style wave. I watched him turn. He walked casually out of the room with one hand in his pocket, scuffing his feet as he walked.

Damn, I thought, I didn't even ask him his name.

12

24th February, 11:30 a.m.

Rehearsals for the show were due to start at 9:00 a.m. with filming at noon. It was to be the first time that a talk show of this type would be broadcast live on the network. The new presenter had been styled, rehearsed and polished. The people who would air their problems and family feuds to the nation had been shipped in. All Paradise TV had to do was sit back and watch raw human emotions pull in the gossip-hungry viewers.

Being simple, although VIP, audience members, Maz and I were not obliged to attend the rehearsal. Not being an early riser at the best of times, several late-night beakers of champagne had made me highly allergic to getting up. It wasn't until 11:20 that I dared go for vertical and face my reflection.

I stood in the white marble bathroom of our exquisite hotel room, wearing the plush white bathrobe I had found in the cupboard. The other had been packed in the bottom of Maz's bag within ten minutes of our arrival in the room, along with two velvety monogrammed bath towels. The harsh lights above the mirror reflected off the marble, highlighting the rather unattractive luggage set that had decided to collect underneath my heavily bloodshot eyes. I felt sick and looked even sicker. I made a meagre attempt to comb my hair and sighed. I liked to describe my hairstyle as 'natural', 'slightly unruly', perhaps even 'Bohemian', but I had to admit that after such influences as swimming, sleeping, bathing, showering, wind or light ruffling, my head looked like it was home to a particularly untidy family of large birds. I patted the curls with water and turned to look at Maz.

She was perched precariously on the edge of the bath with her head poking out of the bathroom window, puffing on a cigarette. Two smoke alarms hovered on the ceiling above her head. Maz called them the nicotine police. The hotel security guard was unimpressed at having been called to our room at 3:00 a.m. to investigate the brain-numbing sound of an activated alarm. Maz had explained it was due to my excessive highly potent gas problem, as she had attempted to swallow a lit cigarette.

She had then asked the man if he could possibly grab us girls some munchies from the hotel kitchen. A few rounds of toast, pudding and anything chocolate would be fine, she explained. I never realised five-star-hotel staff could swear so much.

I heard Maz cough into the brisk Newcastle air. She wobbled slightly on the bath edge but regained her balance. I gazed jealously at her long, thin legs and wondered how it felt to have thighs that didn't meet in the middle. I poked at my own thighs and wondered whether they had miraculously toned up since the last time I had briefly considered exercising. No such luck. Nights of calorific and alcoholic indulgence seem to have repercussions on my body within hours. Let's face it, I was no supermodel waif even on a good day. I felt huge, enormous, of *mammoth* proportions. Of course, I was actually no fatter than the previous day, but it was psychological. It was a definite tracksuit bottoms and baggy T-shirt kind of day.

'What you thinkin' about, pet?' Maz retrieved her head and sat against the white tiled wall with her feet in the bath.

'Tracksuits,' I replied.

'Uh oh, feelin' fat are we?'

'Yup.'

'Totally sloth-like and ugly?'

'Sure am.'

'Completely rejected and unloved?'

'That's the one.'

She could read me like a book. The sign of a true friend.

'I need a man,' I groaned, hauling myself up next to the sink.

'Na, you dain't, woman. You need sex.'

'I need *companionship*.'

'Get a cat.'

'I hate cats, they're boring.'

'Get a dog then.' Maz laughed. 'Aye man, get yerself a dog. If you feed it enough, it'd love you forever. Just like a man but without all the hassle. Apparently dogs look like their owners, ye kna?'

'I feel sorry for it already.'

'You'd need one with lots of hair. Aye, one o' them Durex dogs or somethin'.'

'Dulux.'

'Whatever.'

Admittedly, I'd rather have been likened to a cute, petite breed like a Schnauzer or a Chihuahua, but I took it that we were being realistic.

'So what were you thinking about?' I asked glumly.

Maz smiled brightly and gazed up at the window.

'Hmm, lights, cameras, an audience, Ricki Lake . . . '

'The usual then?'

'Aye.' Her eyes were wide and bright, even

212

after a night of mixed drinks and little sleep. Bitch.

'You kna, Jen, I was just wonderin' how I'd feel if it were my own show startin' today.'

I smiled and nodded, wanting her to continue.

'It'd be lush wouldn't it? All them people watchin' us sort out problems. My name on boards, like, all aroond the studio and everyone cheerin' when I come in with wur massive microphone. Aye, it'd be canny ace man. It could've been me, ye kna. The presenter is that heffer of a woman they picked from my audition, the posh one — lucky tramp.'

Every so often my usually brash and carefree best friend gave me an insight into what really went on in her heart and mind.

'If it were me, I'd have lots of different shows. Like some romantic, some slushy, if I had to, and I'd have geet funny subjects for a laff, and then dead serious ones. Aye. I could help people get together, families and couples like. I could pick people up, help them with their dreams, get them good advice. Imagine it, man.' She took a deep breath. We sat in silence for a moment.

'Maybe one day, hey Maz. I mean, look at me. I didn't think I'd end up being a barmaid, this time last year. You never know what'll happen.'

'Na. I'm too flippin' common.'

'Shut up.'

'Too bloody 'regional' she said. Aye, that was it. Stupid cow.'

She jumped out of the bath and stared past me into the mirror, furiously pulling her hair into a ponytail. 'Howay, man, Jen. Enough of this shite. Get yerself ready, we've only got ten minutes.'

★ ★ ★

'Chop chop ladies!' yelled Petronella, the audience coordinator. She grabbed Maz firmly by the elbow and marched towards the studio, frantically waving her red clipboard. 'Terrible, terrible rush. No time to be dawdling now girls.'

'Sorry, we — '

'Never work with children or animals, they say. Huh! Never work with people at all I say to them. Honestly, you people will be the death of me . . . '

The high-pitched voice continued to bounce along the corridor as I bent down to tie my flapping shoelace.

Suddenly a shiny red court shoe appeared next to my foot. It tapped impatiently. I glanced up to see Torica, hands on her minute hips, staring down at me with an irritated look on her heavily made-up face.

'Oh Julia, Julia . . . '

'*Jennifer.*'

'Quite.' She shook her mane of blonde hair and tutted loudly. 'Honestly dahling, no rehearsal, no make-up. I nearly had you as a no-show.'

'But I'm — '

'Come on now. Busy busy. Let's get in our places shall we? Marvellous. This is live television you know, hon, not a holiday camp. I mean, raylay.'

Her skeletal fingers wrapped around my right hand and I was hauled to my feet. Five nails, filed to vicious points, dug into my sweaty palm as we hurried towards the studio door. Torica's hips wiggled at a violent speed and she glanced nervously at her Gucci timepiece every five or six paces.

'Good, good, almost there,' she muttered. 'Can't let the team down can we, Jemima?'

'It's *Jennifer.*'

'Whatever. Excellent, here we are. Action stations, dahling.'

I was propelled through a set of heavy double doors and emerged into what appeared to be a reject lounge scene from *Anne and Nick*. A semicircle of chairs in the centre of the room were filled, I noticed, by our motley crew of bus companions. One seat remained empty, presumably for the presenter. I scanned the babbling audience for Maz's friendly face but the glaring studio lights made recognition impossible. With my arm shielding my eyes, I stumbled across the stage in search of a seat. Tripping on a large black cable that snaked along the floor, I toppled forward, reached out wildly and grabbed the headphones of a small, hassled-looking woman directly ahead.

'Fifteen sec — aah!' she shrieked, grabbing her ears as we tumbled to the floor. Sheets of paper flew in all directions from her clipboard as we struggled to untangle ourselves.

'Bloody hell,' she shouted, 'these bloody people!'

I felt a strong arm pull me up by my sweater and throw me into the empty seat on the stage. The man then glared at me nastily, before jumping back into position behind camera two.

I tried to stand up but the woman with the headphones ran forward, holding out her left hand and a clipboard in a defensive manner.

'Stay where you are, you fool!' she screamed. 'On in five . . . four . . .'

I looked around desperately for Maz, trying

to ignore the hysterical laughter from the audience.

'Two . . . ' She held up both thumbs, the lights increased in intensity, music blared out from nowhere and camera two zoomed in on my startled face.

'Ladies and gentlemen, please welcome your exquisite host, the answer to all our problems, Miss Julia Juniper.' The voice boomed from somewhere above my wildly spinning head, then was swallowed up by a medley of painfully loud elevator music. The audience members shuffled on the blue plastic seats to get a better view of the stage and the numerous cameras revolved around the studio floor with choreographed chaos. A colossal cheer from everyone present, except yours truly, heralded the somewhat delayed appearance onto the stage of our really not-so-exquisite host Julia Juniper.

I glanced dubiously over my right shoulder. This woman had obviously taken make-up lessons from a master plasterer. Her bright orange foundation was shovelled into the grooves of her prematurely wrinkled face, and set with a further four inches of bronzing powder. Her orange lips, circled with a thick brown line, stuck out like an adult at a Boyzone concert. Her eyelids were barely working under the strain of three sets of false eyelashes. The early-80s bouffant hair-do stood to attention with the apparent aid of half a dozen cans of superhold hair spray, making her head look several times too big for her salmon-trouser-suit-clad body. Frightening was not the word. This woman would scare most drag queens in a dark alleyway at night.

Julia Juniper wafted past my chair and took her position on the yellow cross in the centre of the stage. The audience fell silent as our host lifted the oversized black foam microphone to her enormous lips and set her mouth in a toothy smile.

'Haylay everyone. Welcome to the first ayver live television talk show on this network.'

The small, headphoned woman raised her arms and the audience cheered.

'Where we solve *your* problems and change your life.'

Hands up, another cheer.

'Tayday orn the show, we have a fahbulous variety of guests for you, from the mundane to the bizarre. Wherever you are, whoever you are, we will have a storay to interest you . . . '

I glanced along the line of chairs at my stage companions. They wore the anxious looks of a pack of seals facing a Canadian trawler. Evidently the idea of airing their dirty laundry on live TV was now a less appealing prospect.

'Now I want you to meet George,' Julia continued. 'George says his wife Magenta is showing herself up by gallivanting around with her twenty-three-year-old toyboy Philip. Magenta is fifty-two.'

Hisses and laughter rose from the crowd. Camera one moved forward to focus on George, whom I recognised as beige man from the bus the previous day. George, who had opted instead for a combination of olive green and brown, squirmed in his chair and fiddled with the buttons on his chunky-knit cardigan.

'So, George, do tell us what happened.'

'W . . . we . . . well, Julia,' he stammered, 'Magenta and I have been married for thirty years almost. Everything was fine until that . . . that young punk, excuse me, came on the scene.'

'Oh *puhlease*,' Magenta interrupted, waving her hand in George's face. 'Fine? You call a life of pure boredom fine? George is an accountant, Julia. Honestly, we only had sex once every three months to celebrate the end of a financial quarter.'

'But . . . '

'We went out once in a blue moon with his spectacularly dull friends, and they always ended up discussing debits, credits and capital gains tax over a light ale.'

'They . . . '

'Life with George was less interesting than watching paint dry, Julia. His calculator has more appeal to him than I have. He's dull, he wears Y-fronts, and he's vegetarian. I mean, please, I'm not going to waste my life darning socks and knitting lentils, Julia. Dull, dull, dull!'

Say what you mean, Magenta, I thought. I mean, don't hold back or anything. I felt a sudden pang of sympathy for poor, dull George.

George coughed nervously and touched Magenta's pink-stockinged knee.

'I can change. I love you, Maggie,' he pleaded desperately.

'Get yer bleedin' hands off her,' yelled Magenta's young stud, jumping to his feet and grabbing George's trembling arm.

'She's my wife!'

'She's not your chuffin' anythin', mate. She's mine.'

Philip was obviously blessed with a huge amount of testosterone.

The crowd yelled, 'Deck him man!'

People jumped to their feet and cheered while Julia Juniper looked around nervously.

'Magenta, please,' George wailed.

'I'm warning you, mate!' Philip stepped towards the cowering accountant, puffing out his chest like a Wonderbra girl. George's chances of success were looking slim. Magenta feigned mild distress at the sight of her duelling men.

Bitch, I thought. I couldn't understand how Mrs Plum-hair-do, mid-life crisis could have two men, albeit a hopeless pair, fighting over her 52-year-old self on national television while I, a young, vibrant, not bad looking 26-year-old was forced to live a life of almost total chastity. I vowed to discover Magenta's secret after the show.

It was only after the second punch was thrown that security stepped in and removed Philip from the stage. Our pusillanimous host cowered on her spot amongst the audience shouting, 'Stop! Stop! You hooligan! You're ruining my show!'

The audience became increasingly raucous, hungry for more action from the stage.

'Shut up you imbeciles!' Julia yelled. A particularly feeble display of agony aunt potential, I thought. Finally, headphone girl jumped to her feet and signalled to Julia by thrusting ten fingers in the air.

'Join me after the break,' Ms Juniper whimpered, and the supermarket music filled my ears.

I saw this as my own signal to evacuate the stage seat. Glancing around quickly, I jumped to my feet and made for the audience. Headphone girl was nowhere to be seen and the stout cameraman was busy trying to calm an incredibly red Julia, who was freaking out in the wings. Just as I slid past the frontier of cameras, I felt something pull sharply on my hair.

'Where the HELL do you think you're going?'

I spun round to see my headphoned opponent staring at me with wild eyes.

'Well?'

'I'm . . . uh.' I felt like a school kid who has been caught out of bounds.

'Sit down, NOW!'

'But . . . I'm supposed to be . . . '

'I don't care for excuses, get back to your seat!'

Something about live television made people particularly power happy, I thought.

I gazed at the audience. So near and yet so far. Out of the corner of my eye I saw our host striding towards me, her salmon suit flapping in her slipstream.

'Oh bum,' I muttered, and quickly returned to the stage.

'Now I want you to meet Noreen,' said a newly composed Julia Juniper. 'Noreen says her daughter, Sarah, has an unhealthy obsession with vampires, death and the occult.'

I watched on the monitor as the camera moved in on the young girl dressed totally in black lace and satin. As her picture filled the screen, Vampira reached up to straighten her black veil, revealing an intricate tattoo of the devil on her right forearm. I guessed she wasn't a 'spring' on the Colour-Me-Beautiful scale.

'Haylo, Noreen,' said Julia, smiling insincerely and averting her eyes to the nearest autocue.

'We can all see Sarah's . . . um . . . 'style', Noreen. It's awfully strange. Can you tell me when this all started?'

'Yes, Julia.' The anxious woman touched the silver hair above her ears, pushing it into place. 'Sarah . . . or Bathsheba as she now calls herself . . . was twelve when she started to change.'

'Why was that?' Julia interrupted.

'She saw some horror films . . . '

'At twelve? Were you neglecting your child, Noreen?'

'Heavens no.'

Whispers coursed through the crowd.

'I love my daughter but it's hard, I'm a single mum and — '

'Oh come on, Noreen, that's no excuse now is it?'

'No . . . but . . . um.'

I stared at Julia in bewilderment. She was obviously standing for no nonsense after the last scenario.

'Let's meet Sarah, shall we?' Julia continued unabashed.

'Bathsheba,' the little girl muttered.

'How old are you, Sarah?'

'*Bathsheba*,' she said forcefully.

'Don't be silly, now, little girl.' Julia was beginning to get flustered. 'Just tell us your age.'

The girl stared blankly through her veil then sighed. 'Thir'een,' she replied.

'Thirteen,' Julia replied. 'Thirteen and you dress like this.' She pointed at the girl on the stage who shuffled her feet and looked shyly at the audience.

'Aye . . . so?'

'You should be in dresses at your age.'

'Howay, I hate dresses.'

'What do you like . . . Bathsheba?'

'Me, I like death and stuff.'

The audience giggled. Several people booed loudly. I wondered how our host would solve this little gem.

'Don't be ridiculous,' Julia continued. 'You have no idea how silly you look.'

'I like lookin' different, man.'

'Different! Dysfunctional more like. If you were my daughter I wouldn't let you out of the house, looking like that.'

'If I wur your daughter, I'd kill mesel', ya scraggy cow.'

'Why you little — '

'Please!' Noreen interrupted. 'I just wanted some advice.'

'Advice!' Julia's face was reddening under her coagulated crust of foundation. 'You need more than that, Noreen, you need an exorcist for this little tramp.'

The audience gasped. Headphone woman waved her arms frantically.

'Gettin' in a ragee are ya auld woman?' Bathsheba shouted. 'Watch ya dain't burst oot of yer suit now.'

'You little bitch!' Our delightful host ran towards the stage, arms flailing and eyes blazing. The camera focused on the wall as security struggled to control the situation.

'I think Trisha's approach is a bit more effective,' I muttered to the girl next to me. 'More discussion, less untamed violence.'

I couldn't help but laugh, and took a second to scan the audience for Maz's face. Suddenly a flash of obscenely bright salmon viscose obscured my view.

'What about you then?' Julia Juniper

225

screeched in my face. 'What is your problem?'

She was losing it, I could tell. We were nearing the point of no return on the talk-show scale. This made the infamous Jerry Springer series look like a brownies' gang show.

'I don't have a problem,' I said, instantly aware that my face was now being broadcast live on national television.

'Of course you have,' she squealed. 'All you common people have problems. You're all whingers, that's what you are!'

I held my breath. Headphone lady, Torica and various television crew raced around the studio like a herd of cattle with BSE. Pandemonium would be an understatement.

'Come on then!' she squealed. 'What's your name?'

'Um . . . what?'

'NAME!' she yelled, thrusting her distorted face into mine.

'Um . . . Jennifer,' I stammered.

The audience hooted with delight.

'PROBLEM!'

'I . . . I don't *have* a problem, I told you.'

'Then what the HELL are you doing here, Jennifer?'

'I don't know,' I whimpered. 'I . . . I . . . we only came for a laugh . . . '

'LAUGH! You think this is funny do you?'

People ran in all directions, lights flashed and the audience were on their feet. Julia Juniper was almost sitting on my knee.

'And the free champagne,' I wailed, 'we wanted free champagne.'

'Ah-ha!' she shouted. 'So that's it, is it?'

'Is it?'

'You're an alcoholic aren't you?'

'*No!*'

'And in denial too. That's your problem!'

'What?'

I couldn't believe what was happening. This mentally deranged woman had obviously taken an instant, very big, dislike to me. So, I'd laughed at her inability to control an unruly thirteen-year-old. So what? That didn't really give her the right to brand me an alcoholic on national television.

'Hang on a minute!' I shouted. 'I'm supposed to be in the audience.'

I looked at the crew, begging for help. Headphone girl shook her head disapprovingly and refused to spring to my assistance. Camera two stayed on my frantic face.

'You're a loser!' Julia screamed. 'Admit it, go on!'

'You're mental,' I replied.

'You're *all* losers,' she wailed, turning to face the excited audience.

All of a sudden, it appeared her grasp of

the Queen's English had escaped her as she threw a full-blown tantrum.

'I don't give a *damn* about your pathetic problems. I hate you all!'

The cameras continued to roll as security tried to take control and remove Julia Juniper's witchlike hands from my hair. Magenta and George started to argue while Bathsheba roared with laughter. It was wild.

As all hell threatened to break loose, a loud voice suddenly boomed from the midst of the animated audience.

'Wait just a bleedin' minute!'

Heads and cameras turned towards the direction of the voice. I looked up, past my attacker, straining my eyes against the lights. I saw Maz strutting down the stairs towards the scene of anarchy on the stage. Amid the confusion, my tall, confident friend oozed control and order like a ringmaster in a disorderly circus.

'Now jest hang on woman,' she said loudly, reaching the stage.

Maz towered over the buxom talk-show host and fixed on her a stony gaze. 'Howay, get yer flippin' hands off wor mate,' she said, grabbing Julia's arms firmly, 'or I'll flamin' deck ya.'

Julia spun round, momentarily releasing her grip on my hair. She stared up at Maz, who by now was breathing heavily and shaking her head.

'Get away from me,' Julia wailed. 'This is *my* show.'

'Aye, worst luck,' Maz added.

'Security, please!' Julia screeched.

I waited for the burly guards to drag Maz away from the action but they stood mesmerised. Everyone was waiting to see what would happen.

Maz placed a firm hand on Julia's padded shoulder and forced her into the empty seat, previously occupied by the equally tempestuous Philip.

'Howay, sit doon and shut up!' Maz yelled.

Julia Juniper stared open mouthed.

'And you two can give it a rest an' all,' said Maz to the squabbling George and Magenta.

A strange hush descended on the studio.

'Why-aye lass,' shouted Bathsheba with new-found fortitude. 'I'm gan yem,' she said, and left the stage.

Maz stood in the centre of the stage, her eyes fixed on our host, completely oblivious to the cameras between herself and the audience. 'What a star,' I whispered, suppressing a smile. She looked completely at home in this totally bizarre situation.

Julia began to speak. 'The problem with people like *you* is — '

'The problem, woman,' Maz said defiantly, pointing her finger at Julia, 'is stuck-up cows like you who think you can treat people however you bloody well fancy. You come on here all smiles and foundation, but as soon as the camera switches off yer aboot as friendly and approachable as a traffic warden on a bad day. You're a bleedin' disgrace. You dain't *deserve* the title of talk-show host. You divny give a toss about any of these people, do ya?'

Maz gestured to the remaining guests on the stage and then stepped closer to the quivering host. 'I tell ya, these people *are* the show. Aye, I meybe common in your eyes. I may be too chuffin' 'regional' to get a job like yours, but I kna one thing. Just cos yer a legend in yer own mind, that doesny mean you can gan aroond treatin' people like the dirt on the sole of yer designer shoe. Everyone deserves respect woman, so if you deen't wanna give us any you can piss off!'

Julia Juniper gasped and turned a dangerous shade of puce. A tumultuous cheer rose from the audience. The entire studio was on its feet applauding my fearless friend.

'Howay, Jen,' Maz said, reaching out her hand, 'we're leavin'.' She wasn't even shaking. Maz was as solid as a rock.

At that moment, amid the rapturous applause, which, admittedly, was not for my benefit, I instantly felt like a glamorous heroine in a cheesy Hollywood movie. This would be the heartstring-pulling moment. Good conquers evil, girl gets guy, America saves the world, gathered crowd cheers loudly. It was all I could do to stop myself thumping my chest with my fist and yelling, 'God Bless America!'

Fortunately, we reached the studio doors before I could get too carried away. I was about to push them dramatically when a young man stepped in front of me and held the door open. I smiled at his chivalry and glanced at his face. His green eyes twinkled mischievously. Eyes like pale green glass. I took a sharp intake of breath. It was my drinking partner from the previous night. Of course, I remembered, he was doing work experience on the show. We paused momentarily. He looked even better by day, I thought. Practically edible. Like a family-size bar of Galaxy. Maz and I had probably wrecked his work experience with the last hour's antics. I wanted to say something but I was never very good at awkward moments. I opened my mouth.

'Howay, man, let's gan yem,' Maz yelled in my ear, pushing me through the door.

I stumbled but didn't fall. I knew we should leave quickly before the Julia Juniper protection squad caught up with us. In the background, the elevator music blasted into action. I could still hear the audience cheering as we raced down the corridor, looking for the exit.

As we reached the end and made to turn left, I glanced over my shoulder. The studio door swung slowly on its hinges, but there was nobody there. I sighed heavily. He was gone.

13

3rd March, 10:30 a.m.

'Bad cheese,' said Dave thoughtfully.

'Can you see my knicker-line, Maz?' I asked, going on tiptoe to try and see my rear view in the mirror.

'Na, they look canny, Jen,' Maz replied.

'Are you sure? They don't make — '

'Do NOT say 'do they make my bum look fat?'.'

'I wasn't going to.'

'That's a'reet then.'

'I was going to ask whether they made my whole miserable, pudgy lower half look any less like a stodgy English pudding . . . possibly.'

'Ah howay,' Maz laughed. 'Paranoid low self-esteemed woman in the vicinity. Clear the room of fatty foods before she devours them all in an act of self-hate.'

'Fish,' said Dave.

'I don't hate myself actually.'

'You could have fooled me, pet.'

'I like my good bits, which are few and far between, of course. Actually I can't think of any good bits.'

'Yeah, fish might do.'

'Dave,' Maz said in an exasperated tone, 'what the hell are you talkin' aboot?'

'Fish. Yeah, I wur thinkin' fish might do the trick.'

'What trick man?'

'Shite loads of stinkin' bloody fish. All o'er the place like. I reckon that would get rid of them buyers.'

Dave's wavelength, although generally not of this world, became a little more comprehensible. The sale of the pub was forging ahead. Potential buyers had been found and Dave's mission to temporarily devalue the land was in the pipeline.

'Fish won't work, man.' Maz shook her head and stretched out on the saggy brown sofa. 'The buyers dain't want the buildin', they want the land. They won't give a toss what the place smells of as long as they can flatten it, build their poncey flats or whatever and make a packet.'

Dave looked sullen.

'Hey don't worry, mate,' I said, patting him sympathetically on his broad back. 'You'll think of something good. There's no real rush anyway. Matt said he'd call when the date was confirmed for the buyers to visit.'

'Aye, Matt,' Dave nodded his head. 'That wur 'is name.'

'Whose name?' Maz asked stiffly.

'The guy who rang yesterday.'

Maz and I both sat up straight and stared intently at Dave.

'What did he say?' we yelled in unison.

'Didn't I tell ya?'

'No!'

'They're comin' the neet.'

'Who?'

'Them poncey buyers and their bloody lawyers.'

Dave continued. 'Well not really the neet. More like three o'clock. Aye. That's why I'm thinkin' of wor plan.'

Maz leapt out of her seat and began pacing the room. It didn't take many paces, it was so small. 'Ah shite man Dave,' she said, shaking her hands furiously. 'You could have tell't us, like.'

'I jest did.'

'Aye, I mean last neet!' Maz yelled. 'The chuffin' buyers are comin' today. Ah howay, there's nay chance. I'm losin' the pub and I cannot do anythin'. Ah shite, shite, shite, shite, shite, shite . . . '

Maz continued her prolific monologue while Dave lit a fag and reached for the paper.

This wasn't good. We were totally unprepared for the big visit and only had a few hours to come up with a way of eradicating the threat of an impending sale. Maz was frantic, Dave was oblivious, and my mind went into overdrive. There had to be something we could do.

★   ★   ★

Ever since our farcical television debut, Maz and I had been treated as legends in the realm of the Scrap Inn. Maz was being heralded among our customers as the next Robert Kilroy-Silk while I was simply the infamous alcoholic barmaid. Jennifer Summer, Freak of the Week.

Thinking I could reach no lower point in my mother's eyes had been a misconception. I had, according to Mother Summer, not only dragged the family name through the proverbial mud but also laid it to rest in a coffin of cow dung. Well, that was the gist of what she had spluttered. Mum was ashamed to show her face in the upper echelons of Newcastle society. Rosemary Conley nights were now out of the question. As for afternoon tea in Fenwicks, unthinkable. Oh the shame! She could not bring herself to venture further than her extortionately priced and highly overrated therapist's office. Pathetic really, considering the immense appetite and respect her gaggle of cronies had for a good bit of scandal. Nationally-broadcast scandal was even better. I would have done wonders for Mum's street cred. Evidently she did not agree. I had now been sent way beyond Coventry by my mother, Susie, Sebastian and their two horrible children, which pleased me greatly. I sensed I had been sent to rot somewhere on the outskirts of Swindon.

My born-again dad, on the other hand, found the whole incident highly amusing and seemed to revel in Mum's obvious distress. Despite Mum's protests, he maintained his twice-weekly visits to the Scrap Inn to join Auld Vinny et al. in their quest for the holy ale.

The pub had also now become Maz's main concern in life. The experience with Julia Juniper had left Maz totally disillusioned as far as talk shows were concerned. She still worshipped Ricki Lake, but Maz had given up any hope of fronting her own show after destroying Ms Juniper in front of several million viewers.

It's a strange thing when a lifelong ambition suddenly seems hopeless. In my experience it can be likened to fancying a famous pop star in your oh-so-simple younger years. You dream of an idyllic pop-star life with your leather-trousered man in your pop-star mansion with your two-point-four funky pop-star kids. The dream is absolute perfection until you finally meet the object of your desires and realise he's a rather sad, unwashed, arrogant, brain-dead, suede-leather-tassley-jacket-wearing tosser. Romantic trauma at age nine and three-quarters. Personally I still blame him for my life-long string of useless love affairs. Well, surely they couldn't all be my fault.

Every so often I would catch Maz staring dreamily at the shrine to Ricki Lake above the bar. Nevertheless, she would not admit to feeling upset. All that mattered now, she said, was saving the pub from its threatened flattening. Stuff the quivering Gordon. Maz intended to run the joint and make it successful if it was the last thing she ever did.

Thus, the importance of Dave's tardy message. This could be the day that the Scrap Inn, Maz's new hopes and yet another of my careers were all sucked down the drain. All thanks to the ever-bastardly Jack.

★ ★ ★

'Dave, man,' Maz yelled, 'get your mates round here now! Tell 'em we need a bit of back-up at the pub.'

'Aye.'

'Mention lawyers, man, and they'll come runnin' with baseball bats. Nay offence, Jen.'

'None taken.'

'Aye well, howay then, Dave.'

'What's the plan then, like?'

Even the usually unflappable Dave was beginning to look flustered.

'I've got absolutely no idea man but I tell't you we're gonna have to think bloody fast.'

Dave sprang — as much as a sixteen-stone giant under the influence of marijuana can spring — into action. He left the flat in search of manpower. Grant and Phil Mitchell would have been particularly appropriate. I had always sensed that Jack was petrified of the dastardly duo whenever he dared to watch *EastEnders*.

Maz poured herself a large tequila from a discoloured bottle which lay fermenting in the cupboard behind the sofa.

'Eugh shite,' she muttered, running into the kitchen in search of salt and lime.

★　★　★

Pathetically disguising my voice to avoid recognition, I dialled the number for Glisset & Jacksop and asked to be put through to Mr Matthew Capley.

'Matt Capley.'

'Hi Matt, Jen.'

'Jen? Oh bloody hell, hiya ex-colleague. Receptionist said it was some mad Scotswoman for me. Bloody panicked I did.'

'Disguise.'

'Yes, hon, cunning. So what's up?'

'It's about the pub, Matt. I just heard the buyers are supposedly coming today. Is that true?'

'Yes darling, totally true I'm afraid. Your ex-heart-throb has been racing about like Linford Christie with the runs all morning. You'd think this was his number one client or something. Honestly.'

'Number one vendetta more like.'

'Hmmm. He doesn't take kindly to public humiliation. Bummer eh, hon?'

'Well, as I managed to ruin a live TV show for his *numero uno* client, I reckon I am now officially public enemy number one.'

'Oh yes, darling, I heard. Hilarious. I always knew you were a bit of an alco.'

'Shut up.'

'Soz.'

'Anyway Matt, my major concern is saving this pub. Jack is set on destroying me and dragging the Scrap Inn with me. I've got about five hours to stop him.'

'Three, babe.'

'What?'

'Three hours. He's scheduled for two to two-thirty so you had better get your toosh moving, chick.'

'Oh bollocks. Matt, what can I do?'

Matt paused in thought while I silently prayed for a flash of divine inspiration.

'I can't say too much, Jenny babe. This call is probably being recorded as it is and I don't want to end up in the sequel to Spy Master, I better watch my back.'

'I thought your boyfriend did that for you.'

'OK, clever clogs. Well, all I can say is . . . your buyer is a housing developer. Not from the North-East, so they're fresh to this area. Geordie virgins, of which there are few. Ha, ha, ha. So, babe, just think of ways to surprise them. What would put them off buying? What would put you off buying? Put on your lawyer head, sweetheart.'

'It's a bit rusty. I'd better go down to Kwik Fit for a quick service.' I sighed dramatically. 'OK Matt, thanks anyway.'

'Good luck sex bomb.'

'Cheers.'

'And Jen . . . '

'Yup?'

'I hope you're over him. He's a real arsewipe you know.'

'Huh! Yes, of course I am.' A little

over-exaggerated. I blushed guiltily.

'His jaw's far too square. Pythagoras would have a field day with those angles, darling.'

Matt always had the ability to cheer me up. He usually spoke a lot of sense too, in his own wacky way.

I said goodbye, promised to keep in touch, over and above the obvious impersonal Christmas card, and set about oiling my brain to enable it to produce a solution. I had now assumed the role of Hannibal, leader of the A-Team. Plan-formulator, keeping cool in the face of impending danger. Luckily for Hannibal, he usually found himself being held captive in an aircraft hangar, accompanied by his ever-victorious team and surrounded by enough raw materials and machinery to create an intergalactic anti-bad-guy device. I, in comparison, had only my rapidly depleting collection of brain cells, Derek, Denise, Auld Vinny and the promised assistance of Dave's group of reprobates. To say our chances of success were minimal was wildly optimistic. We were doomed.

★   ★   ★

'Maz, Jen,' Denise screeched from her position at the front door. 'Blurks in suits, man, headin' this way.'

'Jesus,' Maz yelled.

'OK, calm everyone.' I tried desperately to appear in control. 'You all know the score, so get in your places and let's do it.'

For no apparent reason, I suddenly had the urge to speak with a New York drawl. Rousing team talks always sounded better in American, I found.

While everyone chattered excitedly, I ran to the door and stared through the inch-wide opening. Striding down the street were six men. The three in the centre were sporting the less dynamic suits and dodgy Father's Day present ties. These I presumed to be our buyers. The others were clearly lawyers. After four years of study and almost two in practice, I could spot a solicitor at fifty paces standing on my head with one eye closed. On the left was a small, barrel-shaped man, no taller than 5'6". He wore a very dark black wool three-piece suit, topped with a metallic green bow tie. His self-assured stride, shiny shoes and well-fed figure shouted financial success. A good lawyer. The young man at his side looked fresh out of law school. Clean-cut, interested and eager to please, he was clearly a new trainee. Not yet deflated, disillusioned and worn out from all-nighters, he had a lot to learn. This odd couple obviously formed the buyer's legal team.

The vendor's legal hit squad consisted of

only one man. Confident with an insincere semi-smile, the most hyper-dynamic of dynamic city suits and a definite strut. I felt my stomach tie itself in a variety of complex knots as I watched him approach. My head screamed 'Bastard' but my heart began to flutter at the sight of my Jack.

'This is it, Maz,' I whispered conspiratorially as she appeared behind me. I put my arm around her and tried to smile optimistically.

'Where the hell is wor Dave?' Maz gripped a bottle of lager anxiously. She subconsciously throttled the bottle's neck.

'He'll be here, Maz, don't worry.'

We turned and peered outside. The hunters had reached the hunting ground. As the pub fell silent, the business discussion outside the door became audible. Luckily, lawyers were not renowned for speaking quietly.

'Gentlemen, this is our site,' Jack said proudly. 'The measurements you have been given include the location of the . . . public house . . . ' — said with a certain disdain — ' . . . itself, along with a yard area behind the gateway to the side and the parking spaces to the right of the building. All surrounding grassland is common ground.'

Jack paused. The three men in dodgy ties walked slowly out of view, obviously committing every inch of the locality to memory.

Maz and I ran to a barred window to our left and quietly opened the small window at the top.

'The public house has occupied the land for quite a few years, gentlemen . . . ' Jack continued.

'Ninety-five actually,' Maz muttered.

' . . . but the area is changing fast. The drinking hole has become largely redundant . . . '

'Bollocks.'

'Shh Maz.'

'Prick.'

' . . . but this is prime land, gentlemen, as I'm sure you will appreciate. A spectacular view of the river, the great Tyne Bridge in the distance and a stone's throw from the quayside. I'm sure you'll agree, this land will be in great demand in the near future.'

'Howay,' Maz whispered, 'the tosser sounds like he's goin' for the Nobel Prize for bullshit. How you could *ever* have fancied him, Jen, beats me.'

I smiled weakly.

The buyers walked back up the hill. We ran to the door. They stopped, waiting for Jack's splurge to continue. Barrel man scribbled notes furiously in a blue legal notepad. His trainee hopped from one foot to the other, unsure of his role.

'This is one of the fastest developing areas in the North-East, gentlemen. My clients have received significant interest from other parties but are willing to give your corporation first refusal.'

'What a load of canny shite, man.' Maz was like a horse chomping at the bit. I look expectantly up the road for any sign of Dave.

The fattest of the dodgy-tie men finally spoke. 'The scrap yard opposite, is that fully functional?'

'Er yes.' Jack paused momentarily. 'You will notice, however, it is almost completely shielded by the fencing and tree cover.'

'Ooh, cunning,' I whispered. 'You'd hardly notice the enormity of it all.'

'We estimate, gentlemen, that the scrap yard will cease to operate within the next five years as the area becomes more upmarket.'

'Bloody cheek, snobby git,' Maz growled.

'And the local people,' the fat man continued, 'are they largely impoverished?'

'Jesus!' Maz's voice was rising dramatically. 'Who the bleedin' hell are these people?'

I put my arm through hers and raised one finger to my lips. We had missed Jack's response but it wouldn't take a genius to hazard a guess at his words. Fat dodgy-tie man leaned to one side as barrel man whispered something in his ear.

'Hmmm . . . the land,' he continued. 'We assume you are offering us good quality building land.'

'The finest,' Jack replied. 'It is on a steep incline from the river as you will appreciate. There are, therefore, no drainage problems. After demolition' — Maz shuddered at the utterance of this word — 'the land would be immediately available for development.'

The buyers nodded.

Come on Dave, I pleaded silently. Jack ruffled his feathers proudly.

'I must point out the generous offer being made by my clients,' he continued boldly. 'Gentlemen, you are looking at a gold mine.'

'Aye, gis a second and I'll blow you all up,' Maz whispered.

I was starting to fret. I had almost forgotten how convincing Jack could be. After all, I had totally fallen for his charm and incessant lies. Perhaps we were kidding ourselves. How could we, a group of barmaids, punters and ex-cons foil the plans of a powerful law firm? It was hopeless.

'Shall we take a look inside?' the buyers asked in unison.

Jack looked startled.

'Lead the way, Jack,' barrel man said in a deep, Shakespearean voice.

The party moved towards the door. Maz

and I sprinted for the bar and gestured to the gathered crowd of customers to start talking.

'Remember, we don't know anything,' I said. 'Act natural.'

Almost immediately, my order had the same effect as shoving a video camera in someone's face and shouting, 'Just pretend I'm not here.' It seemed to turn our punters into amateur dramatists. Those at the bar stood bolt upright, stiffly sipping on their pints. The crowd at the tables sat in unnatural poses, some laughing loudly, others muttering 'rhubarb, rhubarb'. I felt like the barmaid wench in a low-budget Hollywood Western, only with a less impressive cleavage. The door swung open, the six suits entered and the pub fell silent. All eyes were on the strange new cowboys in town.

'Six pints of your best,' said the happiest looking of the men in the dodgy ties.

'Five and a lemonade for the young man,' barrel man insisted, nodding his head at the trainee. Trainee blushed then glowered at the back of his boss' head.

Those were the days, I thought to myself, and instantly felt a sense of liberation. *I may only be a lowly barmaid to you people but I'm in charge of my life*, I thought.

I put my head down, avoiding Jack's

intense stare, and helped Maz to pull the pints.

'This place is surprisingly charming inside, James,' said fat buyer to happy buyer.

'Yes, Richard, it's very . . . um . . . very *northern*.'

Maz slammed a pint on the bar, spilling half of the contents.

'The service leaves a lot to be desired,' Jack growled. 'Whatever happened to service with a smile?'

Another pint slammed on the bar.

'If you want a cheesy smile, gan to Burger King,' Maz said through gritted teeth. 'If it's a pint you want, shut yer gob and 'you got it'.'

Our customers took their less than full pints uneasily and glanced nervously at their fellow drinkers.

'Nuts?' I said loudly.

The men all whipped round to look at me.

'Do you want *nuts*?' I asked.

'Er . . . no, thank you.'

'Shame, you could all do with some,' Maz muttered loudly.

We giggled and looked sarcastically at the gathered troupe of businessmen.

'H . . . how old is the pub?' fat buyer, Richard, enquired eventually.

'Ninety-five years,' Maz replied.

'Gosh, that long?'

'Aye. Shite loads of history here, mate, but ye kna, easy come, easy go, eh?'

Fat buyer shifted uncomfortably.

'Aye . . . the locals love it,' Maz continued. 'Best pub in Byker.'

'*Really?* I thought it wasn't doing too well.'

'Bollocks man, look at that lot.' Maz gestured to our conspirators around the pub. 'Here al' the time, man. Aye, there'd be a bloody riot if it ever closed, like, it's an institution.'

Our customers nodded in unison. The buyers looked at each other quickly. Their lawyer frowned and Jack shook his head.

'Let's find a table shall we, gentlemen?' he said, looking for an escape route.

The buyers, however, were not to be fobbed off.

'A riot . . . Is this a rough area, then?' asked happy buyer James.

'Oh aye, terrible,' Maz nodded enthusiastically and looked at me.

'Oh . . . oh, yes,' I lied, wracking my brain. 'Riots, burglaries, drugs. You know, the *usual*.'

Happy buyer didn't look quite so happy. Jack glowered at me but I continued.

'There's trouble *all* the time, nobody's safe. We're safe, of course, because all the thugs drink in here. If they didn't behave, they wouldn't get a pint so we can control them, see?'

Jack's five colleagues looked cautiously over their shoulders at the locals. As if on cue, Auld Vinny lifted a tattooed hand and raised his middle finger at them. They looked away quickly. Maz and I smiled. Fat buyer looked puzzled.

'S . . . s . . . so, what do you think would happen, theoretically speaking of course . . . '

'Of course.'

' . . . if . . . if someone built nice flats in this area?'

'Hmmm,' I said, touching my cheek and trying to look thoughtful. '*Nice* flats?'

'Yes, *really* nice flats.'

'Well, with nice flats come nice people, Richard. Can I call you Richard? With nice people come nice cars. With nice cars come radio thieves and twok-ers. It would be a war zone. It all comes with the territory, Richard.'

Jack huffed like an irritated horse. 'This is nonsense!' he said strongly. 'This is a perfectly good area. I've parked my Beemer here before and nothing happened.'

'Aye, but have you checked it in the last five minutes?' Maz said slyly.

'Maybe we should leave,' dodgiest-tie buyer whispered nervously to James and Richard.

'Gentlemen, please,' Jack said.

Barrel man coughed and straightened his bow tie. 'If I may speak, Richard.' His voice was far too dramatic for this century. 'One must consider that one could use such matters to drastically reduce the asking price and one could iron out those small matters afterwards. This could be of great financial benefit to your corporation, Richard.'

Richard nodded approvingly.

Damn. What did he have to go and open his big fat mouth for? And why did people always believe everything their lawyers said? Most of the ones I knew, myself excluded of course, were either dodgy, opinionated, self-obsessed or spoke through their rapidly expanding backsides. They would happily argue black was white one week, and white was black the next, if they thought it would make them a buck or two.

I fiddled with the pump handle and prayed for salvation. Dave was our only hope. I would have been happier relying on someone a little less . . . well, dim . . . but it was a crisis at short notice. What a predicament.

★ ★ ★

Somewhere between fantasising about removing Jack's finely tailored suit piece by piece and picturing him astride me on the bar — so I was a sucker for bastards — I heard a loud rumble coming from outside. Maz and I glanced nervously at each other as the rumble grew louder. The creaks and blackboard-scratching noises of working machinery filled the air and built to a crescendo amid a choir of gruff male voices. *The A-Team* plan, it seemed, was fully operational. Our very own equivalent of BA Baracas had arrived.

'What in God's name is going on here?' Jack yelled, as countless sacks of household rubbish cascaded from the bin lorry, spilling their contents onto the parking spaces directly adjacent to the Scrap Inn.

'Just doin' wur job, mate.'

The rubbish continued to accumulate. Soggy loo rolls, Tampax applicators and three-week-old leftovers cascaded onto the concrete. Denise spotted a curry-stained lampshade in one pile and grabbed it with a proud grin.

Jack ran after the binman in charge, tripping over decaying fruit and empty beer cans in a desperate attempt to 'stop this bloody nonsense now'.

'I represent the owners of this pub and I *demand* you stop right now! Do you hear?'

'Howay man, get lost will yuz and let wur dae wuz jobs.' The binman-in-chief I recognised as Davc's mate, Jez, a regular lunchtime drinker.

'I swear I will have you arrested if you carry

on with this . . . this joke.'

'This is nae joke, mate. This is a designated dumpin' site. I've got papers ta prove it.' Jez handed over a sheet of coffee-stained paper. Jack hurriedly tried to decipher the barely legible contents. I caught Maz's eye and winked.

'This can't be!' Jack shrieked, losing his cool surprisingly quickly.

'Aye well it is,' Jez continued boldly, 'so move yer bleedin' Armani arse, man, before we cover it in shite!'

Jack reddened and looked helplessly at the buyers. Their disbelieving eyes had been diverted, however, towards a white van that had pulled up at the front door of the pub.

The van doors opened and three men in white overalls climbed out. Their heads were completely covered with hats and visors and in their heavily gloved hands they held either clipboards or equipment befitting a chemistry lab. My ever-straying mind flashed back to GCSE chemistry. Mr Jones, wearing his immaculate Daz Ultra white coat. Mmm, what I would have given for a steamy rendezvous with that man by the light of a Bunsen burner. Straight and nerdally scientific he may have looked, but I could have brought out his wild side given half a chance. Miss Bennett, the man-eating music teacher, had just happened to get there first.

The three men ignored the chaos brewing in the car park and made their way to the grassland attached to the left side of the Scrap Inn. Jez and crew were momentarily forgotten as the bemused buyers went to check out the new development, with an agitated Jack hot on their heels.

Maz and I allowed ourselves a conspiratorial smile before joining the party.

'What the devil are you doing?' shouted my usually cool ex.

The three men looked up briefly. One raised a gloved finger and held it to his visor-covered mouth to request silence.

'No, I will NOT be quiet! I demand an explanation.'

Jack's shrieks fell on deaf ears as two of the mystery men prodded the ground with their Geiger counters and the third unravelled a roll of black and yellow tape. When Jack attempted to cross the newly erected perimeter, he was held back by a brisk shove from the third man.

'Get off me you idiot,' Jack yelled. 'I'll have you know this is a five-hundred-pound tailored suit.'

To no avail. The circus continued. The buyers stood, rooted to the ground in amazement, and the negotiating techniques of Jack, the hotshot lawyer, deteriorated rapidly. No amount of intense legal training, bravado or financial puissance could help Jack now. These men were not to be deterred from completing their mission.

'If someone would just tell me what is going on here.' Jack was beginning to sound uncharacteristically despondent.

'That'll be the waste, man,' a voice piped up from the assembled onlookers.

We turned to see Auld Vinny leaning casually against the nearest lamp post. As our highest-ranking regular, Vinny merited an important role in our master plan.

Jack shook his head uncontrollably. 'Waste! What waste?'

'Waste, contamination, shite, like,' Auld Vinny replied. 'There's been rumours of it fer bloody ages.'

'Of what?'

'*Contamination*, man. Not bloody surprisin' mind, in a bleedin' dumpin' ground. Aye, thuz reckon the land is contaminated with waste, man. 'Bout time the chuffin' council sorted it oot like. Bloody shockin' man, I tell't ya.' He was amazingly believable. Probably due to a lifetime of yarn-spinning over a pint.

Jack looked as if he was about to scream, cry, collapse or a combination of all three.

His bright red face oscillated between Vinny's direction and the men in white overalls. Maz and I stifled the laughter that was threatening to erupt from our feet upwards. Dave's friends were giving a fine performance.

'Aye man. I remember when this hill was just fields,' Auld Vinny continued. 'Fields and this pub. I tell't yuz it was stylin'. Nowt but fresh air an' broon ale. They reckon the contamination is eatin' into the bloody land, man. I reckon thur'l be naebody livin' here soon if these lads find what they're lookin' for. I reckon — '

'Yes, yes . . . we don't CARE what you 'reckon', you stupid doddery old fool!'

The crowd gasped dramatically at Jack's outburst. His companions frowned and shook their heads.

Further down the hill we heard the bin lorry pull away, its load discarded in the car park.

'I don't believe this is happening,' Jack wailed. 'Richard, there must be some mistake.'

Fat buyer looked disapprovingly at the crumbling figure before him.

'Richard, I'll sort this out.'

'No need, Jack. I think we should be on our way now.' His team nodded in agreement.

'Just give me a minute gentlemen, please.'

'Thank you for your time, but perhaps you need to do a little more homework next time, Jack.'

'But this is a *mistake*, I assure you.'

'We won't be proceeding any further with this deal.'

'Please gentlemen, *please*.'

'Shame on you, Jack,' tutted barrel man. 'Begging is most unbecoming of a lawyer.'

'Goodbye, Jack.' They turned to leave.

'They did this.' Jack pointed a trembling finger at Maz and me. We feigned surprise. I put my hand on my chest and gasped.

'Oh please,' Richard scoffed. 'Now you're not making any sense, Jack. How could they have done this? They're just barmaids.'

We let this condescension pass just this once, and chose to smile sweetly rather than punch him in the teeth. Maz and I looked on with great satisfaction as the buyers and their legal team disappeared up the hill, Jack wailing pathetically behind them.

As they vanished into the distance, there was a momentary silence until Maz began to laugh. Our customers joined in and the laughter inside me finally erupted. We clutched our stomachs, patted each other on the back, and fell about in the street, roaring hysterically. The contaminated waste team joined in the frivolity. The largest of the three pulled off his space-age visor and wiped hysterical tears from his eyes.

'Dave!' I roared. 'You should have been an actor.'

'Aye, my talents were wasted in jail.'

Maz hugged her brother fondly. 'Thanks Dave, man.'

'Nae problem, sis. It pays to have mates in the refuse business. The rest of the stuff me an' Chip just . . . uh, borrowed. He's security at a lab.'

'Aye well, you better clean that rubbish up bloody quick . . . after a pint or two.' She grinned.

The crowd trooped merrily through the door of the Scrap Inn for an impromptu celebration, Denise still clutching her lamp-shade. Maz and I were left standing alone on the litter-strewn pavement. Maz put her arm round my shoulders. We beamed at each other. I noticed her eyes were brighter than they had been for a while.

'Ah thanks, Jen, yer a bleedin' star.'

'Well, we're not out of trouble totally, Maz, but we've bought ourselves some valuable time.'

She took a deep breath. I hugged her. Over her shoulder I caught sight of a male figure in the distance. He looked familiar but I couldn't be sure. I shrugged and looked up at Maz again.

'Yep. We may be 'just barmaids', Maz, but we're a force to be reckoned with when we put our minds to it.'

'Aye, pet. Never judge a barmaid by her cleavage eh.'

We laughed and headed for the pub door. As we reached the step I turned to replay the scene in my head. I sighed happily.

'Who needs the A-team?' I smiled. 'I love it when a plan comes together.'

14

I awoke with butterflies doing the fandango in my stomach. I instantly sensed that it was an important day, but my mind took a few minutes to catch up with my instincts. Suddenly the mist cleared and I sat bolt upright in bed, whacking my head on the ethnic mobile (made in Sunderland) that was supposed to bring a touch of culture and mysticism to my room. It had seemed like a good idea at the time.

I jumped out of bed, found Victor and Hugo, my furry cat slippers, and cautiously approached the dressing-table mirror. Eugh! These early-morning inspections of my underlying natural beauty were always a big disappointment. Fresh-faced and delicate I most certainly was not. I looked as if I'd spent the night being dragged backwards through very dense hedges. My hair was wildly ruffled on one side and pasted flatly to my face on the other. My right cheek bore the imprint of my watch and my face was red and blotchy. I rubbed my eyes in an attempt to

261

dislodge the several tonnes of sleepy dust (or eye-snot as Maz liked to call it) that had coagulated in each corner. Any man waking up with me would seriously curse the camouflage properties of make-up. Oh to be Worzel Gummidge, I thought, interchangeable heads would be a blessing.

On a stressability scale of 1–10, first dates with men whom I consider to be even remotely good looking, score about 16.5. For me, they are way up there with job interviews, smear tests and 30,000-feet solo free-falls (I imagine). At that moment, any of these options would have been preferable to an afternoon on the flight path of cupid's arrow. What if we had nothing to say to each other? What if he found me, or I found him, excruciatingly boring? What if, when relieved of his beer goggles, he realised with horror that his date was the best living example of a human pear? Damn, why oh why had I said the yes word? Turning *Club Tropicana* up to full volume in the hope that George and Andrew would lift my spirits, I set to work with my Epilady.

The previous night, Maz and I had been passing the time discussing career moves for Jack when *he* had entered the bar. We had almost settled on the idea of a plastic-flipflop seller in Morocco when Maz had suddenly exclaimed, 'Why-aye, check oot the fit bod in them kegs!' His slightly faded blue Levis hugged the contours of his thigh muscles as he walked slowly down the steps into the bar. The black T-shirt accentuated his firm pecs and trim waist. His heavy black boots scuffed the floor as he walked, sending shivers up the creases in my trousers. And those eyes. Sparkling like green pools in the moonlight from behind the dark locks of hair that fell over his face.

'Must be in the wrong pub,' Maz had concluded.

All I had been capable of was opening and closing my mouth like a gormless goldfish. I had instantly recognised him as the work experience boy from Paradise TV. My nether regions had also recognised him as the dishevelled beauty who was really starting to tickle my tastebuds. He was hotter than a stolen vindaloo.

'Ow! Bloody Epi-flippin-lady.'

Ripping three inches of raw flesh from my shin brought me back to reality with a bump. No chance of wearing my pedal pushers now, after falling victim to this twentieth-century instrument of torture. Probably just as well.

★ ★ ★

'Maz, please come with me,' I groaned.

'Jen, man, I'm not coming on a date with you. It'd look reet stupid. Anyhow, he looks lush, you'll be fine.'

'Oh please, I'm shy.'

'Howay Jen, if you're shy Ulrika Jonsson's a bloody rocket scientist.'

'But . . .'

'Jen, you'll thank me I promise. It'll be good for yer self-esteem.'

'What self-esteem?'

'Precisely.'

★ ★ ★

So it was that I boarded the Metro alone, destination first date. Every so often during the journey into town, I caught sight of my reflection in the window opposite. By the end of the short trip, I had decided that my top looked too tight, my make-up was too thick and my hair resembled the aftermath of a bad perming incident. I felt like Limahl from Kajagoogoo in drag. Not a great boost for the old self-confidence.

I got off the Metro at Monument Station, cursing the train's central heating for having successfully disproved the fresh and dry qualities of my deodorant. In a vain last-minute attempt to shed a few excess pounds, I bounded up the escalator and jogged out to the main street. Pausing at Grey's Monument to suffer a mild heart attack, I scanned the people milling around for any sign of my date.

A group of scantily clad girls tottered past dressed in the uniform of Lycra, bare flesh and Spice Girl shoes. Husbands and boy-friends trailed sulkily behind their partners as they were frog-marched from one women's clothes shop to another. Black and white footie shirts dotted among the passers-by made it clear that this was Newcastle, the home of the Toon Army.

Turning to face the monument, I noticed a young, trendy guitar player with straggly blond hair and a Brit Pop attitude singing 'Champagne Super Nova' in a surprisingly tuneful voice. Despite being soulfully engrossed in his music, he managed to give a menacing glare to every person who neglected to see, and add to, the small collection of coins in his open guitar case. Hoping it would make me look less desperate, I positioned myself strategically next to the busker and pretended to be lost in a world of musical appreciation.

Still no sign of old green eyes.

'I've been stood up,' I concluded pessimistically.

OK, I had only given him 3 minutes and 30 seconds grace but I'm a great believer in invoking the escape clause at the first available opportunity. I sighed happily. First date embarrassment had been avoided for that day. No need for stilted conversation, feeble jokes and forced enthusiasm. I could go home, eat doughnuts and wallow in an afternoon of self-indulgence. Call me a coward if you will. I never claimed to be anything else.

Breathing easily for the first time that day, I spun around and headed for the station entrance. Suddenly feeling an uncomfortable tightness across my ankles, I glanced down just in time to see the busker's guitar lead wrap itself firmly around my legs. The pavement came up to meet me at an alarming rate. The busker was instantly unplugged and about £200-worth of amplifier crashed to the floor behind me.

The previously small crowd of music enthusiasts around the monument metamorphosed into a St James' Park-sized throng as everyone in the vicinity came to have a good look at my misfortune. The crowd laughed and hooted as I rolled in the cigarette butts on the ground, clutching my bleeding knee. I briefly hoped that ripped jeans would soon come back into fashion. Busker boy leapt around with one hand on his forehead and the other swinging his guitar dangerously close to my head. His catalogue of swear words didn't appear to be in danger of drying up in the near future. I considered telling him that my real name was Jennifer but, taking stock of the situation, I decided 'You dizzy bitch' would do.

Just as I was completing my third plea to God for an Armageddon-scale natural disaster, an arm was suddenly thrust into my scarlet face from the surrounding mob. I grabbed the hand helplessly and was gently pulled up to face my saviour. The first thing I noticed was the colour of his eyes. They shone like precious emeralds, burning into my own watery iris. My whole body was shouting 'Blush!' but my burning cheeks took the brunt of my increased circulation. Extreme embarrassment coupled with luscious hormonal surges were, I decided, not a good recipe for softly glowing skin. I felt like I had Jupiter on my shoulders.

'Were you waiting for someone, Jennifer?' he smiled. He ran his free hand through his hair and laughed. All I could muster was a giddy smile. For once, I was glad that my date had turned up. Very glad indeed.

★ ★ ★

A hazy half-hour later, we found ourselves in McDonald's on Northumberland Street. The busker had somehow been pacified (I suspected by way of a monetary donation but my saviour denied any such thing) and the crowd had eventually dispersed. I had hobbled away from the scene of the crime, trying to play down the gaping hole in my new jeans and the blood gushing from my knee. I now sat, leg raised on a plastic stool, with a wad of McDonald's serviettes pressed on my injury.

I had originally hoped for a, shall we say, classier lunch destination. A cosy Italian, the arty-farty place above the theatre or, at the very least, a Miss Marple-style coffee shop. At that moment, however, McDonald's seemed just the ticket. No frills, no fuss, just lots of noise and the soothing smell of fast food. I felt unusually relaxed and content.

'To think I was worried we might miss each other,' he grinned, taking another handful of anorexic French fries. 'I might have known you'd stand out in a crowd.'

I blushed. 'I'm not usually that clumsy, it was a momentary lapse of concentration.'

'Aye well, I'm sure I'll find out,' he smiled. 'I can't wait to see what you'll do on our next date.'

His last two words sent a warm glow

through my body. 'Next date.' So this wasn't a one-off in his mind, despite my very public display of lunacy. If we went on another date, then 'me and him' might become an 'us'. Thoughts of a whirlwind romance, rings, churches and fluffy white dresses flashed through my mind. I banished them with a shake of my head before he had the chance to see the glint in my eye, and concentrated on extracting the wilted gherkin slices from my Big Mac.

We gorged ourselves on 30p ice creams, drank cheek-crushing triple thick shake through the same straw and shared stories over sesame-seed baps. When my knee finally stopped bleeding, we walked/limped to Eldon Square shopping centre in search of plasters and antiseptic cream. I had never spent a first date in Boots before but, with him, it felt amazingly natural. Finally, with a Mr Bump wash-proof Elastoplast firmly in place and his hand firmly in mine, we made our way slowly down to the market that ran along the banks of the river.

The stalls were crammed with all manner of things, from hand-knitted pink tea-cosies to Newcastle United condom holders. I spotted a great offer on the underwear stall but decided against openly purchasing three pairs of sturdy thermal knickers for £3.50 at this early stage in our relationship (2 hours and 26 minutes to be precise). We got head spins from sniffing aromatherapy oils, searched the CD stalls for anything other than Whitney Houston compilation albums and were forced to endure a demonstration of an entire set of Tupperware tubs. '*The blue one fits inside the red one, which fits inside the orange one, which . . . um . . . fits inside the green one . . .* ' and so on. It was only when we were threatened with a complimentary demonstration of the Tupperware beaker and jug ensemble that I instantly developed acute pain in my knee and just had to leave.

We sat down on a bench next to the river and he carefully changed the plaster on my knee. I felt a twinge of excitement as his strong, slim hands touched my skin.

That was replaced by a twinge of pain as he ripped off Mr Bump to make way for Mr Happy.

'Ow!' I squealed.

'Sorry, pet.'

He called me pet. I glowed with pleasure. His calm, concerned bedside manner was so attractive. I set my brow in an expression of pain and decided to play the sympathy vote for a while longer.

We sat in silence for a few minutes and gazed at the boats passing up and down the busy River Tyne. For once, I didn't feel awkward not speaking. It was an easy silence and purely by choice. I wanted to savour the moment and, rather than open my big gob, breathe in the stillness that spoke volumes. As his right arm slipped across my shoulder, pulling me closer to him, I knew he was feeling the same way.

'Have you ever been there?' he asked eventually, nodding towards a heavy white ship that was moored to the opposite bank.

The upper deck was emblazoned with the words *Tuxedo Royale*. I wondered at how quiet and empty it looked in the afternoon light, as if nothing ever happened there.

'I have actually,' I replied wistfully, 'just the once, but it was a pretty . . . um . . . memorable occasion.'

His bright green eyes searched my face for more information. He looked so interested, I found myself recounting the tale of my none-too-successful New Year's Eve. Not yet assured of his unconditional affection, I decided to leave out such details as my marathon puking session in the Tuxedo Royale's toilets and my early-morning skirtless gate-scaling episode. He listened so intently that, before long, I had revealed all the details of how the events of that night had snowballed to change every facet of my once-comfortable existence.

I told him about Jack's affair with my secretary and of his heartless plan to ruin my life. I told him about Glisset & Jacksop and the untimely end to my legal career. About my lovely flat on the quayside and my involuntary move to 'Chez Maz' above the Scrap Inn. I then found myself telling him about my new life as a barmaid. The days and nights of endless conversation with the punters. The goals and dreams revealed over a bottle of Brown Ale too many, most of which would never be achieved but which kept us all going. I told him about our 'family' of regulars. Denise and Derek with their marriage-made-in-purgatory, Auld Vinny, the Ultimate International Sex Machine, banging on the door at 10:30 a.m. and demanding to be allowed to start his day's work, and even my dad who had found solace in this unlikely place. I told him about Maz's ambition to be the next Ricki Lake and of her brother Dave's life as a very unsuccessful criminal. He laughed at all the right bits, looked concerned when that was required and assured me that Jack 'had a slate loose' for cheating on me and dumping me so unceremoniously.

When I had finished, I was breathless — partly due to speaking too fast and partly due to how tightly he was holding me. Hearing his breath close to my ear, I turned my face towards his shoulder and looked up at his profile. He felt my gaze and lowered his chin, bringing his face tantalisingly close to mine. His eyes glowed, almost unreal in their vibrancy.

Women would kill for those eyelashes, I thought. They were jet black, thick and breathtakingly long, curling up towards his eyelids. I couldn't help thinking that they wouldn't have looked out of place on a camel. I could almost feel the breeze they created each time he blinked.

My gaze moved down his strong, straight nose to the pair of full, pink lips. As I watched, he parted them slightly and inadvertently moistened them with his tongue. First the top lip, then the soft skin of the bottom lip. The moisture glistened in the light, making me want to drink it in and taste it. In the cold March wind, I felt the warmth of his breath as it brushed across my right cheek. Our faces were so close, I was afraid that my breathing sounded too loud. I hoped that he wouldn't feel the burning of my cheeks or notice how my pupils had dilated with wanting. My stomach began to tighten and I could feel a warm, stirring sensation in my groin. Already my body was reacting to the pleasure and our lips hadn't even met.

Oh God, I thought, *I hope I haven't got food between my teeth.*

Paranoia was replaced by surprise as he cupped my chin in his hand and pulled my face gently to his. I gazed briefly into his eyes and saw the hint of a smile before he pressed his mouth against my lips. A burning sensation shot through my body. As his lips caressed mine and his tongue pushed into my mouth, I felt myself melt in the firm grasp of his right arm. I breathed deeply, absorbing the warm, musk aroma of his skin. His touch, his smell and the passion in a single kiss all felt so right. I relaxed and slowly ran my tongue along his teeth. As his hand slid round to the nape of my neck and his breathing intensified, I heard a low groan escape from the back of my throat.

Spurred on by my sighs, he pulled me closer and we kissed urgently, feeling and tasting each other for the first time. My tongue explored his mouth, my hands explored his body. He leaned towards me and I slid my hand inside his shirt and across the smooth skin of his stomach. His hand grasped my waist and I clutched his solid, rounded pecs. I could feel his ribcage rising and falling as his breaths became deeper. His touch was gentle but passionate as his slim hands moved over my clothes. His knee pressed into my leg and a bolt of lightening shot up my thigh. I could feel the blood rushing to my groin like shopaholics to the January sales and my head was in a spin. I hadn't felt this way for so long. A simple kiss and I was lost in the throws of passion. Wow, he was good.

The booming horn of a passing ship infiltrated our fantasy and dragged us back to reality. The blast made me jump and he pulled back from the kiss. I reminded myself to breathe again before I went into oxygen debt and I slowly opened my eyes. In the midst of my pleasure, I had completely forgotten where we were. The brown water of the Tyne, the tall, dark buildings lining the riverbank and a wintry blanket of grey cloud came gradually into focus. All of a sudden, though, it all seemed much brighter.

I gazed up at him as he caught his breath. His face was visibly glowing and his green eyes flickered over my face. I felt as if I was smiling from the inside out, flushed with pleasure and quietly impressed at having found a man who could kiss so well. He stared at me, as if unsure of my reaction. I smiled at this hint of insecurity and squeezed his hand.

'That was a really loud horny. *Horn* . . . horn

. . . I meant horn,' I stammered.

'I know what you meant,' he beamed.

★ ★ ★

We stood on the platform of the Metro at Central Station, his arms wrapped around my waist. I didn't want the date to end but I had to do a shift at the pub and Maz would have my guts for garters if I didn't show up. It was probably just as well. God knows what trouble I'd have got into if he had kissed me like that again. I felt like the sex goddess of the North-East. Wrapped in the arms of a gorgeous man, fresh from the grasp of passion. I was totally sexy and completely irresistible (despite the Mr Happy plaster and slight limp). I had experienced a rare injection of happy hormone without consuming a single ounce of chocolate and I was determined to make the most of it. I was up there on Planet Janet without a care in the world. It's amazing what a kiss can do.

'I'll call you later then, pet,' he said in his lilting Geordie accent.

'Sure, that'd be great.'

I looked around me to check that people had heard him and that they were suitably impressed. *Act cool*, I thought. *Kiss me again*, my body pleaded.

'Thanks for a great time,' I said, blushing slightly under his gaze.

He didn't reply but bent down and kissed me, gently squeezing my waist with both hands. We were still entwined when the train rumbled onto the platform.

'I better go,' I whispered.

He nodded and let his hands drop to his sides. I stepped back on to the waiting train.

Suddenly, I was hit by a wave of mild panic. I stopped in my tracks and spun around to face him. Jesus, Mary and Joseph, here I was about to leave after an afternoon of total perfection, yet not only did I not have his phone number or his address, I didn't even know his name. In all the chaos, fun and snogging, this minor fact had somehow slipped my mind.

'Damn!' I exclaimed.

I felt like such a slapper. How could I ask him now after having shared a milkshake, not to mention a fair amount of saliva? He'd think I was a right cheap tart.

'What's wrong, pet?' He rushed forward and took my hand.

His face looked so concerned, I momentarily considered making something up — 'Damn I've got terrible amnesia (family trait) so could you just tell me your name again?' — but I couldn't do it. I paused

277

momentarily, not sure of my next move. The train was ready to leave but I stood in the doorway to stop it closing. I was getting vicious looks from my fellow passengers but I was stuck for the right words. This was a delicate subject. His eyes searched my face for a clue. It was only when an eight-foot buffalo of a man with tattoos for skin politely requested that I 'hurry the fuck up', that I suddenly plucked up the courage.

'I'm sorry,' I whispered.

'Sorry for what?'

'It's . . . um . . . it's just . . . oh bollocks.'

'What?'

I took a deep breath. 'It's just, I seem to have forgotten, well I don't know if you actually told me and I would never do this usually but . . . um . . . but I . . . ' (the buffalo huffed impatiently and stamped his hoof) ' . . . well, the thing is . . . I seem to have forgotten your . . . your . . . your . . . '

'My . . . ?'

'Your . . . name.'

His worried expression instantly melted as his face broke into a broad grin. He started to laugh loudly.

'Oh Jen,' he beamed.

'Oh Jesus,' snarled the buffalo.

He reached in from the platform and gently touched my arm.

'I can see it's going to be a mad ride with you, pet,' he laughed.

I smiled meekly as he kissed my hand.

'Randall,' he whispered, 'my name's Randall.'

'Randall,' I mouthed as the train doors slid shut. 'Hmm, I like it.'

15

'Thur's nae such thing, pet,' said Denise emphatically, fiercely rubbing a stain on the front of her lilac velour tracksuit. 'Aye, it meybe al' sweetness and light now like, but it won't be long before he burps, farts, wants 'is socks washed and expects 'is friggin' tea on the table.'

Derek burped loudly and put a flabby arm round Denise's shoulders. 'Howay wor lass, you love it, man.' He winked cheekily at his wife.

'Get off us,' she groaned, shrugging off his arm and reaching for another pickled egg. 'Give us that Julia Iglesus fella any day. Aye, a bit of Italian stallion would do us.'

'He's Spanish, Denise,' I interjected.

'Aye well, it's the same thing. Foreign, and rich. He could bloody well serenade me in his skin-tight shiny trousers any day of the week, I tell't ya.'

'Howay,' Dave interrupted, 'a Geordie man'll give ya better lovin' than some paella merchant, woman. You want a *real* fella, like.

280

Not some poncey git with a lacy top and maracas.'

Derek nodded vigorously in agreement. Denise ordered a tequila and let her mind wander to distant Latino shores.

'I didn't say Randall was perfect,' I said, taking the conversation off its tangent before we got onto Spanish donkeys and matadors. 'He's just really . . . '

'Nice,' said Denise.

'Boring,' said Derek.

'Normal,' I replied.

'Aye well, if you get pissed off wi' 'normal', pet,' Auld Vinny grinned, 'I can show you somethin' better I tell't you.' He touched the peak of his 'Ultimate International Sex Machine' cap and winked mischievously. 'Experience, that's what you want lass, why-aye.'

I laughed nervously and shivered at the thought of pillow talk with the crusty old sailor. Mind you, pillow talk with Randall had so far eluded me. We'd held hands, kissed, fondled, talked all lovey-dovey and cuddled up in front of the TV but there had been no last-ditch attempts to get in my knickers. The first two weeks of our relationship had been proper dating, polite and controlled. Call me pessimistic but I almost found it hard to believe that such a gentleman still existed.

Most of the men I had come into contact with would assume I was frigid if I hadn't agreed to shag, or at the very least give them a blow job, within twenty minutes of being introduced. I was beginning to think that either I had found another Troy, or that Randall found me physically repulsive. My self-esteem was plummeting.

Following our perfect and eventful day in town, our second date had been a movie at the Odeon on Pilgrim Street. Two hours of Mel Gibson, half my bodyweight in popcorn and a vat of Pepsi sucked tantalisingly through the same straw. The third had been a cosy meal in a café on High Bridge Street, where we had consumed enough cake to keep a Weightwatcher in rations for a month. Then followed baltis for two at the curry house and dates over pasta, Chinese and Mongolian barbecue. I had come to the conclusion that relationships are often founded on a wave of gluttony. I wondered what the next stage would be after we had consumed every national dish from around the world.

'Probably comfort eating,' Maz said. 'After he lets you down, like all men do.'

I had a nagging suspicion that Maz would be right; she usually was. But I tried to push it to the back of my love-struck mind. Perhaps the fact that we always met at my flat, never at his, should have set alarm bells ringing. In fact, I didn't really know if he *had* a flat. He always seemed to avoid the question. The truth was, I didn't even have his phone number. He preferred to call me, which he always did, on time. I hadn't even had the nerve to question him about how a chance encounter at a party and an even briefer meeting at a TV studio door had escalated into all this. I mean, how had he found out where I lived? I was sure I hadn't told him the night we first met although too many bubbles had been consumed for me to be entirely sure.

So, perhaps I was being naive. Perhaps an overweight cherub with a conscience was, as we speak, frantically flapping his wings and beating me over the head with his bow and arrow, shouting, 'Look! Open your eyes! Can't you see what he's doing, you mad woman? Are you blind or just mentally retarded?'

But I didn't want to push the issue and rock our little love boat. I didn't want to sound like a neurotic woman, incapable of trusting an independent man. Anyway, maybe taking things slowly was healthier for a relationship, I assured myself. Naive or not, I was happy. Happy in our little boat, rocking gently on ripples of lust, blissfully unaware that, at any time, a freak wave could appear and send me tumbling to the bottom of a cruel sea.

Any time the nagging doubts resurfaced, I only had to look at Randall to be reassured. I loved the way he pushed his hair back from his face when he was deep in thought and hummed when he was nervous. I melted when I saw him lightly scuff his feet in his heavy black boots and sway his hips as he walked. He seemed comfortable in the simplest surroundings and took pleasure in the most ordinary of things. His eyes sparkled when he spoke and he frowned intensely when he listened. He was neither arrogant nor timid, just quietly self-assured and sincere.

I couldn't decide what it was from the whole picture that attracted me to him. All I knew was that every day with him felt like a sunny Saturday and every moment apart was like a rainy Monday morning.

Damn. Thirteen days and I was already beginning to sound like a Mills and Boon book.

'Gis a pint will ya, lover girl?' Dave said loudly, waving his arm in front of my glazed eyes. 'Jaysus, I hope this love thing doesny last long, the service in this joint is canny shockin', man.'

★ ★ ★

'Why-aye, this toon is f'kin' *lush*, man!'

We glanced up from the bar-length game of dominoes to see Maz standing at the entrance to the pub with a look of sheer delight spread across her face.

'Where have you been?' I asked, pointing at my watch.

'Four punters too much for you, lass?' She strode through the pub whacking each person on the back to greet them, then plonked her backside up on the bar. She was clearly buzzing with excitement.

'Where have I been?' she repeated dramatically. 'I'll tell you where *I've* been. I have been to the tele-bloody-vision studios.'

'What for?'

'What for? What *for*? Only to see my very own proflippin'-ducer of *the* most abso-bloody-lutely numero uno show in the North-East.'

Maz reached for a pint glass and gestured to me to fill it up.

'What are you gibbering about, Maz?'

'What I am sayin' is, my fine friends, you are now in the presence of Paradise TV's newest recruit. Talk-show star, presenter extraordinaire, solver of problems, soon to be mega-bloody-famous, *moi*!'

'What? How the hell did that happen?'

We all looked incredulously at Maz's glowing face. I feared I was about to witness first hand a spontaneous human combustion.

'Well, I deen't kna really. I jest got a call this mornin', like, askin' us if I could gan to the studios in Newcastle. I thought someone was tekin' the piss but they said they'd seen us on that live show and they'd recognised us from my audition a while back.'

'So they wanted to audition you again?'

'Aye well, I thought so. I didny hang aboot like. Bombed it doon there, straight into a meetin' with this posh producer fella.'

'So what did he say?'

'Well, apparently, the big boss had seen me on TV and decided he'd like a local lass presentin' their new show, after the last one flopped. He said someone had put a good word in fer us, I deen't kna who like, and they wanted *me*. Me, *moi*, yours truly.'

'How did they find you?'

'Deen't kna. Dain't care really. Get this, the fella says, 'We were hoping, Marilyn, that you would consider joining our team.' *Consider*. Bloody hell! 'I dain't need to consider it, mate,' I said. 'Count us in!''

'Maz, I can't believe it. This is *fantastic*. It's, it's amazing.' I felt completely shell-shocked. Maz's dream had just materialised out of nowhere, just when she'd decided to give up on her lifelong ambition.

'Aye,' Dave added, raising his pint glass. 'Yer a f'kin' legend, sis. Good on ya.'

We all grabbed a drink and toasted Maz while she recounted every detail of her visit to Paradise studios. We were told everything from the colour of the socks the producer was wearing to the price of custard creams in the staff canteen.

'So, what's the format?' I asked, trying to gather my thoughts enough to formulate a sensible question.

'Well, I deen't really kna yet, like, but they said it's gonna be different from all the others. 'Relaxed and vibrant,' he said, fer the younger end of the market.'

'So you won't need to wear them poxy pink suits like that Julia Juniper woman?' Denise asked.

'I don't think so. If they expect us to look like the power woman part of Kays Catalogue, I'll jest tell 'em to piss off. Anyhow, it's gonna be mint I reckon. We'll have rehearsals and then it's roll the bleedin' cameras and away we go. I'll get you all tickets of course. You'll all be bleedin' VIPs.'

'Well, I like the sound of that, like,' Auld Vinny added.

'Abso-bloomin-lutely,' roared Dave.

'So what about the pub then?' I asked, kicking myself for sounding sour.

'What about it?' Maz asked.

'Aye, will you be pissin' off to fame an' fortune and forgettin' about us?' Dave added.

'No chance.' Maz sounded resolute. 'I'm not stupid, like. It's only one show and it's early days yet. I'll still be doin' shifts here an' all. You never kna, maybe I'll earn enough cash to buy this place.'

Maz put a firm hand on my shoulder and gave me a heart-warming smile.

'Deen't worry, lass, we'll still be flatmates, and this place'll need you more than ever.'

I hugged her tightly. 'Wow, Maz, I'm proud of you, you silly tart. You'll be a star, I'm sure of it.'

★   ★   ★

'Her own show, just like that,' I said the following evening as I concentrated on rolling up my chicken fajita. I sealed it with an immense globule of guacamole. It can't be fattening, I told myself, it's only fruit. We had now reached Mexico on the relationship scale.

'Is she pleased?' Randall asked.

'Pleased? God, she's over the moon. I don't think she's stopped smiling since yesterday.'

'That's great.' He hummed quietly as he carefully dipped tortilla chips in a tub of salsa.

'You never know,' I added, 'you might end up working together on the show, wouldn't that be weird?'

He smiled and concentrated on squeezing a slice of lime into another bottle of Sol.

'So how is your work experience?' I asked after a brief pause.

'What? Oh, aye, fine.'

'You don't talk about it much.' A second beer had made me feel uncharacteristically brave.

'Hmmm? Well, aye, it's OK. I'm just learning the ropes. It's not that interesting to talk about.'

'Let me be the judge of that.' I touched his hand across the table. *Don't be fobbed off,* my mind warned. 'I want to hear about what you do, Randall. You hardly tell me anything about yourself . . . I . . . I feel like I hardly know you.'

I could sense the beginning of a burning issue between us. I didn't want to cause our first argument, but I didn't want to be brushed off again. Either he'd tell me why I wasn't allowed to get too close or I'd have to turn into Jeremy Paxman to force the answers out of him.

'You do know me, Jen.' He was humming again. Nerves. 'You know the stuff that matters.'

'Like what? I know you like beer, wine and prawn cocktail crisps, your favourite colour's green and you hate Jeremy Beadle with a passion. Hardly ground-breaking stuff, is it? That could go for most of the population.'

The beer was rushing to my head faster than I could think and I was beginning to feel strangely agitated.

'God, I don't even know your surname.'

'Pettifer,' he replied curtly.

Pettifer. Jennifer Pettifer. Ooh, I didn't like the sound of that, but we'd work something out. Funny, it sounded familiar.

'I didn't realise it was important,' he mumbled.

'*Important?* For all I know, Randall, you could be a serial killer with a fetish for size twelve barmaids.' OK, so I was getting a little carried away. It's a particular talent of mine.

'Don't be ridiculous.' He agreed.

'Well. For a start, you don't tell me anything about your job. You're only on work experience, for God's sake. I know TV people can be uptight, but it can't be that top secret.'

I could feel the tension mounting but I was on a roll. Inwardly I vowed not to mix beer and Tequila on our next date, if we had one.

290

He stared at me across the table, saying nothing. In my tipsy state I found his mellow reaction to my pointless outburst even more infuriating.

'Oh just clam up, why don't you!' I spluttered. All eyes in the small Mexican restaurant were now on Table 8. *Shut up, Jennifer*, I urged myself. 'Why are men so incapable of talking about things?' I continued. 'Give them football, cars or tits as a subject and the conversation flows doesn't it? Give them anything remotely personal and it's, sorry, no can do.'

He took a sip of beer and looked away. A hushed snigger coursed around the room.

'Tell me something, Randall, please. We've been going out for two weeks and I've never even seen where you live. What are you hiding? If you've got a wife and eight kids, I'd rather know now.'

He stood up suddenly and pulled his jacket from the back of the chair. His hand reached into his pocket and pulled out a wad of notes. A slim, exquisite hand. The one I had been holding as we had entered the restaurant. The notes scattered on the table in front of me.

Bollocks, I thought. *Motor mouth does it again.* We had been having a great night until I'd done the unreasonable woman thing. Now he was going to walk out and leave me sitting

291

alone like Norma No-mates at the cactus-shaped table.

I glanced around the room and saw embarrassed faces turn away hurriedly. Even the waiter had his head buried in a menu, a look of desperate concentration on his face. My heart sank. I wanted to beg 'Don't go' but I was too proud. Drunk and pig-headed — always a dangerous combination.

I watched Randall shrug the soft black leather jacket onto his shoulders. He pushed back the lock of hair that fell over his face, all the time avoiding my gaze. I watched him walk slowly past my chair without saying a word, and waited for the footsteps to disappear behind me. Shit, shit, shit. Me and my big gob. I sank into my chair feeling miserable as the Gypsy Kings hollered in my ear.

Suddenly I felt a hand grasp my left shoulder. Expecting to see an irate waiter, I looked up shyly and was surprised to see Randall's sea-green eyes burning into me. I wondered what he was about to do. Perhaps the serial killer quip had been a bit too close to the truth. I opened my mouth to speak.

'Ssh,' he said, gesturing to me to stand up. He took my coat and slipped it delicately over my shoulders. There was a hushed silence in the restaurant. Even 'Bamboleo' had been turned down to a low wail. We walked towards the exit, his arm firmly round my waist. As we reached the door, he turned his face towards mine.

'You want to know me?' he whispered enticingly in my ear. 'Maybe it's about time.'

16

'This place is like an Ikea catalogue,' I said, hunting for the on switch of a metallic green designer fan.

'Do you like it?' he asked.

'Hmm? Oh yeah . . . yes, it's really nice,' I said. Unlived in, I thought. Needs a woman's touch.

I picked up an expandable fish-shaped gadget and looked at it curiously.

'Bottle opener,' he explained. 'Red or white?'

We stood in the kitchen of Randall's flat, a small room painted stark white. It was clinically clean like the rest of the rooms. I had to admit, it was stylish and filled with every gadget known to man. Bodum coffee maker, wine cooler, ice maker, thick-slice/thin-slice/multi-slice toaster and baffling chrome banana holder. A gigantic flat-screened television dominated the living room. All he needed was a popcorn machine and an ice-cream lady and he could have sold tickets to watch it. The only other furniture in the living room was a Japanese futon, an art deco rug and a glass triangular-shaped coffee table. A metallic silver CD rack stood in one corner, piled high with all tastes of music from Kula Shaker indie to sleazy listening. A matt grey hi-tech sound system with enough flashing lights to illuminate Blackpool played Moby at a gentle volume. Knowing that men like to think they have a Masters Degree from Dixons, I declined to comment on the size of the sub-woofers, the levels of the graphic equaliser or the possible English translation of EON RDS, Ms Seek, Dolby BNR. Better to nod knowingly and enthusiastically hum the tune.

The fitted kitchen was quality pine and lit from all angles by discreet silver spotlights. A green Aga covered most of one wall, the remainder of which was filled with a stack of green Le Creuset pans and a rack of sparkling utensils. I wondered whether they had ever been used. Everything looked so new and glistening. There were no dirty dishes in the sink, no odd socks lying around the washing machine or mouldy take-away curries in the fridge. I was sure every bachelor pad contained at least one pin-up of Melinda Messenger, but there were no 'it' girls in sight. Perhaps I should have been pleased about the absence of *Loaded* magazines and postcards from Ibiza, but it was strangely impersonal.

'Don't you have any pictures?' I asked.

'What sort of pictures?' He looked puzzled.

'Pictures, photos of your family, things in frames . . . '

He looked at me blankly.

' . . . to brighten the place up a bit,' I added.

'I hadn't really thought about it,' he shrugged. 'Aye, maybe I will.'

Very strange. I felt as if I'd stepped into a Homes-R-Us showpiece and was about to be flogged a fitted kitchen with free set of matching luggage.

'Biscuit?' he asked, holding out an olive-coloured pottery jar stacked with ginger cookies.

'You're very organised,' I said, taking two. 'My guests are lucky to get a few broken bourbons and a stale chocolate digestive.'

He smiled and handed me an enormous glass of Jacob's Creek Riesling, my choice from the well-stocked wine rack. At £4.59 a bottle, it was my idea of a middle- to high-class bottle of plonk.

'I want to drink it, not keep goldfish,' I laughed, grasping the stem of the huge glass for dear life.

'Cheers, pet,' he winked, and led the way back to the living room.

Feeling like a fourteen-year-old about to get her first taste of a fondle and a French kiss, I sat awkwardly on the edge of the futon, fiddling with the tassel on a semi-ethnic cushion and intermittently gulping my vase of wine. I half expected my mother to come into the room at the most inopportune moment like she used to do at school discos.

'Jennifer Summer!' she'd yell across the dance floor, packed with raging adolescent hormones, '10:45 p.m. we said, young lady. What is it now, hmm? 10:58 p.m. Thirteen minutes, madam, *thirteen*. Now take that young man's hand off your bottom and get it to the car, Daddy's waiting.' At which point I would scurry out, snog-free, praying to every conceivable god to strike my loud-mouthed mother dumb in the very near future.

OK, so it wasn't likely to happen in Randall's flat, but I had learned never to underestimate my mother. I knew we were building up to *it*, to much more than a snog, and the anticipatory small talk was killing me. Jacob's plonk was doing little to calm my nerves. Just shag me, I wanted to shout, *let's get it over with!*

I'm not saying I didn't want it to happen, neither am I saying I wasn't looking forward to it, but a first time with someone is always steeped in anxiety. That first moment of nakedness, the first few minutes of nervous fumbling, and the apprehensive excitement. The questions: 'Will he be good?' 'Will I be good?' 'Will we be compatible?' 'Will he regret having got intimate with a sack of overboiled spuds?'

The problem was I did really like him. In fact, I was falling for him faster than a 19-stone bungee jumper from a suspension bridge. Perhaps I was placing too much emphasis on this one evening of carnal knowledge but I wanted it to work. Frankly it was all getting too much for me to bear.

★　★　★

'Everything OK, Jenny?' he asked, placing a hand on my twitching thigh and stroking it gently.

'Yep ... hmmm ... great.' I nodded fiercely and took another huge gulp of wine.

'What was I saying then?'

'Saying? Um ... ooh. Can't remember now but it was very interesting.'

'Aye, must have been.'

He smiled broadly and reached forward, slowly peeling my entwined fingers from the stem of the wine glass. I let him take it and watched the way his lean body moved as he walked over to the coffee table. Placing the glasses gently on the shiny surface, he turned to face me, clasped his hands together and hummed quietly. *Nervous*, I thought. *At least I'm not the only one.*

My heart began to race faster as he moved softly towards me and knelt on the floor in front of the futon. His breathing sounded deep and hollow. In my mind his breaths drowned out Moby's lyrics as I concentrated intensely on Randall's every move.

You're gorgeous, I thought, as I grasped the hand he reached out towards me.

'Come on, Jen,' he breathed, pulling me tenderly up from floor level, 'there's one room you haven't seen yet.'

★ ★ ★

'It's wonderful,' I gasped, trying to take in every inch of the spacious bedroom. No black silk sheets, no full-length mirrors around the bed, no pretentious stacks of dumbbells sitting unused in a corner. The room was painted a warm terracotta above a varnished wooden floor. Deep red drapes framed the one bay window, matching the voluminous duvet that covered the bed. The few pieces of furniture were delicately carved in dark pine.

The bed had four carved posts stretching up to a stiff pelmet and thin voile curtain. Any sharp edges were softened with colourful scatter cushions and huge bowls of fruit and *pot pourri*. A solitary picture hung next to the bed, a vibrant scene in reds and yellows of a summer's day in Venice.

I felt his arms wrap round my waist from behind and his warm cheek touch my face.

'No, you're wonderful,' he whispered, and gently kissed my neck.

My usual reaction would have been to shrug him off with a 'Yeah right, piss off and stop winding me up', but the way his lips caressed my neck and his arms held me tightly, I could feel myself getting lost in the moment of fantasy.

I turned slowly to face him and ran my fingers down his cheek. His eyes were intense, flickering across my face and down to my chest. He pulled me to him.

Our eyes met instantly. I didn't allow myself time to think as he moved me gently over to the bed and ran his hands down my body.

'God, I want you so much,' he sighed, taking my head in his strong hands and kissing me passionately.

Do you? I thought, but restricted myself to a loud sigh. 'I really want you too.'

We kissed urgently, both of us sensing the other's desires. He moved his hands towards my waist and pushed my top up to reveal the white skin of my stomach. I gasped as he pulled my top over my head and cupped my breasts gently in his hands. He stared at them for a moment before sliding his hands around my back and unhooking my bra. He pulled it off my arms in one effortless manoeuvre. My chest raised up and down as I tried to control my breathing.

Please like them, I begged inwardly.

'You're beautiful,' he whispered.

I groaned deeply as he bent down and took my nipple in his mouth. He sucked gently and carefully massaged my breasts with his warm hands. My thighs felt weak and a wave of immense pleasure washed over my body. I threw my head back as his lips moved down towards my waist. Kissing, licking, feeling, his hands were unbuttoning my trousers and pulling them down over my thighs. I could feel his breath on my stomach as he knelt at my feet. I sucked it in sharply with one of the few muscles I had, hoping he hadn't noticed.

Now! my body shouted. *Please.*

'Sit on the bed,' he said, softly pushing on my waist.

Damn blasted boots and socks. I had forgotten about them. He deftly unlaced them, pulled off my incredibly unglamorous blue socks, and dropped my trousers on the floor beside them. He stood, looking down at me as I sat on the edge of the bed in my white lace knickers. I smiled at my cunning plan to invest in new, foxy lingerie after the first week of our relationship. My usual over-washed sensible pants would really have spoiled the moment.

I blushed under his gaze but my body felt warm, flushed and sexy. I wanted to feel him naked beside me.

He urgently unbuttoned his shirt and pulled it off to reveal a firm, flat stomach and solid, rounded pecs. His skin was golden with a light dusting of dark hair across his chest and around his nipples. Fit, I thought. Thank you, God.

His shoes were off in a flash. I watched, mesmerised, as he whipped off his belt and undid the button on his trousers.

I reached for his zip, pulled it down and moved his trousers down over his hips. His bum felt smooth yet firm to my touch, tensing as I stroked the naked skin. My eyes were on his groin. I whimpered without meaning to, and pulled him on top of me.

I felt a rush of heat as my skin touched his, feeling his nakedness for the first time. We kissed and moved slowly together. I moved my hands over his shoulders, down his long, lean back, over his bum to the hair at the top of his thighs. I pulled him closer to me, grinding his penis against my groin.

His hand moved to my stomach then down to my knickers. His eyes flashed like precious emeralds as he pulled them down towards my knees. I was naked, he was naked, and we were both filled with wanting.

Take it slowly, my mind insisted. *Take me now*, my body screamed.

His knee moved between my thighs and pushed them slowly apart. I was writhing with pleasure and groaning loudly, all paranoid inhibitions gone in the glint of his eye. I felt his hand move between my legs, and shivered as he clasped his hand over my clitoris. He stroked me firmly, getting gradually faster.

That's it, I thought, no messing.

I was losing control with every touch. The feeling was so overwhelming I realised that battery-operated sex could never be as good, no matter what the feminists claimed. He made me feel so good. I caught my breath as he pulled his hand away.

No, I thought. *Don't stop now!* But I sensed his next move as he looked into my eyes as if for reassurance.

I wasn't going to debate the issue. I smiled

and nodded as he reached into a drawer by the bed and pulled out a small, red packet. Feeling like an amateur sausage maker on *The Generation Game*, I fumbled with the condom until it rolled into place. I clasped his waist, pulling him to me. In a second he was inside me, pushing deeper. Our eyes were locked in a silent conversation as our pubic bones ground together. He felt wide and firm as he moved in and out. I groaned louder, and held him close, arching my back and rolling my hips. His bum raised up and down under my grasp as he thrust himself deeper into me. I let out a strangled yelp as the rhythm got faster. Droplets of sweat filled his forehead and he wrinkled his brow with effort and determination.

'Yes,' I sighed.

'Hmm, yes,' he murmured.

We moved naturally, unable to stop, faster and faster. Stronger and firmer.

I squirmed as his bone rubbed the sensitive skin on my clitoris, sending shock waves of desire through my body. I'd almost forgotten how it could feel.

Then it hit me like a bolt of lightning. My groin was on fire and my body shook uncontrollably. He thrust harder as I quivered under him.

'Wow!' I yelled.

'Oh Jenny,' he groaned and exploded inside me. We clasped each other tightly and I bit my lip to stop myself biting into the soft flesh of his shoulder. The orgasm was intense. I wanted it to last for ever, wave after wave of glorious pleasure. Finally it subsided and I felt the weight of his body on mine. Trembling and sweating, we held each other and breathed deeply together, savouring the moment encircled by it. I stroked his back and smiled inwardly, bursting with emotion.

It was over, but it was so good.

Again! I wanted to shout. Again, again, AGAIN!

17

'How many times?' Maz yelled over the chorus of 'Super Trooper'. 'Ya little slapper, man. It's nae wonder yer glowin' like, yer circulation's gone mad, lass, all that bumpin' and grindin'.'

We both let out a shriek of laughter and I wiggled my hips in mock sex motion as I sat on the sofa.

'Aye, he's nice like,' Maz said, referring to the newly crowned superstud Randall. My official boyfriend, since last night and this morning's marathon of desire.

'He's kinda . . . different,' Maz continued, gnawing thoughtfully on a beer bottle, 'like, a . . . oh, whaddya call it . . . an enema?'

'An *enigma?* How do you mean?'

'He just looks a bit mysterious ye kna. Doesn't give much away when he talks. Pretty quiet.'

'Yeah,' I agreed, thinking back to the close-call in the restaurant, 'he's a bit shy, I s'pose . . . but he definitely comes out of himself at the right moment!'

We laughed again until our stomachs hurt and sighed, 'Oh dear,' until one of us thought up the next line.

★ ★ ★

I was glad our shift was over. I'd only just got to the pub in time for work and had been desperate to tell Maz about my hours of indulgence. She knew, of course, and had winked obviously as I poured Randall his one drink before he left for work.

'Good on you, pet,' she had muttered as I flounced around behind the bar. I was feeling sexy and wanted, and exploiting every minute of it.

Of course, on the one night I had hoped for a girlie chat, the pub had been uncharacteristically busy. The lesbian darts team had brought their 'partners' along to their training session, hence a batch of frustrated husbands from the estate, with an idyllic view of female homosexuality, had come along to 'watch'. Corduroy dungarees, DM boots and builders' bums had been rife in the vicinity of the dartboard.

A raucous hen party, unfortunately choosing the Scrap Inn as their final destination, had filled the opposite corner for the second half of the night. The group of Liverpudlian slappers — no other word would be appropriate — were decked out in white lacy angel costumes adorned with multi-coloured condoms and pictures of naked men, that is when they weren't auditioning for the female version of *The Full Monty*. Saint Peter would have had a full-scale security system fitted to the pearly gates if he'd seen this lot of angels coming. Of course, I was pleased for 'Paula's gettin' married on Saturdee — poor cow', but I vowed if I heard 'We're really mad, we are' one more time, I'd shove their tinselly halos where the sun don't shine.

My father had also popped in for his twice-weekly dose of medicinal whisky and one or two stories from Auld Vinny's sea-faring days. Apparently my mother had tried to put a stop to his regular alcoholic encounters with the wayward daughter by announcing that her therapist had advised they partake of a 'joint hobby'. Tupperware parties had been scheduled for the offending evenings with Dad playing host to gaggles of Mum's highly pretentious friends. In a moment of unprecedented bravery, much to my amusement, Dad had told Mum an unrepeatable alternative use for the interlocking plastic tubs and had caught the first Metro to Byker.

Auld Vinny had been on fine form,

expostulating over Robson's latest football team signing ('Bloody six million poont, man, 'bout as useful as a fishnet bathtub'); the standard of British TV ('Load o' canny shite, man, feckin' grown men in cuddly suits wi' coathangers oot of their heeds') — the Teletubbies; and female equality ('Flash in the pan load of bollocks').

Only when he asked Randall, 'Did you give 'er one, then?' did I decide to point out that his lesbian friends were leaving and 'surely they'd want him to escort them all home for a *party*'. I'd never seen him move so fast.

★ ★ ★

'Mars, Snickers or Bounty?' asked Maz, waving a handful of fun-size chocolate bars in front of my glazed eyes. Convincing myself that four mini-Snickers didn't quite add up to one whole one, I reached for the fifth and sixth of the night and cracked open another bottle of Bud. I was on a well-earned short break from guilt trips about my six-figure daily calorie consumption.

Randall's hormonal appreciation of my naked body had done enough to persuade me I was beautiful. I knew I shouldn't be relying on him for reassurance but, let's face it, it helped. Perhaps I was a slim baguette-legged,

'I eat so much and can't put on weight' nimble beauty after all. To think I'd been living in denial for the past 26 years. Shocking.

'You soppy cow,' Maz smiled, noting my smiling indulgence. No groans of 'Oh I really shouldn't' or 'But my thighs are so massive' before shoving the chocolate in my gob. (I never actually refrained from devouring it.) Just happy, silent troughing.

'Takes you home fer a bit of hinky kinky,' Maz continued, 'and you gan al' loved up on us.'

I smiled. 'Piss off, I'm not loved up, I'm just happy.'

'Aye, ga-ga more like.'

'Rubbish. I am not ga-ga, or loved up. I'm not 'in love' either.' I was doing my best to convince myself, although the soft focus, hazy dreams in my head said otherwise. 'Anyhow, you're just jealous.'

'Of what?'

'Of me having one of the few remaining gentlemen in this world for a boyfriend.'

'Me? No way man.'

'I'm sure you'll find someone soon, Maz.'

'Piss off,' Maz tisked and tutted, slamming her feet on the coffee table. 'I dain't want a boyfriend. Come the day my body clock's tickin' fer stretch marks, mornin' sickness and a life of naggin' some useless fella, then I might get a boyfriend. There's plenty fellas oot there when a girl's gaggin' for it if you kna what I mean. I won't go without.'

We laughed loudly. Maz certainly had no shortage of men willing to take her out and show her a good time, as it were. They stuck to Maz like flies to a car bonnet when she wanted a date. She was living proof that the 'play hard to get' and 'don't give a stuff' theories worked like a dream. Without fail, the dedicated philanderers, infidels and arrogant tossers, most of whom were ridiculously good looking — loved by all but mostly by themselves — would be reduced to quivering celibate wrecks, willing to die for their woman, as soon as they realised they had been filed in the one-night stand cabinet by my gorgeous best friend. 'I love you', 'Please marry me', 'I'll buy you a car . . . a house . . . a small planet' were heard by Maz on an almost daily basis but she kicked them to the kerb with an 'I'll call you, maybe never' or 'Pull yerself together man and piss off home'.

Mmm, come to think of it, she really didn't seem to want a boyfriend. Realising I was in danger of becoming one of those very boring 'I'm in a relationship, it's fabulous, you must be thrilled for me' type people, I decided to shut up and change the subject.

'So have you heard any more news about your show?'

'Oh aye, they were ganna write us a letter. Was there any mail today? I forgot to look.' She jumped up enthusiastically and headed for the hall.

'Knowing Dave, he probably filed it in the microwave,' I called over my shoulder.

'Aye, I'll check the washin' machine.'

I laughed and dreamily undressed, I mean unwrapped, a Bounty.

'What the bleedin' buggery bollocks is this like?' Maz stomped into the room, eyes bulging, face redder than a chicken tikka masala, frantically waving a piece of paper in her shaking, outstretched hand. It came to rest two inches from my nose. Lucky — paper cuts are pitifully small but they bloody well hurt.

'They're jokin' man,' she yelled, 'it's a wind up, must be.'

'What? What is it, Maz?'

I tried to grab the paper but her grip was steadfast.

'Bloody tossers. It's an April fool. What's the date, eh?'

'What? Just tell me what it is, Maz.'

'I'll give 'em bleedin' 'yours sincerely' and all that crap. So bloody up themselves they can't speak chuffin' English man.'

'Maz.'

'Flippin' legal bloodyistic waffley shite. What the hell stunt are they trying to pull eh? They can't do this.'

'Do *what*?'

'They can't. Not that easy can they?'

'I don't *know* do I? I haven't got the faintest idea what you're drivelling on about have I?'

I jumped up from the sofa and wrestled the piece of paper from her hand, peeling her fingers off one by one. It was a letter. Good quality, sturdy cream paper. Typed and headed. The bold heading I recognised immediately. I experienced a sudden sinking feeling and started to sweat as I read the words. I hadn't even reached the main body of the letter. In bold black type across the top of the page were the words 'Glisset & Jacksop Solicitors'.

More often than not, an unrequested lawyer's letter is an ominous sign. Either we had been named as sole beneficiaries in a mad recluse millionaire's Will or, the more likely option, this was going to be very bad news. Feeling like a teenager about to read the dreaded A-level result slip, I cast my eyes unwillingly over the print and began to read.

I could hardly believe my eyes. What I read

was a notice to quit the premises. The flat had been sold, along with the pub, to an unnamed buyer, and both were to be vacated within a fortnight. All our efforts had been in vain. Evidently, Jack had managed to push a sale through quickly, without us ever getting wind of the transaction. The very formal letter was signed at the bottom, 'Jack xxx'. The bastard. I lowered the piece of paper with shaking hands and stared at Maz. I could tell she was gobsmacked. The three lit cigarettes in her right hand were a fairly solid indication.

'Maz ... they've sold the pub,' I stammered.

She took a long drag of nicotine.

'Aye well, it doesn't take a genius to work that out.'

'Buy why didn't Gordon tell us? He's the bloody manager.'

'Gordon, aye fat chance. He's too friggin' scared to give me bad news, flippin' proof. He'd rather I heard it from the lawyers than him havin' to come here and tell us face to face. He knas I'd probably deck 'im, that's why.'

I thought for a moment, turning everything over in my head. Maz chain-smoked and drummed her feet on the coffee table.

'Have you got a signed lease?' I asked eventually.

'Have I bollocks,' Maz retorted, 'it were all just casual, us livin' here.'

'But you must have *rights*,' I stressed. 'I know I was here just as a favour, but you were the real tenant. You were practically running the place. We can fight it.'

'Fight what? There's nay point, pet.'

'Of course there is. You'll have *rights*. They can't just chuck us out!'

'Rights my arse! That's what you learned at law school, pet. It doesn't work like that in the real world. They can do whatever they bloody well like. Remember what happened with your landlord.'

I felt defensive and angry at being thought of as naive by my best friend.

'They can't,' I muttered tearfully.

Maz looked at me, almost pitifully. She was now amazingly calm and collected, resigned to the fact that we were being chucked out on our ear.

'Anyway, Jen,' she sighed, 'there's nae point in fightin' it. The pub's been sold so we'd only be delayin' the inevitable if we caused a scene.'

Inevitable. Maz never said words like inevitable. The whole situation just seemed so unreal.

We sat in silence for a while, me staring at the wine and beer stains on the carpet from many a raucous evening, Maz working her way through a pack of twenty fags with amazing speed. She produced more smoke in an hour than a steelworks' factory chimney. Eventually, when she could bear the mortuary atmosphere no longer, Maz stood up.

'I'm gan to bed . . . '

'Right, OK.'

'While I've still got one.'

Sitting alone in the flat, with only *Crimewatch Update*, a subtitled French B-movie and two incomprehensible documentaries for company, I felt very alone. My heart had sunk to somewhere below my knees and my head was pounding with the sound of my own pulse.

Suddenly I remembered that Randall had, at last, given me his phone number. How could I have forgotten? I jumped up excitedly and bounded to my room to find the piece of paper with the number on it — or rather, the *pieces*. I had copied it out on about twenty different Post-it notes and placed them strategically around my bedroom. Well, I didn't want to risk losing it, did I? It was my lifeline. I glanced at my watch. 12:05 a.m. It was late but at least I knew he would be there. I had to call. I had to get him to cheer me up, maybe even pop round to comfort me. He'd definitely be in.

He wasn't in. I stared menacingly at the receiver as the answering machine clicked into action. It wasn't even his own voice, it was some *woman*. She claimed to be a BT recorded message and, to be fair, she sounded particularly robotic, but how could I be sure? I couldn't. Where was he? How *dare* he not be in when I needed some sympathy. Where could he possibly be at this hour of the night? I gripped the receiver tightly, hoping it would change its mind and say, 'Oh, I'm sorry, actually Randall *is* in and he will be round in no time for a shag, beep.' But the message stayed the same. I built myself up to shout, 'Where are you? I need you *now*.' But when the tone sounded I took a deep breath and said, 'Randall, darling, it's Jenny. Um . . . I've just had a bit of bad news and . . . um . . . I wanted to speak to you. S . . . orry it's so late . . . I'll call you again. Sweet dreams. Bye.'

Sap.

18

20th March, 5:00 a.m.

I hardly slept at all that night. Every time I
closed my eyes I had visions of waking up in a
cardboard box with only a discarded copy of
Hello! magazine for warmth. Surrounded by
tramps, drunks, and addicts of one sort or
another — not unlike our customers, come to
think of it — and occasionally kicked or
sworn at by passers-by. Now and again one
would throw me the odd coin. *Odd* being the
operative word — ten pesetas, two francs,
three Indonesian rupiah, worth all of one
hundredth of a penny. I would never know
where my next meal was coming from. A bin,
the gutter, a half-eaten meal on a pavement
café table. I would dream of hot food. What I
would give for a chicken Pot Noodle. Oh,
how low had I sunk?

Finally I could take it no longer. I threw
myself out of bed and began a frantic search
through my wardrobe to find an outfit
befitting of a squatter. Not too tarty, they'd
think I was on the game. Not too expensive
looking, I'd never be a successful beggar that

way. Not too Oliver Twist-ish, I was sure things must have progressed since then. God, I was never going to survive on the streets, I didn't even know what to wear.

The early hours of the morning took about a month to pass by and I became increasingly panic-stricken. I sat down, stood up, paced the room, stood still, lay on the floor, lay on the bed, jogged on the spot, even read a book — *Newcastle A — Z Street Atlas*. Anything to make me feel like I was doing something useful. I know people always say 'things will seem better in the morning' but how could they? No job, no money, no home. Things were terrible now and they'd still be terrible when the sun finally decided to get up. Not just terrible, but bad, apocalyptically awful, stunningly dire, life-threateningly traumatic. But at least if it was daytime I could *do* something about it. I could phone people, moan, bitch about Jack, talk to Randall. This 5:00 a.m. business was just such a waste of time.

★ ★ ★

Finally I woke to the sound of Maz slamming doors, unaware of ever having fallen asleep. My head was resting on the bottom shelf of my bookcase, my body slumped on the floor.

I had a crick in my neck the size of Ireland, and a heavy, grey cloud perched ominously over my head. Amazingly, though, I awoke with an intelligent thought in my head — first time for everything. 'Call Matt,' said the sensible voice, 'he'll know who bought the pub.'

'Nice one,' I nodded. 'Thanks!'

Anything was worth a try. I needed more information.

★ ★ ★

'Matthew Capley is not available at the moment.'

'Bloody machines!'

' . . . leave a message . . . '

'I hate you. Hate you, hate you, HATE YOU, HA . . . '

'Hello?'

' . . . um . . . '

'Hello. Who's that?'

'Oh . . . um . . . Matt?'

'Yes, Matt Capley speaking, who are you?'

'Jen, Matt, Jen . . . it's Jen, *Jennifer*.'

'Jen. *Jen*. Oh, bloody hell, hon. You get nuttier by the minute,' he guffawed. 'How are you?'

'I thought you weren't there.'

'Soz. Popped to the wee-wee house for a second.'

'Nice.'

'Anyway, babe. Is this a social call?'

'Yes.' I felt guilty for only phoning him when I needed a favour.

'Great!'

' . . . and . . . and . . . er . . . no.'

'Oh.'

'I need a favour, Matt.'

'I guessed.'

I launched into my tale of woe. The sale of the pub, the letter from Jack, losing my job, losing the flat, the cardboard box, the rupiah, the Pot Noodle. Matt oohed and aahed and 'no-way'ed in all the right places, having quickly recovered from his initial disappointment that I wasn't ringing for a girlie chat. This was much more exciting.

'Well, you *know* what I said about that Jack,' he said dramatically when I had drawn to a close. 'Never trust a man with a — '

'Square jaw. Yes I know.'

'He would do *anything* to secure a deal, darling. Sell his own children if anyone was mental enough to make some with him.'

I blushed.

'*Anything* to make Partner, Jen. That's what he lives for. Well, that and waking up every morning to see his own beautiful reflection.'

'This is a lecture isn't it?' I sighed.

'Yes,' Matt said, surprisingly sternly, 'a lecture to any poor cows out there who can't see that black is white, I mean, black is black. Oh . . . you know, a spade's a . . . whatever.'

'It's OK, Matt. I don't like him any more. I've found someone.'

'Ooh!' he squealed. 'Tell me, tell me, tell me!'

'Not now, later. Right now I need to know who . . .'

'Tell me, *please*.'

' . . . bought the pub.'

'Tell me.'

'Matt, please, I — '

'TELL ME. How tall?'

'Six foot. Now — '

'Mmm, tall! Hair?'

'Brown. Can — '

'Long or short?'

'Shortish.'

'Bod?'

'What. Oh, lovely, yes now — '

'Occupation?'

'Matt, come on.'

'Name, then. Name?'

I sighed dramatically. Of course, I wanted to tell him everything about Randall. About his eyes, his soothing voice, his mannerisms, his shoe size. Matt would take in every word, tell me that I had the catch of the century and assure me that it would last for ever. But, there would be time for all that later. I needed information.

'Name!' he shrieked again, before I had time to speak.

'Oh, OK then. It's ... it's' — even his name made me breathless — 'it's Randall.'

'Randall?' Matt repeated. 'Lovely name.'

'Thanks.' As if it were my doing.

'Funny though.'

'Why?'

'Cos that's the same as the name you're after.'

'What?'

'The man who bought your pub.'

'What about him?'

'Randall. His name was *Randall*. We didn't represent him cos we were for the sellers but it was definitely Randall because ... '

I heard the sound of cracking glass somewhere inside my head. My mouth was suddenly very dry. 'R ... Rand ... all. Randall what?' I cleared my throat.

'Pettifer,' Matt said triumphantly. 'Randall Pettifer.'

The bottom fell out of my world. The glass shattered into a million pieces. I heard the sound of falling, the bottomless sound in a cartoon when Wile E Coyote plummets at top speed into a vast chasm. Only, this wasn't funny. This wasn't the figment of an animator's imagination. This was real, horribly, horribly real. My body shook with fear and rage. Matt was still waffling in my ear.

'You know him, he's . . . '

A bastard.

'His dad . . . '

Has a lot to answer for.

' . . . always on the lookout . . . '

For a gullible sap. I was in despair. I couldn't bring myself to listen, until something he said caught my attention.

'What?'

'What, what?'

'What did you say then?'

'When?'

'Just then.'

'Um . . . '

'About a flat or something.'

'Flat . . . oh yeah. I was just saying we did a flat for him a couple of weeks ago.'

'*Did?* What do you mean, *did?*'

'Arranged it, hon. Fully furnished from taps to tapestries. He didn't care which flat it was, just that he wanted one and fast. We got one, rushed it through and hey presto! He didn't even have to buy the loo roll, honestly. Funny these people aren't they, darling?'

He laughed. Wile E Coyote hit the floor. Dead.

'Jen, I was saying they're funny, aren't they? Rich folk.'

No answer.

'Jen?'

A quiet sob.

'Are you OK, Jen?'

Tears. Lots of them. The Aswan Dam had burst.

'B . . . b . . . bye . . . M . . . M . . . Matt.'

'Jenny babe, are you . . . '

'M . . . mus . . . must go.'

'Are you OK?'

'G . . . g . . . go n . . . now.'

'Jenny . . . '

'Bye.'

★   ★   ★

I slammed the phone down and ran up to my bedroom. Throwing myself on the bed, I buried my face in the duvet and sobbed uncontrollably. My shoulders shook, my eyes exploded, my nose ran and my mouth contorted in agonised expressions. All I could think was Randall. Pub. Flat. Don't. Understand. I was so confused and shocked, I could think of nothing better to do than wallow in the pain. Then I thought of something.

'I'm sorry, but Randall cannot come to the phone right now . . . '

Stupid posh tart.

' . . . a message after the tone . . . '

Oh hurry up. *Hurry up* with your Queen's English!

' . . . as soon as possible.'

Snotty bitch.

' . . . the tone.'

Gulp.

'Beep.'

'*Bastard*. You no-good, worthless piece of scum! How *could* you? How *dare* you? I hate you. Hate you as much as I hate people with Walkmans on trains! Hate you as much as you hate Jeremy Beadle. Ha! I hope you're happy now you . . . you *man*.' I was running out of insults. 'I never want to see you again you . . . *bastard!* Go to hell . . . By the way, it's Jenny.'

Well, he might not have known it was me. We hadn't had a proper row before, he might not have recognised me in my new role as the She-Devil. I slammed the phone down, picking it up and slamming it down again several times for effect. I was so outraged, so angry, so *furious*, so . . . miserable. I slumped in a heap on the floor and continued to cry.

19

20th March, 11:00 a.m.

'I'll break his legs!' Dave roared.

'No you won't,' Maz yelled. 'I will!'

'And 'is arms.' Dave mimed a snapping motion with his monstrous hands.

I shivered.

'His neck!' Maz shouted. 'I'll break his bleedin' neck, man.'

She punched the air with staggering force. I heard the molecules of oxygen whizz past my ears and career into the wall behind me.

'Maybe I got it wrong,' I pleaded meekly. 'Maybe it wasn't him after all.'

'*Wrong*,' Maz repeated. 'Yeah, you got it wrong. The minute you started seein' him, that's when you got it wrong.'

I frowned and fiddled with my fingernails. Dave punched the wall.

'I never liked him.' Maz growled.

'Yes you did!'

'No I didn't.'

'Yes you did. You said he was nice and canny and an enigma.'

'Didn't!'

'Did.'

We scowled at each other and looked away huffily. Dave kicked the table.

Things had been escalating since Maz and Dave had come out to the hall to investigate what all the slamming and unslamming of the telephone was about. Of course, I hadn't had the good sense to keep my big mouth shut. Instead, through the tears, sobs and heaving of shoulders, I had relayed every detail of my phone conversation with Matt. I should have known. Maz was already feeling fragile and Dave needed very little excuse to throw his weight around — there was so much of it, it had to be put to some use. My story had only served to exacerbate the situation and we now stood precariously on the edge of World War III. A gang of hooded Geordies could soon be on their way round to Randall's flat to give him a good lynching and it was all my fault.

'Listen,' I said loudly above the wailing, shouting and gnashing of teeth, 'there's no point getting carried away until I find out exactly what happened.'

'Aye there is,' Dave protested, headbutting the door frame.

'No. Let me go round there and find out.'

'Why?'

'Because there might be a perfectly logical explanation.'

'Aye right, ha!'

'It could all be a big misunderstanding.' I forced a smile.

'Misunderstanding,' Maz tisked.

'Misum ... gin ... don.' Too many syllables for Dave at this time in the morning.

'But you'll go all ga-ga,' Maz groaned.

'No I won't.'

'Yes you will. He'll tell you what he thinks you want to hear and you'll believe him.'

'No I won't.'

'Yes you will.'

And so on.

★　★　★

Somehow I managed to convince Maz and Dave that it would be best if I visited Randall alone. The problem was I had been so caught up in arguing my point and averting a murder that I hadn't even thought about what I would say to him. So it was that I found myself standing in the street outside his flat, too afraid to ring the bell, but too outraged to run away, without an iota of a plan.

It was then that it began to rain. I don't just mean light, slightly dampening, refreshing rain. I mean gallons and gallons of the stuff. Multitudes of torrential, drenching, hair-frizzing, sock-soaking rain. One minute it was dry and the next, totally without warning, the heavens opened, the clouds burst, God emptied the contents of his Olympic-sized swimming pool and it *pissed* down. Of course, with rain, there always comes commotion. People ran in all directions, squealing and cursing, as if hydrochloric acid was being poured over their heads. The organised few produced brollies, and Pac-a-macs from the depths of their bags, the brave pulled out oversized plastic ponchos. People scurried for shelter holding carrier bags, newspapers, small hankies, wallets, chairs and tables above their heads in a vain attempt to keep two square inches of their hair dry. All down the street, windows and doors slammed shut as people dived into the nearest house or car. A skinny blonde girl, with long brown legs up to just below her eyebrows, and a skirt the size of a stamp, ran down the street towards me, shrieking as if the rain would melt her tan.

I often think I'm invisible to beautiful people. Either they ignore me completely or they walk into me, step on my toes, or push me out of the way if I dare to take up more than the airspace of a small moth. Sure enough, she careered into me, sending me flying into a puddle which filled my shoes with water, and soaked the bottom of my jeans.

'S . . . s . . . sorry,' I stammered in response to her icy glare, and immediately kicked myself for having apologised when it was totally her fault. It's a self-esteem thing — she had some and I didn't.

'Are you OK?' I pleaded.

'No thanks to you!' she huffed.

Tell her to piss off, my mind hissed.

'Sorry,' I begged.

She strutted away and folded her endless legs into a sleek red sports car. Screeching away, she made sure not to miss the puddle in the gutter which tidal-waved over the kerb and almost washed me away.

'Bitch!' I yelled, as she disappeared from view. I was all for venting my anger after the event. Less trouble that way. 'Stupid slag! I hope you crash. I hope your engine floods on a level crossing and an Intercity 125 flattens your stupid poncey car. I hope you break both your scrawny legs, you rich, bulimic little COW! And . . . and I hope all your hair falls out and you get spots and cellulite and club feet and . . . '

I felt a hand on my shoulder and whipped round, expecting to see Little Miss Rich Bitch ready to scratch my eyes out. But it wasn't her, it was Randall. Gorgeous, irresistible, lightly soaked Randall, and he was smiling at me. I gasped visibly at the sight of him. Shit.

What was I going to say?

'Jenny, you're soaked,' he frowned. 'What are you doing standing in the rain, pet?'

'Um . . .'

'And who were you talking to?'

'Er . . .'

'Why didn't you come in?'

'Oh . . .'

I shuffled my feet and tried to wipe my dripping hair from my face. He stared at me curiously.

'Let's get out of the rain,' he said, wrapping his arm round my shoulders and leading me across the road to his flat. I was powerless to refuse.

Once inside, he took my coat, wrapped me in a warm, soft towel and made me hot chocolate. I had wanted to say no but it was made with milk and it had whipped cream on the top, and it came with four chocolate digestives for dipping. Any girl would have done the same. Of course, it was perfect. Not too sweet, just enough cream, not too burny on the tongue. Perfect. Just like the rest of his faultless flat. In fact, he probably kept a small Chilean woman in the kitchen cupboard, specially trained in the art of hot chocolate making, next to the one who cleaned, the one who cooked and the one who specialised in how to deceive your girlfriend. The flat had all been created by someone else, why not the hot chocolate? I felt the resurgence of my rage and glared at him across the room. It served to break the silence.

'Jenny,' he said, 'I've been so worried, I didn't know what was wrong.'

'Huh!' I sneered at him, slamming down the empty cup.

'I got your messages and I didn't understand what was going on.'

'Hmm!'

'I . . . I was about to come round and see you, pet.'

'Yeah right.'

'Aye, but then I saw you standing outside in the rain and . . . '

His voice trailed off uncomfortably. I looked at my fingernails. He hummed nervously.

Don't let him get away with it. Maz's words reverberated in my head. *Don't be a bleedin' walkover.*

'What is it, Jenny?' he asked.

I pursed my lips.

'What have I done?'

'Huh.' I lifted my nose in the air.

'What?'

'You know.'

'I don't.'

'Yes, you *do*.'

'I *don't.*'

'Yes y . . . ' Fearing we could get stuck in an endless rally of dos and don'ts, I decided to be a tad more direct.

'You *do* know. You deceived me.' Just a tad.

'*Deceived* you. How?'

I paused and looked him in the eye. My heart leapt at the sight of his beautiful face. Beautiful in my eyes, anyway. But I had to find out. I couldn't be a 'bleedin' walkover'. Anyway, maybe all the worry would be for nothing. Maybe it was all a mistake.

'Everything, Randall,' I replied. 'Your flat, your life, the pub. Everything.'

His eyes narrowed. 'The *pub.* What do you mean by that?' His voice was weak.

'I know,' I said firmly, 'I found out. The pub has been sold, I'm out of a job, Maz and I are going to be thrown out on the streets to live in cardboard boxes and eat chicken Pot Noodles and it's all your doing. You, my boyfriend. Why would you do that?'

His eyes widened. My breathing was short and sharp. Deny it, I pleaded, tell me it's not true.

'H . . . how . . . ?' he stammered.

My heart missed a beat.

'Wh . . . who . . . ?' he croaked.

I almost threw up. Tell me I'm wrong.

'Who told you?' he said.

Wanker.

'Who told me!' I screamed. 'Who told me! What the hell is that supposed to mean?'

'You weren't supposed to know about it yet.'

'Not supposed to know . . . ' I sucked the air through my teeth. 'And when exactly was I supposed to know, hmm? When they came to take my bed away or maybe when they came to drag me out of the door by my hair. Or maybe just when the demolition truck pulled up outside the door, hmm, would that be a better time? Would it?'

'No!' he wailed, reaching for my flailing arms.

'Piss off!'

'Jenny,' his eyes looked pained, 'I was going to tell you.'

'Oh well thank you very much but I've saved you the trouble . . . or the *pleasure* perhaps.'

'It was supposed to be a surprise.'

'A *surprise*. A sur-fucking-prise. Oh it was a surprise all right. 'Jenny, you're losing your job,' oh cool, 'and you'll be penniless and homeless too,' ooh goody, what a surprise. Are you completely mad? Are you certifiably *insane*?'

I sprang up from the futon. He lunged towards me and tried to pull me to him.

'Don't touch me!'

He looked hurt. 'Who told you?' he asked again.

'Jack told me, that's who. He wrote a lovely letter. The person who despises me more than anyone in the world, even more than my mother.'

'I didn't ask him to write it.'

'Oh, so you know each other then?' I growled. 'Ooh, let me guess, he's your half brother.'

'No.'

'Your boyfriend?'

'No!'

'Well, whatever it is, nothing could surprise me now.' I glared at him.

'But Jenny, you don't have to move out.'

'Oh, don't be stupid.'

'I'm not, I — '

'What am I supposed to do, live in the rubble when you demolish the place?'

'But I'm not — '

'You make me sick.'

'But — '

'How *could* you, Randall?'

'But I — '

'I trusted you.'

'Let me — '

'*I liked* you.'

'Please let — '

'I even let you see me naked.'

'Jenny please — '

'I had sex with you.'

'Jenny — '

'I let you lick chocolate spread out of my belly button!'

'But — '

'God, I'm so stupid. You were probably laughing at me all the time.'

'No! I — '

'Fun was it, your little game?'

'Jenny!'

'Enjoy yourself did you?'

'Jenny, *Please!*' he yelled.

'Don't shout at me!' I screamed back.

'But I can't get a word in edgeways.'

'I don't care. I don't want to hear it.'

'Please, just let me explain.'

Randall insisted on launching into a lengthy explanation, but I wasn't listening. Something behind him had caught my attention. His words faded into oblivion. My eyes opened wide with horror and my jaw almost hit the floor.

' . . . and so I decided to . . . what, what is it? What are you looking at me like that for?'

'So you got some photos then?' I said nastily.

'Pardon me?'

'*Photos*, Randall. You decided to put some photos around the place like I suggested.'

'Oh, oh yes.'

He followed my gaze to the silver photo frame over his shoulder. Cautiously he lifted the frame and held it out towards me. 'They . . . they do brighten the place up,' he said gently, trying to smile.

'Who *is* that in the photo with you, Randall?' I asked firmly, already knowing the answer.

'Wh . . . who?'

'Yes, Randall, *who?* Who is that person you have your arm round?' I could almost feel smoke coming out of my ears. Thick, black, choking smoke and flames.

'Who. Oh um . . . that's Troy,' he smiled.

Smile once more and you'll be having your teeth for lunch, I thought.

'Oh, Troy,' I snorted. 'Now would that be the all-American, physically perfect, white-toothed, very tanned, extremely homosexual Troy?'

'Yes, that's right. Oh . . . '

'*Oh*. Would that also be the Troy I thought was going to be my boyfriend until I discovered that's exactly what he was looking for.'

'Oh, of course, you — '

'Don't say anything!' I said hotly.

'But . . . '

He looked uneasily at my outraged expression and edged closer towards me. He was so close I could smell him, the warm, musky smell of my man. I wanted to cry.

'Please, Jenny,' he pleaded, reaching out a shaking hand to touch my shoulder. 'I can explain everything.'

'I swear, Randall,' I said, shrugging off his hand, 'if you touch me again I'll break both your arms.'

He took a sharp step backwards, his eyes flickering over my face.

'I don't want to hear your explanations. What are you going to do? Tell me even more lies?'

'No,' he shook his head vigorously. 'You don't understand.'

'No, I don't. I can't.'

There was an uncomfortable silence as we stood apart, staring into each other's eyes. I wanted to punch him yet, at the same time, I wanted to kiss him. I just felt so disappointed. *Why me?* I thought sadly. *Why do these things always happen to me?*

'Jenny,' he said softly. His eyes filled up with water.

Oh God, don't cry, I begged inwardly. I'll end up sleeping with you if you cry.

'Jenny darling,' he said again. One heavy

tear rolled down his cheek.

'No don't please!' I could feel my resistance crumbling like a digestive biscuit.

'I can explain,' he insisted. 'You've just reacted a bit . . . well, unreasonably to it all.'

'*What?*' I shouted. Cry all you like, you bastard. 'Unreasonably! Un-bloody-reasonably! You stupid, insensitive, brainless wanker! How the hell do you think I'm going to react, hmm?'

He stared at me blankly.

'You're pathetic,' I continued. 'You and your stupid games. Was it a conspiracy, hmm? You, Jack and your boyfriend Troy. Or did you think it up all by yourself? God, you're such a bastard, Randall. To think I could ever have thought that I . . . I *loved* you. Shit, it makes me feel sick.'

His eyes opened wide and he gasped loudly. He lifted both hands to his head and pulled his fingers through his hair. 'But Jenny,' he whispered, 'I love you too.'

My heart leapt into my mouth and my stomach tensed. He'd said it, the 'L' word. The word that sends most men into violent convulsions and usually causes them to have a severe attack of the unfaithfuls. Yet Randall had said it, plainly and simply. No visible sweating or trouble getting the words out, he'd just come right out and said it. I should

have been leaping around the room screaming 'he loves me!' for the whole street to hear.
We should have been popping champagne
corks and having wild, passionate sex all over
the flat in celebration of his honesty. Yet that
was just it. How could I believe that anything
he said was the truth any more? He had lied
about everything just to get what he wanted,
so why would he stop now? For all I knew, he
had been sleeping with . . . with Troy. Tears
welled up in my eyes and cascaded down my
face. I turned away from him and dragged
myself towards the door. I could hardly
breathe, I had to get out of the flat.

'Please, pet,' he called after me.

I whipped my head round to look at him.

'I'm not your pet,' I hissed. 'Why don't you
go and find some other poor cow whose life
you can ruin?'

He didn't retaliate. I threw the door open
and stepped out into the hallway. My face
was burning from a combination of rage and
fresh, hot tears. I couldn't turn to look at
him, it hurt too much.

'Goodbye Randall,' I choked, and ran
down the stairs to the safety of the pouring
rain.

20

It wasn't just the Holly Hobby wallpaper that pissed me off. It was a combination of the wallpaper, the matching Holly Hobby bedspread, lampshade and bean bag set and the bunk beds. They were a constant reminder of all the years I had been forced to share the room with Susie, under the pretence of being sisters thus wanting to spend every minute together in a room the size of a bedside cabinet. I had wanted the Wombles. Nothing would have made me happier than having Uncle Bulgaria and his furry family on my bedroom walls, but, even at 15, Susie had wanted Holly Hobby. A miniature, flouncy dress-wearing cutie pie with an enormous head. Very much like Susie actually. Holly Hobby she wanted, so Holly Hobby we got. It had been a daily source of tension between us while we were growing up and the subject of many an argument with my mother.

'But I hate Holly Hobby.'

'I don't care.'

'What sort of role model is she for today's woman?'

'I don't care.'

'Furry animals who live in holes and pick up litter are much cooler.'

'I don't care.'

'It can be damaging for a child to live in surroundings which she finds offensive, you know.'

'I don't care.'

'I could be scarred for life.'

'I don't care.'

And so on, etc.

My mother had never been one for explaining herself, despite my inventive arguments. In fact, my continuous demands for a referendum over the decor only made her more determined. As a result, I had lived in a Holly Hobby world until the age of eighteen, when I had finally left home for university. How I managed to avoid developing a liking for frilly dresses and large bonnets, I'll never know. A lucky escape, I believe.

I say 'finally left home' because I had thought at the time it was final. All those years ago, I had escaped from the clutches of Holly Hobby and my mother to embark on my own, independent adult life. I had so many hopes and ambitions. Get a good job, earn lots of money, buy my own place and decorate it however I wanted. It had all gone to plan at first, yet here I was back in Holly Hobby hell living with my parents. I couldn't believe how it had all gone so wrong in just four months. I felt as if my life had gone full circle and I was right back where I had started eight years before with only a broken heart to show for it.

I had now been back at home for almost a month and was plunging deeper into depression every day. I hadn't seen Maz since moving out of her flat above the pub and I couldn't bring myself to go and see her. She had moved into a luxurious apartment provided by Paradise TV, with Dave in tow, and had embarked on rehearsals for her new show. She had offered me one of her five bedrooms to stay in. She even said that her new employers had encouraged her to bring her friend along. Of course, I didn't believe her. She was just being kind, as Maz always was. Perhaps telling her that she was a stuck-up media cow who liked to treat people like charity cases wasn't such a good idea. I couldn't help myself. I was seething with jealousy. I was so jealous, my skin had turned a permanent shade of green and I was unable to perfect any facial expressions beyond a scowl. I was supposed to be the successful one, not Maz. All through school, it had been the same, but now, just when it mattered, God had turned the tables and put me on a helter-skelter to insignificance. I didn't like his sense of humour.

Over the weeks, the jealousy had subsided, and I had kicked myself for having offended my best, most loyal friend. I missed our nights in together, discussing sex over a few bottles of cheap white wine. I missed our nights out together, discussing sex over cheap white wine. I had no one to have a laugh with, no one to cry with and no one to moan to when I felt like the Hunchback of Notre Dame's uglier sister. My social life was a barren landscape, the only movement being the odd tumbleweed blowing across the foreground. The highlight of my evenings was trying to decide which bunk bed to sleep in. Do I go for the top bunk and risk plunging to my death in the middle of the night, or do I choose the claustrophobia of the bottom bunk and suffer from the sensation that the roof is caving in on top of me every time I open my eyes? I never realised life could be so dull. Even *I* found myself intensely boring, so how could I possibly expect my friends to like me? I was desperate to make it better, but pride stopped me from making that single life-saving telephone call to civilisation. I chose, instead, to wallow in my own despair. I had always been a very capable wallower. At least I was still good at *something*.

Pride, of course, was irrelevant when it came to earning a living. My father would have happily loaned me some money until I was back on my feet but my mother held the purse strings so tightly that even the pennies were gasping for air. She would rather have scooped her own eyes out with a spoon than give me anything for free. I was sure she had supersonic hearing. If I opened the fridge, Mum would be by my side in a flash relaying the cost of a slice of wafer-thin ham. The slightest rustle from the biscuit tin and up she would pop to ensure that I hadn't dared to take more than one Rich Tea. Jammie Dodgers were out of the question and, as for chocolate Hobnobs, they were gold dust, reserved for 'paying members of the house-hold only'. She would rub my nose in my failings at every opportunity, even going so far as to inform me in front of the neighbours that I was squandering loo roll.

'Four sheets are enough for anybody,' she had shouted across the front garden, 'even for someone with a bottom the size of yours, Jennifer!'

After three days of endless ridicule, I could take it no longer. Fearing that she would start counting the cornflakes in my cereal bowl, and the grains of sugar in my coffee, I caved in. I swallowed the rest of my dwindling pride and accepted a job with Sebastian. My life was over.

Now I'm not saying I was too good for the job, after all I was unemployed, penniless and living at home, but compared to my colleagues, I was a veritable genius. The Carol Vorderman of our department, the only one with an IQ above single figures. Mensa had nothing to worry about, Densa reigned supreme in our office.

I had been naive to think that Sebastian would give me a proper job. His offer of a position at the bank, I realised, had been another attempt by my mother and Susie to put me in my place at the bottom of the pile. No chance of keeping any self-esteem down here, noo siree, it was impossible to be self-assured when such tasks as operating the photocopier were considered to be well beyond my capabilities. Training to be a hotshot lawyer was a relic of my distant past, working as a barmaid at the Scrap Inn was a fading memory of a previous happy existence. My responsibilities now included stamp-licking, envelope-sealing, pencil-sharpening, and coffee-making. If I showed potential, I was told, I would be promoted to answering the telephone, but only a hallowed few had ever reached such dizzy heights. At this rate, it could take years. I would be having a weekly blue rinse and going to bingo on a Tuesday night before I could even *think* of applying.

The stamp-licking department occupied the basement floor of the bank building. So unworthy were we, my 'colleagues' and I were ordered to use the back entrance, for fear of being seen by any members of the public. I shared a small, dingy room with Simon, the sixteen-year-old nephew of one of the directors, whose brain had obviously been removed at birth, and Kim, who had the intelligence of a flat-packed coffee table. I hoped Kim was joking when she boasted on my first day of having slept with Simon's uncle to get such a 'great job'. I prayed she was pulling my leg when she asked which side of the stamp to lick. I gave up all hope when she mistook the coffee grinder for a pencil sharpener and served the powers-that-be a special blend of wood shavings and lead at coffee time. Kim's only asset to the company was a pair of sleek forty-inch legs which were open for business longer than a twenty-four-hour service station. I was surprised she didn't suffer from bed sores, the amount of time she spent flat on her back. Sleeping her way to the top would be an understatement, she practically ran the bank. If Kim was off sick, the men moped around the building unable to function. Business slumped if they didn't get their daily fix of Kim's legs and long blonde hair. She oozed sexuality but was too thick to realise. Talking sense into her would be like trying to teach a brick to recite poetry. For the first few days, I had made it my mission to teach Kim about self-respect. *If I have to do this awful job*, I thought, *I can at least save a soul while I'm here*. I gave up when I stumbled across Kim giving the stationery boy a blow job next to the water dispenser.

'But he said he'd get wur al' the highlighters in the wurld,' she had whined. 'Imagine that, Jen, eh, wouldn't that be *ace*? Al' them pretty colours!'

God help us.

Simon, on the other hand, lived his life in a strange vacuum. Every so often, an inkling of common sense would penetrate his haze of stupidity, but such instances were very rare and only lasted a matter of seconds. Somehow, he managed to turn up for work at least two days a week but his presence was rarely noticed. Conversation was a definite no-no, sometimes I even had to prod him to make sure he was still breathing. The only time he showed any visible signs of life was when Kim walked within a foot of his desk. He would instantly blush, often drool, and shift uncomfortably in his chair. Then the moment would pass and he would return to his inanimate self. As far as I could tell, Simon existed only for Playstation and consuming inordinate amounts of illegal substances with his friends. Anything else was a total waste of time.

I never realised I would miss my job at the Scrap Inn so much. I longed to hear Auld Vinny's endless exaggerated stories about life at sea. I dreamed of listening to one of Derek and Denise's many vocal arguments across the pub. I imagined standing behind the bar with Maz, pulling the odd pint, eating scampi fries and fantasising about our futures. I even missed listening to Dave's latest madcap schemes to get rich in less than twenty-four hours. I hadn't really understood how special the pub had become in my life. I had been happy there and the people had become my friends. At least they were capable of entertaining conversation, which is more than could be said for Kim and Simon.

When I had realised what Randall had done, I had left the pub almost immediately. I couldn't bring myself to say goodbye to everyone, knowing I'd broken my promise to them that I would help to save the pub. Since then, I hadn't even gone back to Byker to find out what had become of them all. I couldn't face seeing the Scrap Inn razed to the ground and I didn't want to risk meeting any of our customers. I had let them down, the pub was lost for ever and it was all my fault. The trouble was, I missed it all so much. I had a gaping hole in my life where the Scrap Inn had been and my new job at the bank only made it bigger. It was so humiliating.

After a particularly awful day at work — Simon had taken an E in his lunch break and metamorphosed into a hyperactive loving machine, and Kim had spent hours filling in her application form for *Supermarket Sweep* (spelling 'Kim Carroll' had taken long enough) — I begged my dad to go for a drink with me to the nearest pub. One more night sitting in front of the QVC shopping channel — Mum's favourite — and I would have had to commit suicide. I hoped Dad would agree to come as there were only five paracetamol left in the bathroom cabinet and I couldn't really be bothered to track down the late-night chemist. Luckily, Dad jumped at the chance and we legged it to the pub before Mum found us something better to occupy our time, like dusting the 'good room' or cutting out money-off coupons from her *Woman's Realm*.

We skipped down the road like children let out of lessons for a fire drill, so happy were we to have escaped for a couple of hours. It was pitiful.

'Dad,' I said curiously over my second pint of Caffreys, 'why do you stay with Mum?'

He looked shocked by the question and paused to consider it before trying to answer.

'I don't know really, Jenny.' He shook his head and frowned in a peculiar way, as if he'd never thought of the question before. 'I guess it's just habit,' he answered.

'*Habit?*' I repeated. 'But Dad, some habits are good and some kill you, like smoking fifty cigarettes a day. Some habits you should give up.'

He smiled. 'It's not that bad, Jenny, we get by OK.'

'But are you happy, Dad?'

'Happy, hmm, sometimes. I'm happy when I see you.'

He reached across the small, round table and patted my hand tenderly. I felt a tear roll down my nose.

'But you deserve to be happy all the time, Dad. She's such a . . . such a cow.'

'Now don't talk like that, Jenny, she *is* your

mother and she does love you . . . in her own special way.'

'Huh! If that's love, I'd hate to be in her bad books.'

We both laughed uneasily. We had always had a special connection but we had never spoken this openly before. My dad was a quiet man and tended to keep his problems to himself. I felt sorry for him but that made me feel insecure. I wanted him to be strong, to make me proud, I wanted him to be *a man*.

'Why don't you leave her?' I asked gingerly.

'I couldn't leave her,' he said sadly, 'it wouldn't be right.'

'Why? She doesn't respect you, she doesn't love you . . . '

'But what would she do? She doesn't work, Jenny, and I wouldn't want to abandon her.'

I stared at him pitifully. He was such a genuine, reliable person. He had supported my mother since the day they met and had got nothing in return, but he would never break his vows.

'You're too soft,' I said gently.

'I know,' he agreed, 'but so are you. That's why I love you so much. Just make sure you don't get taken advantage of . . . like I have been.'

His words hit me sharply and bounced

around inside my head. 'Don't get taken advantage of.' Huh! In the previous few months I had done nothing but be taken advantage of: Jack, Troy, Randall — they had all had a shot. I was beginning to think they were collecting points. 'Take advantage of Jennifer five times and use your advantage card to claim your free canteen of cutlery!' Memories of recent events came flooding back. It was still so confusing. I knew I had been used but I still couldn't work out the connection between the three. How had Jack known Randall? How had Randall known Troy? (I dread to think.) Why had they picked me as their victim? Had Randall really liked me at all? Why are men such bastards? It could have been the alcohol, it could simply have been the emotional situation between myself and my father, but I was suddenly overwhelmed by a feeling of deep despair. I was such a failure, such a loser, so alone. It was never going to get any better. This was it, this was my life. The pressure in my head built up until I could hold it no longer. It had to escape somewhere and it did, through my eyes. Floods of tears burst for freedom and every sob shook the foundations of the pub, rattling the glasses and turning the beer sour. A space appeared around me as the punters stepped away from the blubbering wreck, afraid they might catch something if they happened to get too close.

'I . . . I'm . . . I'm such a . . . such a f . . . failure,' I wailed. 'Turn down the music!' a voice shouted.

'I . . . I've m . . . messed up everything,' I sobbed.

'Aye, we wanna hear what she's sayin',' someone shouted.

'I'm a . . . a loser,' I groaned.

'What did she say?' said a voice.

'She's a loser,' shouted another.

'You're not a loser,' my dad insisted.

'I thought he loved me,' I whined.

'Who?' my dad asked softly.

'Who?' someone shouted.

'R . . . Randall,' I answered.

'Randall of course,' they replied.

My dad moved closer and put his arm around my shoulders. His affection only made me even more emotional.

'He . . . he hasn't even called,' I wailed.

'Who?' asked someone.

'Randall,' the crowd replied.

'Git!' said another.

'But of course he has,' my dad said, holding me closer to him.

'Has he?' I asked.

'Has he?' the pub repeated.

'Every day,' my dad replied.

'Every day!' the crowd yelled.

'Shut up will you,' my dad shouted.

The audience stepped backwards.

I stared, open-mouthed, at my dad. What did he say? Did he just say that Randall had called me every day for the last four weeks? I asked him to repeat himself.

'Yes,' he assured me. 'Your mother took most of the calls while you were at work but I spoke to him a couple of times.'

I couldn't believe what I was hearing. 'She said she had told you. She said you weren't interested and not to bother you.'

Not interested! The bitch, the stupid interfering, heartless cow! Here I was, trying to make head or tail of what had happened, believing I had been used up and thrown away by someone I had actually cared for, and there she was, hiding the fact that he had called me at least twenty-eight times! That was the limit. Who did she think she was? I jumped up from the table, knocking the rest of my pint onto the floor. The crowd gasped. I grabbed my father's arm and marched him towards the door. I was furious. If my mother had managed to conceal a score of phone calls, what else had she been hiding from me? It was time to find out.

★ ★ ★

Luckily for my mother, she was nowhere to be seen when I stormed through the door with my father hot on my heels.

'Perhaps she was just trying to protect you,' my father protested.

'More like humiliate me,' I replied, 'cut me off from my own life. Where *is* she?'

I was disappointed. The beer had warmed me up for a good argument, and twenty-six years' worth of tension was about to emerge. It was typical of my luck that she had decided to go out just at the vital moment. It was only the letter addressed to me that I found lying beside the front door which stopped me spontaneously combusting.

It was an invitation to a party. Party — I had a vague recollection of what one of those was — music, Twiglets, snogging, but would I remember what to do when I got there? The party was to celebrate the launch of a new talk show, *The Maz Way*, destined to be Paradise TV's 'hottest new project'. A lump appeared in my throat as I read the invitation.

'Meet the star of this new, exciting show. Mingle with the cast and party in this extraordinary location.'

'Bloody cheek,' I croaked, looking at the impersonal typed piece of cardboard, but I couldn't help but feel pride for my once best friend. She had made it, she had achieved what she had always dreamed of. At least one of us had. I was tempted to throw the card away, but the words 'extraordinary location' caught my attention. I looked for the address — just out of curiosity, of course — but couldn't find the words. I turned the invitation over. On the back was a map, marked with a large red cross. The location was instantly recognisable. I stared at the words next to the cross: 'The Talk Inn pub,' it read, 'previously the Scrap Inn.'

I almost collapsed.

'Wh . . . who?' I exclaimed. 'Wh . . . what? Where? How? Umm . . . ' My grasp of the English language escaped me momentarily. What was Maz doing holding a launch party at the pub we were evicted from? Anyway, the pub had been demolished, hadn't it?

My eyes raced over the words again and again until they finally settled on a handwritten message at the bottom of the invitation. 'Jen, please come, love Maz xxx'.

'Yeah right, as if,' I said huffily. 'No way am I going to some stuck-up media party at my old pub so I can be humiliated even more. Nope, nope, noo, absolutely *no* way, José!'

21

21st April, 8 p.m.

I went to the party. Of course, it was against my better judgement. I didn't really want to go at all. In truth, I only went to satisfy my dad's curiosity about the pub — or so I tried to convince myself. My mind had been in turmoil since receiving the invitation. I was sure it was someone playing a joke on me, after all, Maz and I had been thrown out of the Scrap Inn, so why would she go back there? Nothing made sense any more . . . finally, I understood what it was like to live in Kim's world.

At work that day, I was even more distant than Simon, which was quite an achievement as Simon wasn't even there. Rumour had it that Playstation had brought out a new game so Simon had stayed home to practise. We probably wouldn't see him for weeks. In fairness to Kim, she was very enthusiastic about my invitation to a media party — or medium party as she called it. I had been bursting to tell someone, in an effort to get things clear in my mind. On a scale of helpfulness, it had come down to a choice between talking to Kim or talking to the filing cabinet. Kim had won on sheer eagerness. To be honest, she hadn't really served to clear the confusion, but she had offered to lend me a dress for the occasion. I gratefully declined the offer but assured her that if I happened to shed four stone during the course of the day, I'd get back to her.

Dad agreed to accompany me to the party, so at 8 o'clock, we caught a cab to Byker. In honour of the glamorous occasion, Dad had somehow managed to squeeze himself into his 1960s tuxedo. The trousers were at half-mast and the edges were slightly moth-eaten, but I had to admit he looked good. The darkness of the suit contrasted vibrantly with the whiteness of his hair, and his face glowed with excitement. He didn't get out much. I had opted for a plain black velvet cocktail dress, simple black shoes and pearls, which made me feel a bit like Selina Scott, but my glamour wardrobe consisted of only two outfits and I didn't think my turquoise satin bridesmaid's dress would be particularly appropriate. Since seven o'clock my hair had been up and down more times than Kim's knickers. My styling decision was finally made for me when my curls collapsed with exhaustion around my ears and refused to go anywhere near a hairpin. The 'relaxed, tousled' look it was then.

Luckily, Mum was absent again when the cab arrived. Her usual compliment, 'What *do* you look like, Jennifer?' would not have been greatly appreciated.

As our 'C' reg beat-up Ford Escort banged and clattered its way along the quayside, I felt a knot form in my stomach. By the time we had turned left to begin the steep ascent to our destination, I felt as if my intestines had been crocheted into a small tank top. Visions of our party entrance flashed through my mind. Here I was, about to turn up to Maz's star-studded event with my dad as my date in a barely-roadworthy car which suffered from a greater rust problem than the *Titanic* (post-sinking). The other guests, meanwhile, would glide to the door in chauffeur-driven stretch limos, oozing glamour and wealth with gorgeous escorts on their arms. Maz would die of embarrassment. In fact, she had probably only invited me out of sympathy. She would never have expected me to actually turn up. Damn, what an idiot.

'Stop!' I yelled.

Pedro, our Spanish cabbie, slammed on the brakes. A short while later, the mechanism kicked in and we ground to an unsteady halt. Two miles stopping distance . . . not bad for a 'C' reg.

'Wha?' he exclaimed to the space where the rear-view mirror should have been.

'Wha madder miss?'

'I can't go,' I screeched. 'I can't do it.'

'Do it?' he repeated. 'You wan' do it?'

'No!' I shouted.

Pedro shrugged his shoulders.

'What's the matter, Jenny?' my dad asked gently.

'I can't go to Maz's party,' I wailed.

'But why?'

'I'll embarrass her.'

'Don't be silly.'

'She doesn't want me there.'

'Of course she does, why would she invite you if she didn't want you to come?'

'I don't know!'

Pedro watched the exchange over his shoulder.

'I can go mees?' he asked.

'No!' I yelled.

'Yes,' replied my dad.

He started the engine then thought better of it when he saw the murderous look in my eyes.

'No worries mees,' he said quickly.

'Look, Jenny,' Dad said firmly, 'we're

almost there, so let's just go and see what it's like. We can always leave.'

'I can't,' I groaned.

'You can,' he said.

'Since when did you get all masterful?' I asked grimly.

'Since I decided you should get off your backside and stop feeling sorry for yourself,' he replied.

I gasped. How dare he? I wasn't feeling sorry for myself, I was just, just . . . indulging in self-hate.

'But the *car*,' I whined.

'Wha' madder wi' car?' Pedro asked angrily. 'She supadoopa. Pedro passion wagon.'

'See!' I screeched, turning to my dad.

'OK, we'll walk,' Dad said strongly.

He almost threw me out of the door before paying the obviously offended Pedro.

'Bloody weemeen,' said the cabbie, raising his eyebrows at my father in a 'you're a man, you know what I'm talking about' kind of way.

Dad shut the door, sending the left wing mirror crashing to the ground. The cab wheel-span into the distance.

'Come on,' said Dad, 'time to party.'

'Blimey,' I groaned. 'I think I preferred you when you were boring.'

My heart fluttered when I saw the pub again.
From the outside, it looked pretty much the
same only cleaner, as if it had had a good
wash and the paintwork had been re-done.
The most obvious difference was the new
wooden sign across the front of the building.
'The Talk Inn' it read, in bold green letters. A
crowd was gathered outside, admiring the
enormous balloons and banners that pro-
claimed the launch of the new show *The Maz
Way*. A red carpet covered the pavement,
leading the guests to the bustling party inside.
I held my dad's hand, took a deep breath and
stepped up to the door.

'Ticket please,' bellowed one of the two
enormous doormen. Both were dressed in
sharply cut black suits and wore Blues
Brothers style shades. I nervously handed
over my invitation. Bouncers invariably had
the effect of making me feel hideously
insignificant. I was forever dreading the day
when one would say, 'Sorry, you can't come
in, you're too ugly,' or, 'Sorry, no fat people
allowed'.

'Na miss,' he said after a brief silence. 'This
is fake.'

'What?' I exclaimed. 'What do you mean,
fake?'

A murmur coursed through the waiting crowd behind me.

'Fake, like, not real,' the bouncer answered sarcastically.

'Rubbish,' I fumed.

'Aye,' he replied, 'that's aboot the size of it.'

'Well . . . well, what are you going to do about it?' I cringed.

'Nowt lass,' he laughed. 'Yer name's not down, yer not comin' in.'

'Oh God, you don't actually *say* that do you? Next you'll be telling me to move aside or you'll knee-cap my granny.'

'Aye,' he choked, 'maybe.'

Something in the voice suddenly sounded startlingly familiar. I stared up at the doorman, who removed his dark glasses with a gigantic hand.

'Dave!' I beamed. 'What are you doing here?'

He laughed so loud it almost caused a landslide.

'New job,' he said proudly. 'Security. Me an' Chip.'

He pointed to his team-mate. Chip removed his glasses and nodded politely. I forced a smile.

'Howay get in there,' Dave continued, ushering Dad and I through the door. 'Yer missin' a lush party.'

The atmosphere inside the pub was electric. Music, laughter, chatting, it was a far cry from the media party Maz and I had been to previously. I noticed instantly that the pub had been redecorated. It was light and airy, the walls had been painted a rich green and the floor and ceiling were a highly polished wood. The bar had been moved to the far wall and replaced by tables, green leather seats and a small stage. A sparkling new juke box stood in the centre of one wall and the bars had been removed from the windows which were now stained glass. I had to admit it did look fantastic.

'Wow,' I gasped.

'It's great,' my dad agreed.

'I need a drink,' I added.

My dad fought his way to the bar, while I scanned the crowd for a familiar face. I was desperate to see Maz again after our time apart, to apologise for having offended her, but the star of the show was nowhere to be seen — oh, the price of fame and fortune. Four weeks out of the social scene had already had a dire effect on my ability to make small talk. I 'hello-ed', 'how do you do-ed' and 'I'm Jennifer Summer-ed' in apologetic tones to various strangers in an effort to feel like less of a social leper. Their puzzled glances only made me feel more isolated. A fleeting desire to have Randall on my arm then sent me into a blind panic. This was *his* pub, he was *bound* to be here, what the *hell* would I do if I saw him? The swiftly downed vodka and Cokes eased my alarm, temporarily of course.

While my reborn social butterfly of a father chatted to anyone and everyone in the room, I did a great job of merging with the paintwork. I felt so unworthy, so unsure of myself, that I almost struck up a conversation with the cigarette machine. At least, I would have if I could have thought of anything to say. I kept my head down, fiddled with my pearls, and consoled myself with the free alcohol. It was only the sound of a familiar voice that saved me from total self-destruction.

'Jen, honey,' Matt hollered from the other side of the room.

My incredibly camp friend wiggled through the crowd, knocking drinks over and sending canapés flying in all directions as he rushed to greet me with outstretched arms.

'Matt,' I smiled as he grabbed my face and kissed both cheeks, 'I didn't expect to see you here.'

'Ooh, I snapped up the firm's VIP ticket. I wouldn't miss it for the *world*,' he giggled, 'free alcopops, lots of lovely media men. It's *fantastic* babe.'

I nodded a little too enthusiastically. 'Hmm, it's great,' I mumbled.

'So, what's new?' he asked loudly.

'Not much,' I whispered, not wanting the whole party to hear of my demotion to the stamp-licking department. 'This and that, you know.'

Luckily Matt was too hyper to be even remotely interested in my tale of woe. That meant only one thing . . . love.

'Wow, Jen,' he said excitedly. 'I think I'm in love.'

'I'd never have guessed.'

'But honestly, hon, he is *such* a dish.'

He wiggled his bum inadvertently and pursed his lips like he was sucking a lime.

'American . . . *gorgeous* bod, I mean, de-lish, pearly white teeth. So important, you know, I hate men who could mine their molars for food. Lovely hair . . . oh he's just perfect,' he purred.

'What's his name?' I asked, forgetting my own problems for a moment.

'Get this,' he replied. 'Troy. I mean, wowza, how American!'

'Oh.' I felt sick. The photo of Troy and Randall that I had seen in Randall's flat was catapulted to the forefront of my mind. So Troy was here. That simple fact confirmed it for me. Troy and Randall were lovers. I realised Matt was still jabbering excitedly in my face.

' . . . *and*, get this, his cousin owns half of Paradise TV. His uncle owns the other half. Glam, eh?'

'Look Matt,' I said seriously, 'I think you should steer clear of . . . '

'But of course, you know the big boss, don't you, hon?' he continued, oblivious to my advice. 'You caused all the hoo-ha in his big meeting with your orange hair and drug-taking. That was hilarious!'

I smiled insincerely as Matt exploded into fits of laughter.

'There he is over there,' he chuckled.

I followed his pointed finger to the tall, attractive, middle-aged man who hovered by the stage. I instantly recognised the shock of white hair, the tanned, friendly face and the large, extremely well-dressed frame which positively glowed with wealth and success. Glisset & Jacksop's number one client, the owner of Paradise TV. So that was Troy's *uncle*. I stared at the confident, auspicious-looking man whose meeting I had destroyed a few months before, and tried to think of his name. It was on the tip of my tongue when a cheer from the crowd interrupted my chain of thought. I whipped my head round to the door to see what all the fuss was about.

Maz looked gorgeous. Her red hair was pulled neatly up onto her head, accentuating her delicate face and long neck. Her clothes were obviously chosen to compliment her surroundings. She wore a dark green chiffon, spaghetti-strap dress which clung to her tall, slim frame and made her seem elegant and classy. Her feet peeped out from beneath the soft folds of the skirt, revealing a pair of emerald velvet mules. Even her toenails were perfectly painted, I noticed, a task which Maz herself had described as 'more of a pain in the bum than washin' lettuce'. I hardly recognised this beautiful, feminine woman as my best friend. I felt a sudden surge of pride which turned to nausea when my brain registered the identity of the man by her side.

22

I had to get some fresh air. Thumper had taken up residence in my head, and the vodka was doing funny things in my stomach. The front door was blocked by the press trying to get their shot of the beautiful couple and the back door was being guarded by two more bouncers who would make Mike Tyson look like Barry McGuigan. I made for the loos, battled my way into a cubicle and stuck my head against the smallest excuse for a window I had ever seen. I wouldn't exactly call the air fresh, but at least I had escaped the horrible scene.

'How could she do this?' I muttered to myself, breathing into a disposal bag in an attempt to curb the hyperventilating. 'She knew how much I liked him. I even said I *loved* him. Bloody hell, I must have a sign on my back saying 'Gullible Idiot', right above 'Break my heart — it's fun'.'

I shook my head fiercely and rubbed my eyes, hoping I would wake up from my nightmare. Chunks of mascara coated my

371

fingers, which told me it was real. If I had been dreaming, I would have made sure I was wearing waterproof.

'Go out and confront them,' said a determined voice on my right shoulder.

'No don't! Hide in here till they've all gone home. It's too shameful,' said the shaky voice on my left.

'But you don't know the full facts,' said the right voice.

'Of course you do. She's your best friend and she's sleeping with your boyfriend,' retorted the left.

'Ex-boyfriend,' replied the right.

'Smart arse,' I said aloud.

The left won. I sat on the loo, put my head in my hands, and started to cry.

★ ★ ★

Randall had looked so attractive as he entered the pub. He was wearing his black dinner suit but it was teamed, as always, with his ever-loyal black boots. His hair looked softer, even styled, but still fell over his forehead in his unique, dishevelled way. His face was cleanly shaven. It looked so smooth, I had wanted to reach out and stroke it, then I had looked to his hands. I wanted to see the slim, piano-player hands that had felt their way over my body, touched my face and caressed my hair. The hands that made me tremble with pleasure. The hand that was now clasped tightly in Maz's hand. It was then I realised what I was witnessing. OK, so I was slow on the uptake, but it was a bit hard to concentrate when my hormones were reaching intergalactic proportions.

Not only was Randall at the party but he was at the party with Maz. It seemed Randall had bought the pub and sealed the deal with the love of my best friend. The bastard. He was even two-timing Troy.

It was only the offer by a very highly strung party-goer to 'shove my head down the U-bend' if I didn't 'get out of the bleedin' cubicle now' that made me leave my hiding place. I would happily have stayed there, perched on the toilet, for weeks if I thought it would have spared me a whole lot of emotional turmoil and embarrassment. My aim now was to reach the exit faster than the speed of light and slip away into obscurity. My father could find his own way home. I should have known life was never that simple.

'Jen, lass, you made it!' boomed an unmistakable voice as I crept back into the throng of the party.

My whole body tensed as a radiant Maz

ran towards me and scooped me up in a smothering hug.

'It's lush to see you!' she shouted, keeping her hands on my shoulders.

I looked at her coldly. 'Hello Maz,' I said through gritted teeth.

'D'you like the party then?' she beamed.

'Yeah, it's just fantastic.'

I bit my lip to stop it trembling.

'Great place for a show eh?' she continued. 'I couldn't believe it when they told us they were gonna run the show from *here*, from *our* pub.'

I looked at her curiously, my fury subsiding for a moment.

'The show is going to come from *here*?' I asked.

'Aye, pet. I've been desperate to tell you but I thought I'd wait, like, till it were all sorted.'

My rage returned as I remembered whose pub this now was. 'This isn't *our* pub, Maz,' I said firmly, 'this is Randall's pub, remember? Or perhaps it belongs to you and Randall now? That would be cosy, wouldn't it?'

She was taken aback by my stern tone. Maz let go of my shoulders and stepped back, holding my gaze. 'Jen, are you alreet?' she asked.

'Oh yeah, Maz, I'm just brilliant. Absolutely fucking great!'

She frowned and looked quickly around her.

'Oh, afraid what your fans might think, are you?' I said loudly. 'Afraid they might not like you once they find out what you're *really* like?'

'Jen,' she said, signalling with her hands for me to keep the volume down, 'you've got it all wrong, lass. We were gonna tell you but you wouldn't answer our calls.'

'Tell me what, Maz?' I replied, my voice growing louder with each word. 'Tell me how happy you are in your new poncey apartment with your swanky new job. Tell me how pleased you are that I spend my days doing a job that a PG Tips monkey would find boring. Tell me how happy you and MY boyfriend are now that he's bought you everything you ever wanted. What about *friendship*, Maz? What about the years we spent together, don't they mean anything to you or have you sold out completely?'

My voice was loud and trembling and my whole body shook as the emotion came pouring out. First Jack, then Troy, then Randall, now Maz. Everyone I had ever trusted had let me down. Now I was all alone. I didn't care who heard me. I was aware that the room had fallen silent and all eyes were on us, but I had no pride left.

'You were my best friend, Maz,' I sobbed. 'How could you *do* this?'

Maz was crying too. Maz never cried. 'Jen, listen!' she yelled, but I was running for the door.

I felt like Moses parting the Red Sea as the crowd dispersed to let the mad woman through. I could almost taste freedom when my vision was suddenly blurred by the outline of a man standing in front of me. I skidded to a halt, sending particles of vodka careering through my bloodstream at an alarming rate.

'Randall,' I mouthed.

The sight of him almost made me faint. We were so close, I could see the pores of his skin and feel warmth of his body. His pheromones danced like space invaders before my eyes.

'Jenny,' he said, piercing my rage with his electric eyes.

'I . . . I can't talk to you,' I spluttered.

The crowd turned to Randall.

'Then just listen,' he replied.

They turned back to me.

'But I'm so confused,' I answered.

They looked at him.

'Of course you are,' he smiled.

Back to me.

I made no response. That ruined their game of conversational tennis.

'I bought the pub to save it,' he explained.

'Bollocks,' I spat.

'I thought it would make a good venue for a show,' he continued.

'What's that got to do with you, Randall? You're just the work experience boy.'

A ripple of laughter moved around the room. I glared at our audience.

'Oh Jenny, you're so adorable,' he smiled.

'Piss off,' I retorted. 'Don't mock me, Randall, we all know who you find adorable.'

'Who?'

'Maz of course. Why else would you be so secretive and holding hands and . . . oh you make me want to puke. Not to mention Troy of course.'

I thumped his arm.

'Ow!' he laughed.

'Stop laughing at me, you insensitive git.'

'I'm not,' he laughed.

'You *are*, look at you. You're smiling now. I suppose it's because you're in love or something pathetic.'

'I am.'

I wanted to die. 'Well, good luck to you,' I croaked. 'I hope you'll both be very miserable together.'

'Who?'

'You and Troy or you and Maz. I don't know!'

'But I don't love Maz.'

'Yes you do.'

'No I don't.'

'You *do*.'

'No I don't.'

'Well, who the Jesus, Mary and Joseph do you love then?' I screamed.

'You!' he shouted. '*You*, Jennifer hole-in-the-head Summer. You!'

My head raced to absorb this new information. Rational thought battled for space among the alcohol.

'What are you talking about, Randall?' I asked, frantically waving my arms around.

He grabbed my shoulders.

'I love you!' he shouted. 'I love you so much I can't sleep at night. I daydream at work about spending time with you. I love you so much I long to hear your voice and see your beautiful smile and run my fingers through your gorgeous hair. I love you, you fool!'

I paused for breath. I could feel the tension in the air as the whole party waited for my reply.

'Bullshit,' I muttered.

'What?' he said desperately.

'If you love me so much, what are you doing holding hands with my best friend?' Explain that one, Mr Smooth Talker.

'I'm her boss,' he insisted.

'Oh, is that what you young people call it these days?' I scoffed. 'Her *boss*, how nice.'

'Jennifer!' he replied, then he stopped. His eyes darted around the room then he walked away. He just walked away and left me to the mercy of the gathered crowd. Damn.

In an instant he was back, dragging behind him the man I had recognised as the owner of Paradise TV. I cringed with embarrassment. Oh shit, he's going to have me forcefully removed, I thought. I cowered under the watchful eye of Glisset & Jacksop's number one client. Randall spoke first.

'Dad,' he said loudly, 'I want you to meet Jennifer, my *girlfriend*.'

The big, attractive man held out a firm, tanned hand.

'Delighted,' he said.

'*Dad*,' I repeated, retrieving my hand from the strong handshake. 'What do you mean, *Dad*? This is Mr . . . Mr . . . um . . . well, this is the boss of Paradise TV. He's important, he's loaded, it's Mr . . . damn, what is it?'

'Mr Pettifer,' the man said.

'That's it!' I said triumphantly.

'Pettifer! Pettifer, Pettifer, Petti . . . ' My voice trailed off at the sound of the name. I stared at the man. I stared at Randall. They stared back. *Two* pairs of vibrant green eyes.

'Bloody h . . . ' was all I could manage.

Come to think of it, they were very alike. Tall, quietly confident, attractive in a not classically good looking sort of way. But it couldn't be true, could it? I looked around for Jeremy Beadle and his crew of practical jokers, but of course he wouldn't be there, Randall hated Jeremy Beadle with a passion.

'Are you serious?' I asked eventually.

'Deadly,' said Randall.

'But . . . but what about your work experience?'

'I made it up, so that you wouldn't be scared off.'

'And . . . and your little flat?'

'I got it just so that you would think I was normal. I wanted you to fall in love with *me*, not with all this.' He looked so sincere.

'What about Troy?' I asked.

'My cousin,' he replied.

Out of the corner of my eye, I saw Troy step out of the party crowd. He smiled. Matt, who seemed to be attached to Troy's hip, smiled even wider.

'Troy told me about you,' Randall said. 'I gave him the tickets for the talk show, and he left the rest up to me.'

My mind was swimming. I had to stop and tread water before I ran out of energy.

'So you bought this place,' I said, thinking aloud.

'Yes,' he replied, 'I wanted to help out you and Maz. I knew the show could be a success and I wanted to save your pub. It was supposed to be our project.'

'So why did you make me move out?'

'I didn't. That was Jack. He was representing the sellers so I had to get another lawyer to represent me. I suppose he took it upon himself to break the news. He wasn't aware of our . . . relationship.'

'Bastard,' I smiled.

'Ditto,' he laughed.

I took a step closer to him.

'I wanted to explain,' he insisted. 'I tried calling every day but . . . '

'My mother didn't give me your messages.'

He stared at me so intently, I nearly had an orgasm on the spot.

'Oh Randall,' I sighed, 'I've made such a mess. How could I have got it so wrong?'

'Because you're stubborn,' he replied.

'Yes.'

'And you jump to conclusions.'

'Yeah, maybe.'

'And you don't give people time to explain.'

'Right, well . . . '

'And you sulk for weeks.'

'OK, but — '

'And you fly off the handle without thinking.'

'Well, perhaps . . . '

'And you — '

'OK, all right! I get the message.'

He laughed loudly and smiled at me with his eyes.

'But I've ruined Maz's party,' I mumbled.

Maz appeared at my side and wrapped her arms around me.

'Gis a hug,' she said, pulling me to her.

I hugged my friend, burying my head in her shoulder.

'I'm sorry, Maz,' I whimpered.

'Me too,' she replied. That was the closest she would ever come to an apology.

'You're not a stuck-up media cow,' I added.

'Thanks mate,' she grinned.

Randall stepped forward and took my hands in his. The firmness of his grasp sent shivers through my body. I could almost hear my pearls rattling. The party guests faded into oblivion as I focused on his face. All of a sudden, I was very sober.

'So you're not a work experience boy?' I asked.

'No.'

'You *own* Paradise TV?' I said.

'Half of it, aye.'

I screwed up my face and paused for a moment.

'Oh, I don't care.' I shrugged. 'I still like you.'

He laughed and stroked my face with his hand. Our bodies were almost touching.

'*Like* me,' he repeated, 'is that all?'

'Tell me the bit about me having a beautiful smile again, and I might reconsider.'

His face broke into a heart-melting smile. 'You are beautiful,' he said.

'Pardon?'

'You are beautiful.'

'What?'

'You are b . . . '

I beamed. 'I just like hearing you say it,' I giggled.

He lifted my chin with his hand and planted a warm, firm kiss on my lips.

'I love you, Jennifer Summer,' he smiled. 'Let me take you to Paradise.'

'Wait a sec,' I replied, kissing him back. 'I'll just get my toothbrush.'

Epilogue

We watched the wedding video for the umpteenth time. It was unbelievable. The flowers, the dress, the confetti, the cake. The emotion of it all got to me every time.

'Look at Troy!' I roared. 'He looks like he's going to vomit when Matt says, 'I do.''

'Watch,' Maz choked, holding her side and rolling on the floor. 'Here's the bit where Matt faints and headbutts the celebrant.'

We laughed hysterically, slapping each other on the back and stammering, 'Ooh, oh dear,' in between guffaws.

'You're so cruel,' Randall smiled as he scuffed sexily into the room. 'I think they make a lovely couple. Champagne anyone?'

★　★　★

The video of Troy and Matt's Californian wedding ceremony had arrived that morning. Their romance had blossomed since the night of the launch party and Troy had used his discount flights as an air hostess, sorry

384

steward, to jet them off to a Christmas wedding. Of course, I was pleased for them. It was just the sight of Matt in a white satin frock and veil that made me slightly uneasy.

* * *

Kim gave up her promiscuous ways to move in with the stationery boy. Rumour had it that business slumped after she lengthened her skirts but Kim was happy. She never made it to telephone-answering but she did have every colour of highlighter in the world.

* * *

Simon reached Level 3 on Playstation's 'Resident Evil 2' and turned up for work, occasionally.

* * *

Susie and Sebastian upgraded their dishwasher and bought a Volvo. Apart from that, life in the rut stayed pretty much the same.

* * *

The Scrap Inn, a.k.a. The Talk Inn, became the permanent location for the most popular talk show on TV, but maintained a working bar. Regulars were issued with VIP passes to escape the crowds that travelled for miles to sample a bottle of Brown Ale from the most popular pub in Britain. It was soon clear that our pub would remain standing for at least another 95 years.

★ ★ ★

Derek and Denise took over as head bar staff at the pub and often featured on the show. Their advice to troubled couples was usually along the lines of ''Ave an argument, that'll sort oot yer problems.' 'Howay woman, na it won't.' 'Shut yer bleedin' trap you, they asked me.' 'No they didny ya tramp . . . ' and so on.

★ ★ ★

Dave took great pride in his job as head of security at the pub for Paradise TV, with Chip as his right-hand man. Apparently, Torica asked him out as her 'bit of rough' at least twice a week. He turned her down. He 'couldny understand a chuffin' word she said, like. Too bleedin' regional.'

★ ★ ★

My mother left my father, of course, and moved in with her therapist. He turned out to be Scrooge-like in his stinginess — not to mention overpriced — and drove my mum to distraction every time she did a simple act like reach for a biscuit:

'But do you really need a biscuit?'

'Yes.'

'Why do you think that is?'

'I don't know!'

'Lie down on the couch while we discuss this issue.'

★ ★ ★

My dad was initially surprised by the separation. His period of mourning lasted about three weeks until the money for the house came through. He bought a boat, signed Auld Vinny up as First Mate and set sail for worldwide adventure. These two made Captain Pugwash look proficient. The last I heard, they were shark fishing off the west coast of Ireland. They had decided to wait until the Guinness ran out before moving on.

★ ★ ★

Maz was a roaring success as a talk-show host. Her dazzling personality, Geordie accent and no-messing attitude made her a big hit almost immediately, but she was still just Maz. She bought the flat next door and we spent many a night drinking *better* bottles of wine, eating *bigger* bars of chocolate and gossiping about her latest run of marriage proposals. Maz's real moment of glory, though, came when she sieved through her mountain of fan mail one morning and happened to stumble across a letter of praise . . . from Ricki Lake.

★　★　★

Randall, gorgeous, adorable, dishevelled Randall, finally introduced me to his *real* house and asked me to move in. I said that any house which needed a cross-country train service to take you from the bathroom to the kitchen was too big for me and opted, instead, to move with him into his flat. I redecorated it, of course, and made a bit more mess to feel more at home . . . and put take-away baltis in the fridge, and sat my Argos ghetto-blaster next to his £2000 stereo, etc. I also convinced him to give me a job at the TV company. He said as the fiancée of the owner's son, I didn't really need to work, but I had to have something to erase the memory of working in the stamp-licking department. I took over as a legal adviser — to use the term lightly — on Maz's show. Luckily, his dad didn't ask me for a reference and kindly erased my previous misdemeanours from his memory. Oh, and Randall asked me to marry him. I said no at first, low self-esteem apparently, I didn't trust the fact that I could be so happy, but I changed my mind. I *am* happy and I deserve to be.

★   ★   ★

'The Chimes!' Maz yelled, jumping unsteadily to her feet.

We listened to the countdown, gripping our glasses of champagne with excited anticipation, then Big Ben let rip. We cheered. Maz ran off to kiss everyone in the room. I looked into Randall's eyes. What a difference a year makes, I thought happily.

'Happy New Year, pet,' he beamed. 'Let's hope it's a good one.'

We kissed.

'Happy New Year,' I smiled. 'Here's to twelve months of Summer time.'

★   ★   ★

Oh, wait a minute. I almost forgot Jack. Actually, I have forgotten Jack completely. After Paradise TV took their business away from Glisset & Jacksop, Jack's desk was cleared faster than he could say BMW. The lovely Vicky left him for the head of corporate finance and Jack soon discovered the meaning of isolation. The last I heard, he was a plastic-flip-flop seller in Morocco . . . or was that just wishful thinking?

CHC
VV
100F

R.P.P.